Darker than DEATH

Richard Allen

RICHARD ALLEN

Richard Allen is a retired senior police officer who, in addition to
uniform duties, saw service with the CID, the Vice Squad, the Drug
Squad and Special Branch.
Richard is the author of two bestselling works dealing with police
management and leadership,
which were listed as recommended reading by both the
US Department of Justice and the Police Staff College.

'Darker that DEATH' is the third in a series of
Mark Faraday adventures.

By the same author

Non-fiction:

Effective Supervision in the Police Service
Leading from the Middle

Fiction:

DIRTY Business
DIE Back

Darker than DEATH

Richard Allen

Published by MARS Associates

www.richard-allen-author.com

Member: Crime Writers Association (UK)
Member: International Thriller Writers (USA)

To our son, Mark -
one of the good guys

Acknowledgement

I am particularly grateful for the friendship and advice given to me by the acclaimed Bristol artist, David Rowlands BSc (Hons); also to Hugo Pike OBE, BA, lately Assistant Chief Constable, Avon and Somerset Constabulary, for his family insights and sharing with me details regarding his great-uncle Theodore William Henry Veale VC.

In writing the Mark Faraday adventures and, when thinking of character and example, my father Clifford (1914-1997) and my mother Vera (1918-2002) are rarely far from my thoughts.

As always, little would be achieved in my world without the love, support and loyalty of my wife Ann.

'To forgive wrongs darker than death'
Percy Shelley 1792-1822

Prologue

Monday, 23rd November 1914.

Boesinghe, Belgium.

EDWARD HAYNES always liked this place, a safe and private place. He was at ease here in his world of the great rolling parkland with its ancestral house and uninterrupted, magnificent views of the estuary and, of course, the horses. Like father, like son.

His father, Thomas, had passed away one-year back, consumption they said. He had been a burley fellow, with a ruddy smiling face, a mop of untidy ginger hair and of strong arms and stocky build. As head horseman he had a team of horses and men under him.

Sunday afternoon was Edward's time – once he had taken care of the horses. Up here in the loft, lying out amongst the sweet smell of apples and hay, he could dream of Lottie – Lottie, caring, understanding, gentle Lottie; once beyond his reach, now so near. He squeezed her hand, comforted, reassured.

After a week of rising at before six and working well into the evening, these Sunday afternoons were as often as not full of fretful sleep. He began to stir. It was a little chillier now he thought, the distant rumble of thunder from the Blackdown Hills across the Severn Estuary disturbing the horses in their stalls below, their restless metal shoes grating on the well-worn cobbles. He felt her hand in his again, much firmer now, as if urging him from his stupor.

The metal hob-nailed boots ground on the cobbles again. The heavy bolt was drawn back firmly and the wooden door swung open to let in a draft of cold morning air.

'Come on lad,' said the chaplain as he gripped Edward's hand even tighter. 'I'll be with you.'

Strong hands helped him off his make-shift bed of straw. They weren't unkindly people, they just wanted to get it over and done with, and then to forget. The rumble of yet another early morning artillery barrage was much clearer now, the methodical, regulated, unstoppable madness of hundreds of guns propelling 18-pound shells towards the enemy.

Edward managed to shuffle into his stride, fighting against the effects of the drink his mates had plied him with late the previous evening - his last evening - to ease him on his way. As Edward and his helpers went by, the horses shifted in their stalls again, the whites of their eyes registering their unease.

It had only been four days past that it all began, a night so dark and so quiet, when the Boche opened their lethal fire. Through the swirling grey-white smoke the enemy in their Prussian-blue uniforms appeared like a ghostly mass, growing larger and larger as the noise of battle grew harsher and harsher. It was dusk and so the British were at *stand-to*, but still, the attack was unexpected and the defenders unprepared for its ferocity. Forward trenches were engulfed and overrun; Edward's part of the line wavered, then buckled and broke. There were calls to retire from a multitude of unknown voices. New positions were hastily established further back in the support trenches, but then the retreating troops, pursued by the enemy and the hideous cries of the dying, became entangled in the relief battalions already coming up, their heads and shoulders crouched down, mindlessly pushing forward along the congested communication trenches. In the nightmare of confusion, Edward followed whatever orders appeared to have been given. The terrified screams and muffled cries of the dead and the dying, the crump of the 5.9 howitzer shells and the sharp crack of rifle fire competing with the mechanical cranking of machine guns, all conspired to confuse and terrify. As the acrid smoke gripped his throat, the earth, like an erupting volcano, trapped him against the trench wall. He desperately clawed his way free but when he tried to stand heavy boots trod on him, their owners cursing; men tripped over him; more cursing. Breathless, shaken, he scrabbled forward, slipping and sliding on the slimy duckboards, winding his way with others along the zig-zag of the communication trench and into the gloom.

As Edward approached the reserve trench, a whistle blasted the warning of the approaching *minenwerfer*. The explosion was devastating as it made a crater more than twenty-five feet wide. The ground shook, then seemed to tremble in the after-shock. For Edward, it was as if he had run headlong into an invisible wall. Terrified, virtually incapable of taking a breath, he crawled away on his stomach across the churned up, stinking earth only to become entangled in coils of rusting barbed wire, trapped as if caught in a hideous spider's web suspended from bent metal posts. He tried not to panic although by now he was involuntarily trembling with fear, but he was able to cautiously feel his way towards the top of another crater, only to roll forward into the glutinous black hole, star shells signalling his presence to the enemy snipers and their Maxim guns. He buried his head in his hands, driving his fingernails into his skin, trembling and sobbing, but he did not move, in fact he could not move, and so the exploding star shells and machine guns moved their attention slowly to Edward's left in search of more promising targets. How long he remained in this grim, shallow hole he did not know, but he lost track of time and when he stumbled forward he had also lost all sense of direction.

At daybreak, Edward woke. He found himself resting against a red brick wall on the outskirts of an abandoned village of collapsed roofs, shutters hanging loose and tumbled down walls, the smell of cordite and the trenches replaced by the stench of rotting corpses and smouldering homes. In the distance he could hear another early morning bombardment and, across the broken tiled-strewn and empty square, he saw the wounded mare on her side, the only movements a twitching hind leg and the swarms of greedy black flies. He levered himself up, aching, and shuffled slowly towards the stricken animal, her entrails brown upon the uprooted cobbles, teeth bared in pain, her wide eyes white with fear. Desperately he looked around for what he did not know. He spotted it, hanging on a broken down wagon across a grimy track, a flattened canvas water bucket. He snatched this up and from an old stone trough and a muddy crater, Edward was able to collect some brackish water, but when he returned to the horse she had mercifully died.

Hours passed. At about 11 o'clock a patrol of the Military Foot Police found Edward sat down between the horse's head and the forelegs, stroking her main. The charge was 'Desertion and Discarding his Weapon'.

The Assistant Provost Marshall mouthed out the offence and the sentence of the Field General Court-Martial: 'to suffer death by being shot'. Edward looked at the officer's face, a round face with a huge moustache and a mouth moving up and down, up and down. He barely recognised the words spoken and only noticed the officer's crooked front tooth. Edward gave a confused grin as he glanced about him in his stupor and saw that the six men of the firing party were already at their position along a line scratched by the sergeant in the dirt that lay on the grey concrete, the wooden post a matter of a few yards in front of them.

Chaplain David Patterson could hardly imagine the thoughts of the young soldier as they prepared him for his death. He hoped that Edward Haynes was preoccupied with thoughts of his love, his

Lotte, but he also wondered whether he had other thoughts, those thoughts that are darker than death. 'Think of Lotte, my son,' urged the chaplain, 'think of her. Just think of her all the while.' And Edward Haynes did – until the very end.

Those same powerful hands that had carried Edward from his happy thoughts and dreams, now pinioned him to the rough post. A rather rotund Medical Officer pinned a white card to his chest, close to his left breast pocket in which he kept his favourite photograph of Lottie. At 5.46am the white hood was pulled down over his head.

Another order was quickly given followed by a shattering volley. The nineteen-year old groom from Gloucestershire bucked backwards then slumped forward held by the ropes. Blood poured from Edward's mouth and a dark red stain spread over his shirt where the bullets had entered his chest, here in the village of Boesinghe, less than three miles from Ypres, names that Edward Haynes could neither pronounce nor spell, for reasons he would never comprehend.

Private Haynes, now suspended by the ropes, his knees just inches above the earth, convulsed, blood seeping through the weave of the hood as he coughed. A lieutenant hesitated, looked around and, responding to a nod from the Assistant Provost Marshall, marched quickly forward drawing his service revolver. He pressed the muzzle of his weapon to the soldier's head and leant backwards as if to distance himself from what he was about to do. He squeezed the trigger and there instantly followed the sound of the single shot like the crack of a rawhide whip. The starched white hood covering the soldier's head seemed to instantly change shape and colour like a red balloon slowly deflating. The Medical Officer strode forward. A perfunctory examination followed.

'Quite dead,' he said in a clipped but strained voice, and then nodded to the burial party.

And, as they dug behind the low wall of the abattoir, the distant artillery barrage increased its elevation for the *fourth lift*.

The war that had started with such patriotic fervour and high hopes would go on.

Chapter 1

Sunday, 4th March (more than 90 years later).

Bristol, England.

HE PRESSED both his clenched knuckles over his ears; he screwed up his eyes and grated his teeth together, but nothing could block out the recurring nightmare and the noise of blood dripping onto the wooden floor.

Throughout the previous day he had been completely preoccupied with the mechanics of the after-phase of the murder, shocked at the implications of what he had done but elated with the adrenalin rush of its achievement. But now, as the hours passed and the dark evening drew in around him, he drifted in and out of a restless sleep. He was surprised that the haunting noise of the dripping blood was so loud and so regular – a constant reminder of death. He struggled with a thousand thoughts, thoughts distorted by tiredness and the fear of discovery. He attempted to block out the repetitive noise but, if the sound did lessen his fearful thoughts increased.

Whether in his dreams or in his waking moments, he was drawn back to the evening just forty-eight hours before. He had assumed that one blow to the man's head would have been sufficient to kill him stone-dead, but the fool had started to turn around with an unsuspecting grin on his face. He wrestled with his thoughts again. He just couldn't understand why he had turned around. He had not startled him or been noisy, he reflected reasonably; there had been no reason at all for the fool to have turned, but at least his first blow had been sufficient to cause his victim to fall side-ways then down face-first, and so he didn't see his victim's marble-like eyes as he hit him again, then again, so as to be absolutely sure.

But now this blood-soaked, battered face kept grinning at him from every shadow of his bedroom or every time he closed his eyes to sleep.

In his late evening numbness, panic gripped him again as the sound of the dripping blood persisted and he reasoned that if the noise didn't stop, interfering neighbours would be alerted to his crime. His hands clawed at the duvet as he instinctively pulled the covers up and around his face, but the grotesque grinning images remained as he trembled at the thought of what he had done. – an act easy to conceive but difficult to perfect, an act that he knew could never now be undone.

The panic attacks returned. In the darkness of his bedroom and alone, with his woman away, his heart seemed to grow inside his chest, to pound as if determined to drown out the sound of the dripping blood. He tried to take deep breaths as his moods swung between panic and smugness. He tried to reassure himself that he had cleverly anticipated every eventuality and had covered his tracks. Yes, he thought as he drifted back into sleep, he had indeed been cunning and to confuse any police dogs he had back-tracked, crossing and re-crossing roads at the busiest points, deliberately walking past the distracting scents of the bars and restaurants of Princess Victoria Street. As planned, he had walked down into Goldney Avenue, taking a left into Goldney Road and left again up the steep Goldney Lane to complete the circle and got into his parked, dark blue estate car. When he had arrived home he was absolutely sure that no one had seen him and he had been able to make his way unnoticed from his garage, along under the vine-covered pergola, to his kitchen door.

He was a little calmer now as he comforted himself with the thought of the clever ploy of using a thin, plastic *Raincape* in its 3" x 2" pack, brought to the artist's house in the pocket of his black cashmere coat, then soaking it overnight in his forty-gallon rain butt so as to remove all traces of blood. He had deliberately ripped the shoulder joint of the *Raincape* then discarded it along with the cardboard tube at the rubbish tip early this very morning, the plastic casually thrown in with untraceable general household rubbish and the cardboard tube for re-cycling. He forced a contemptuous smile as he moved in his bed and thought of the city's largest rubbish tip, what the city council pretentiously called their 'premier refuge disposal facility'. But his weak smile began to fade as he thought of the approach road to that very facility at Avonmouth, past the sewage treatment works and its smell, a smell that reminded him of his own revulsion as the blood had splattered onto his face as he beat his victim's head again. As always at these grisly thoughts, the dripping sound seemed to grow louder and louder.

Now fully awake again, he desperately tried to remain positive, to think of his cleverness to cover all the angles. An anxious and weak smile acknowledged that the use of the cardboard tubes with their plastic end-caps had been a simple means of taking the weapon to the house and removing the blood-splattered *Raincape*. His smile became more relaxed as he thought of the cunning little touch he had shown in switching the painting on the artist's easel and then there was the entry to the house itself. The entrance to the victim's house by way of the front door had been so easy, and the breaking of the glass in the basement door from the outside should convince investigators of the means of entry, although the noisy teenage couple outside the front door had delayed his exit much longer than he had hoped. Always noisy, bloody irritating teenagers he thought. Nevertheless, he had made up time and had eventually been able to slink away along Royal York Crescent towards Sion Hill, like a cunning wolf in the night.

He liked that, the thought of being like a cunning wolf in the night, but these thoughts brought only temporary comfort as he became tormented again as he began to think more about the wolf. Wolves in the night, he remembered, always seem to be anxiously glancing behind, an activity necessary for their survival. His heart rate increased again as he thought of his survival and his future, a future now uncertain. He knew that from this moment onwards he would always be glancing behind.

He began to drift into an exhausted and confused sleep, a sleep disturbed by his neighbours rumbling another wheelie-bin noisily along the pavement ready for the Monday morning collection. He mistook the banging of the bins' lids as the police bursting through his front door. He sat bolt upright in his bed, startled, gripped by panic. His heart pounded and he was bathed in sweat. He looked around his bedroom, fear his only companion, and started to sob, not at the death of the artist, of course, but at his own lonely vulnerability. He sobbed, maybe for fifteen minutes, thinking back upon his comfortable life and what should have been, wondering how he had ever been drawn into the killing.

Then his mood changed again and he became resentful. He tossed the duvet cover off, angry at himself for his weakness and stumbled towards his bathroom and the tap dripping water into the sink.

Chapter 2

Monday, 5th March.

Police Headquarters, Bristol, England.

SUPERINTENDENT MARK Faraday closed the door of his apartment behind him, a comfortable but empty apartment without her. Dressed in shirt-sleeved order under a fawn, belted trench coat, he walked along the carpeted hall that gave him a panoramic view across the neat gardens of Avon View Court, the tips of the bulbs already seeking the sun's rays on this bright, but crisp, early morning. He avoided the lifts and descended the sweeping staircase of bright steel and polished wood to the entrance hall below.

'Good morning, Bill,' said Faraday to the fifty-six year old concierge.

'Good morning, sir,' he replied as he unnecessarily ran his cloth over to top of his desk for a third time. 'It's going to be a fine day by the looks of it.'

'It *will* be a good day, Bill,' he replied optimistically, standing in front of the light oak, curved desk. 'And how is Mrs Drake?'

'She up and about now, sir,' he replied, his strained face looking much older than his years. 'That lovely bunch of flowers you sent her last week really cheered her up, that they did.'

Faraday ignored the compliment, compliments he always found for some reason embarrassing, adding encouragingly: 'I think we've seen the last of the cold, Bill, let's hope that the Spring will allow Mrs Drake to get out little more.'

'We'll be fine, sir,' he said, resigning himself to the inevitable care that his crippled wife would always require. Faraday nodded an understanding nod, then turned towards both glass doors which opened at Bill's touch of the green button. But, for all the optimism of Faraday's replies, he was dreading another week at the headquarters of the Severnside Police.

As he drove his metallic quartz-grey Audi A5 coupe out into Julian Road, he knew that he had little to be disappointed about. Not yet thirty-five years old, he had already held superintendent rank for three years; he was fit and enjoyed excellent health other than some mild discomfort in this lower spine as the result of being thrown over the bonnet of a car in St. Pauls nine years earlier; he had achieved a master's degree against the odds; had been awarded an MBE; owned a country cottage and lived in a luxurious apartment with spectacular views over the River Avon which he was sometimes able to share with the beautiful and alluring Kay Yin.

His journey took him into Stoke Hill and along Shirehampton Road, skirting the golf course, to descend into the village of Shirehampton itself so as to join the M5 motorway at junction 18. The lightest touch on the accelerator pedal created a discerning purr-like growl from the V6 engine as Faraday increased speed along the four-lane, south-bound carriageway to junction 19. Here he turned off, then right onto the Portbury Hundred and travelled the final few miles to the modern headquarters of the force that provided policing services to the counties of Gloucestershire and Somerset, the cathedral cities of Bristol and Gloucester; the Georgian city of Bath and the Regency spa town of Cheltenham.

The Severnside Police covered an area over one hundred and twenty miles in length, dissected by the M4 and M5 motorways with their direct connections with London and Birmingham, and into the heart of Wales and towards Land's End in Cornwall. This whole area included five universities, Bristol International Airport, the Rolls-Royce aero-engine and Airbus factories at Filton, the international transit port at Avonmouth, four royal residencies and one of the UK's principal banking centres, all cosseted by the beauty of the Cotswold hills to the north and the Mendip hills to the south. Faraday knew very well that his force was one of the few that provided its officers will the fullest range of policing experiences. Yet, he struggled to generate enthusiasm as the head of Operational Planning.

Ops Planning occupied a large, open-plan office. It was oblong in shape, the right-hand wall of which was glazed and gave oblique views towards Clapton in Gordano and Prior's Wood beyond the M5 motorway. At the very far end of the office and to the right was Faraday's L-shaped desk; to the left, separated by their lockers, filing cabinets and the map cabinet with its rows of shallow drawers, the desk of Chief Inspector Geoff Fowler. Running down the length of the left-hand wall were desks for the two sergeants and two constables, together with their lockers and filing cabinets. In the middle of the office was what Faraday jokingly, but deliberately, referred to as 'King Arthur's Round Table', a large, circular planning table. Every morning at 09.30, Faraday's team moved their chairs from behind their desks and placed them around this planning table for 'Morning Prayers' – the daily fifteen-minute briefing, thirty-minutes on Mondays.

Faraday drove the coupe through the entrance gate, acknowledging the wave of the security guard, and parked in his bay. He knew perfectly well how lucky he was and he tried to view his appointment as developmental, providing him with a broader under-standing of policing, but he knew that this posting seven months before had been the spiteful response of Assistant Chief Constable Wynne-Thomas. He had said as much: 'you are a loose cannon, Faraday' and 'we consider that you need to be brought to heel and Ops Planning will serve to kerb your maverick tendencies'.

Mark knew that experience at headquarters would be beneficial, but he wasn't comfortable at all in an open-plan office which was always full of distractions and an agony for any dyslexic. He had always relied on utterly loyal secretaries in the past, but Ops Planning didn't qualify for one. The absence of a good secretary made his role increasingly difficult. He thought of one of his secretaries, the pretty and petite Jane Hart, her Audrey Hepburn eyes and their 'Breakfasts at Tiffany's', then his thoughts drifted to that incompetent clown, Inspector Gordon Trench. Trench had been transferred from Bristol Central to Ops Planning at the same time as Faraday and seemed to spend a disproportionate amount of his time reporting to Wynne-Thomas, the ACC Ops.

Mark Faraday walked into the headquarters' entrance foyer, smiling at the receptionists. They liked Faraday, not only because he was dark-haired and handsome with penetrating dark-brown eyes, but more because he always took time to talk to them and didn't treat them as 'just Scale 2 clerks' as they had once heard a senior officer describe them. Faraday walked past the potted shrubs, up the stairs under the magnificent portrait and ever-attentive gaze of Her Majesty, through sterile corridors to his office. He swiped his card at the door, there was a buzz and a click as he pushed open the door and entered the empty office. Immediately to his left were the two desks of the civilian clerks who also acted as gate keepers. To his right was a large Y-shaped desk for the three inspectors. He strode passed the round table to his desk and checked the clock. 07:40.

He switched on his desk computer, but as always, Faraday used the first twenty minutes of his day to check his desk diary, his personal *Bible* filled with mind-jogging notes and colour-coded highlights and tags. He checked his *Action This Day* tray and removed some files from a drop-drawer, examining the red *Action* slips on each. Satisfied, he glanced at one of the three faces of the ceiling-mounted, electronic display board hanging immediately above the round planning table, one segment listing the department's on-going projects, a second segment highlighting the day's commitments, the third displaying staff dispositions and contact details and the fourth the digital clock.

At a few minutes past eight, Chief Inspector Fowler entered the office. Aged forty-two, his hair was nevertheless a silver-grey, yet he had a young, clean-shaven face. He was dapper and had an energetic walk. They waved the index finger of their right hands in a rotating clock-wise direction, their usual greeting, their agreement that their approach was always to be positive and, if plans began to unravel or someone made a mistake, they would turn it around and move on. They got on well and made an excellent partnership.

The other members of Faraday's team were a mixed bag, the next of which to arrive were Inspector Hogkiss and Sergeant Purcell who usually travelled together from their homes in Kingswood. Forty-nine year old Ray Hogkiss, the oldest of the group with a Special Branch background, tended to oversee all royal visits – four already this year, another twenty-seven scheduled; whilst Peter Jean Purchell, whose mother was French and was usually referred to as 'PP', was working with Geoff Fowler on the planning for the Glastonbury Festival scheduled this year for the 22nd, 23rd and 24th June.

Inspector Silvia Glass and Sergeant Max Weber arrived at about 08.15, Miss Glass with a swagger and a hearty 'Good morning everyone'. There were nods of acknowledgment, but the thirty-two year old, who had a particular responsibility for the planning of the St Paul's Carnival, was not popular and her arrival with Max Weber was simply a coincidence. Weber spoke with Inspector Hogkiss then walked to his desk with a slight limp, a result of a recurring rugby injury.

Constables Blanchard and Haverlock entered the office about ten minutes later. Both were giggling as they smiled around the room. The stunning Phillipa Blanchard glanced towards the red-haired and stern Inspector Glass who made an unnecessary point of checking her wrist watch and glaring over her computer screen disapprovingly. Inspector Glass resented Pippa Blanchard who had studied full-time for her BSc at the UWE, whilst Silvia Glass had obtained her BA through the longer Open University route as a part-time student. Glass didn't care too much either for Steve Haverlock's laid-back approach to his duties. Born at Wagga Wagga in New South Wales, Haverlock had come to England with his parents fourteen years ago and they had stayed. Twenty-seven years of age, he had been a policeman for six years and was now working with Inspector Trench on the operational order for the Badminton Horse Trials to be held in just two months time between the 3rd and 6th May.

Gradually the tempo of the office increased as staff opened lockers and filing cabinets, pulled open drawers and began the daily round of phone calls, lights blinking on desks as lines became engaged. On time, exactly at 08.30, a bespectacled Inspector Gordon Trench arrived wearing his NATO jumper with peaked cap under his arm, followed by the two clerks. Trench clattered through the door with his briefcase which he bumped down onto his desk, then stood at the round table looking up at the electronic display board, with a fixed grin and hands on hips.

The 09.30 'Morning Prayers' was routine. There were no surprises, each member of staff presenting their up-dates for the forthcoming operations, together with brief resumes of their Monday and week's commitments.

'I was able to see the ACC on Friday,' said Faraday, who always presented last of all. Whilst Faraday had 'the buck stops here' responsibility for all the operations orders produced by his department, he had taken specific responsibility for the forthcoming Royal International Air Tattoo. 'There will be three one-day exercises before the RIAT at RAF Fairford on the 14th and 15th July, although during the proceeding week aircraft from all over the world will be coming in as well as practice displays by the *Red Arrows*, the US *Thunderbirds* and the Jordanian *Falcons*,' he said. 'And so, May, June and July are going to be pretty hectic for us all. We have all the operational orders from previous years, but these must only be seen as templates. Every year, from what I understand, there have been changes which, if not noticed, throw everything off-balance. Attention to detail is key. Anyone at all who has a concern, a reservation, about anything, then stick a note on the "worry board". Any questions?' Faraday glanced around his team in turn, all of whom shook their heads. 'OK, we're done. Thank you.'

They all rose from the round table and returned to their desk, but Faraday wasn't finished.

'Silvia, a moment if you would please,' he said gently.

Faraday walked back to his desk and sat down, waving Inspector Glass to a chair at the side of his desk.

He came straight to the point. 'You don't like the "worry board"?'

'I haven't said that, sir,' she replied crisply.

'You didn't have to. You might not have realised it, Silvia, but you pulled a face.'

'I'm sorry,' she said defensively, 'it wasn't intended.'

'I'm sure it wasn't, but you don't like the idea, do you?' he persisted.

She hesitated for a moment before replying petulantly. 'I think it's childish, that's all.'

'There's a *purpose* in it, Silvia, as you know. It is simply a mechanism which allows staff to jot down worries and nagging doubts they might have.'

'But they can tell me … well, us, if they have *worries*. That's what the chain of command is for.'

'They could, and, maybe, they always would, but it encourages them to think and it generates some healthy competition. We've already had some good ideas. Let's just run with it for another month and I will then be happy to review it.'

Faraday changed tack for what he hoped would be a less confrontational topic. 'Meanwhile,' he asked, 'how's everything going with the carnival?'

'There should be no problems at all,' she replied dismissively, then added unnecessarily, 'It's been running since 1967.'

''Yes, I know,' he replied, 'but it's attended by 60,000 people and, whilst it normally goes off without a hitch, you only require the arrival of racist yobs, a misunderstood or clumsy police officer or a knifing to convert a glittering and enjoyable festive pageant into a very unpleasant riot.'

'But it's not until the 7th July,' she replied, raising her voice an octave, 'Meetings with the Highways' people and others are not even scheduled yet.'

Faraday lent forward so as to emphasis the point he was trying to make. 'The local council will sort themselves out and, you are quite right, that can be dealt with later. What I'm keen to ensure at this early stage is the constructive liaison with the District Commander and, when necessary, the carnival organisers, so that they know that we're on-side and will do everything we can to ensure that *their* carnival is a success.'

'But surely that's a matter for the District Commander.'

'It is,' agreed Faraday, controlling his impatience. 'I certainly don't want to interfere with his well-established channels of communication, but I know that he will shortly be meeting with the chair of the carnival organisers and the residents association and so you should liaise with him and offer to attend meetings with him so you understand first hand the latest thinking, developments and issues.' Inspector Glass made no reply. 'Humour me, Silvia,' continued Faraday. 'Just give him a call and offer to attend any planning meetings he has scheduled...'

He was going to continue but a red light flickered on each phone on every desk. It was Line One. Trench's hand was like the strike of a rattle snake. He grabbed his phone then spoke ponderously before he called across to Faraday.

'It's for you, sir. Detective Chief Inspector Kay Yin.'

Chapter 3

Wednesday, 7th March.

Chelwood House, Bristol, England.

HE AWAITED her arrival with a glass of Glenfiddich, not the best single malt, he thought, but adequate enough. He took another sip, savouring slowly the smooth liquid as he looked out through the French windows of his study towards the old banqueting loggia in the distance amongst the trees, the final rays of the setting sun brushing the pink hues of Penpole stone.

He understood the reason for her enquiry of course, it was natural enough, although her visit was very likely to disturb his dinner. But, he reasoned, better to get it over with now and avoid the prospect of the police bumbling around the offices of Chelwood Kilbride.

When the bell sounded, Gribble, the butler, crossed the Stone Salon of Chelwood House, one of the lesser-know masterpieces of the great architect, Sir John Vanbrugh. He pulled open both of the glazed inner doors, then opened one of the outer doors under the great south-facing portico.

'Good evening, madam.'

'Good evening. I'm Detective Chief Inspector Yin. I have an appointment with Lord Chelwood.'

'You are expected, madam, If you would care to step this way and kindly follow me.'

Gribble closed the door and walked across the black and white marble salon floor, family portraits silently staring down upon them, although their echoing footsteps were impossible to silence. They passed underneath the fine stucco ceiling and the vast brass chandelier and entered the Wooden Hall.

'If I may take your coat, madam, I will inform his lordship of your arrival. If you would care to take a seat,' he said, pointing towards a comfortable chair near a very grand fireplace.

The butler took her black cashmere coat and disappeared along a long corridor beneath an arch to re-emerge, without the coat, to re-cross the Wooden Hall and to tap gently on a door to the right.

Kay Yin waited, seated by the fireplace, taking in her surroundings. True, this house was much smaller than Vanbrugh's Castle Howard or Blenheim Palace, but it was significant and certainly imposing, the hall giving a sense of spaciousness. Above the petite figure of Kay Yin were two galleried floors supported by four great rectangular columns and, leading off from these galleries were a series of rooms, every one of which gave views across the estate on all four sides of the building. The top floor contained the servants' quarters, access to which was gained by a discreet side staircase out of view, but access to the first floor was gained by way of a magnificent 'hanging' staircase, supported by three of the pillars as it wound around and upwards. This engineering arrangement, worthy of any bridge builder, gave the staircase the appearance of floating or hanging unsupported.

She heard a phone ring somewhere on the first, or was it the second floor, then voices. She looked up across to the right as two people, a tall woman in her late forties and a tall man, maybe in his mid-twenties, descending the staircase. The lady looked towards her and smiled warmly but with Caligula-like, penetrating eyes.

Her pink suit was elegant and expensive, her walk gracious. Kay Yin stood as Lady Chelwood extended her hand as if it could be touched, but not shaken.

'I'm Cecelia Chelwood,' she said as she assessed the quality of Kay's bright red single-breasted suit and pencil skirt, 'you must be the detective here to see my husband?'

'Yes ma'am. It was kind of your husband to see me at such short notice.'

'He's very busy, of course. In fact, off to a meeting of the UN's Economic Commission for Africa shortly, but he has a very keen sense of social duty, don't you know. But never mind, you will be something of a surprise for him. I think he was expecting a much older, male colleague,' she said, as if sharing a joke at an afternoon tea party. 'Allow me to introduce our son, Charles.'

Lord Charles Chelwood, confident and handsome, said nothing but took Kay's hand which he held a little longer than necessary. His eyes locked on to her fawn-like brown eyes as he seemed to survey every aspect of her wide mouth, exquisite teeth and almond-coloured neck.

'Well, I think that will do for the introductions,' said Lady Chelwood to her son, as if reprimanding and doting upon an irascible child at the same time. 'Come on, Chief Inspector, we can go straight through.'

They approached the room on the right, Charles Chelwood moving in front of his mother to tap upon, then open, the door to his father's study, a rather gloomy room, the walls of which were lined with books. The 7th Earl, banker and diplomat, was seated behind a large desk. He stood, slightly over-weight and shorter than his wife, and extended a hand.

'Ah, Chief Inspector, I'm Miles Chelwood,' he said charmingly shaking her small hand, clearly taken aback. He gestured towards an easy chair; she paused before sitting, waiting for Lady Chelwood to sit first in a chair opposite, a gesture not unnoticed by Cecelia Chelwood, whilst her son stood behind his mother. 'My PA tells me,' continued Lord Chelwood in a low, even voice, 'that you are investigating the murder of Nicholas Fry, the war artist?'

'That is absolutely so, sir. We are interviewing anyone who has had contact with the artist and your name was listed in a little book he kept.' She smiled and Lord Chelwood was already finding it difficult not to be captivated by her smile, at the same time uneasy at her deliberate reference to a little book. Kay Yin continued. 'It would be helpful if we knew why?'

'It's very straight forward really, Chief Inspector,' he replied, his voice almost monotone. 'A cousin, my grand-uncle's son, Lord Tatton Chelwood, was a VC, awarded posthumously after Passchendaele in 1917, and Nicholas Fry had been commissioned by the board of the bank to paint a picture of the whole business. Fry asked me if we had anything that might help his research. Well, of course we have. Come along, Chief Inspector, I'll give you the grand tour,' he said, then turning to this family asked: 'Are you two coming along?'

'Oh, no, Miles,' replied his wife. 'We'll stay put, I think, dear,' adding, 'Chief Inspector, please don't keep him too long, he will just go on and on until breakfast.'

'I'm sure that we won't be long, ma'am.'

Miles Chelwood ushered DCI Yin out into the Wooden Hall and up the staircase. At the top they turned left, along the landing, past one of the great pillars and through an archway. The door was marked 'Master Tatton's Bedroom'. Chelwood opened the door and switched on the four ceiling lights.

The room was bright, more like a military museum than a bedroom. All the original furniture had been removed except a glass bookcase, a large chest of drawers and a small wooden child's seat in which had been placed a fawn-coloured teddy bear. In the middle of the room were six glass display cases which took the visitor's eye to the far wall and a large painting of a young lieutenant in military uniform, the badges of his rank on each sleeve and cane under his left arm; Sam Browne belt polished as thoroughly as his brown leather riding boots, a slightly misshapen cap on his head. He had a black moustache and looked rather superior, or maybe amused, as if about to ride to hounds. Kay Yin wasn't sure whether she liked Master Tatton or not. She glanced around the room, Lord Chelwood remaining silent as the cross held her attention, awaiting her reaction. Against the wall where the bed would probably have been was a wooden crucifix, about four foot high. The wood was very old and the bottom of the cross had rotted, although clearly treated with preservatives. Carved, crudely, into the top part of the cross were the letters 'RIP' followed underneath by the words 'killed in action', each word following immediately below the other. On the arms of the cross was the carved inscription: 'Major Lord Tatton Chelwood DSO, MC' and, on the lower part of the cross, the figures '26.10.1917'. Kay moved a little closer to read the words in the glass frame under the Royal Coat of Arms:

He whom this scroll commemorates
was numbered amongst those who
at the call of King and Country, left all
that was dear to them, endured hardness,
faced danger; and finally passed out of
the sight of men by the path of duty
and self-sacrifice, giving up their own
lives that others might live in freedom.
Let those who come after see to it
that his name be not forgotten.

After a few moments, Lord Chelwood broke the silence. 'These crosses were grave markers, later replaced by the Portland Stone headstones, I think some as late as 1932 or maybe even later. Beastly business all round. As you can see,' he said, pointing towards the painting, 'he was a handsome, fine fellow. Anyway,' he said as if to steer the conversation towards a more positive aspect, 'over here are his medals.'

Kay Yin turned towards the island of display cases and peered at the row of medals in the first case, five medals in total, the one on the extreme left, a Maltese cross in bronze with the royal crest and the simple inscription 'For Valour', suspended by a crimson ribbon.

'This must be the Victoria Cross. I've never seen one before, sir. I thought that they were all locked away or in museums.'

'Then your visit has had an added bonus, my dear. Not all VCs are locked away, of course, and we have a first-class alarm system here too. Not made of gold or silver, of course, just of bronze taken from a Russian cannon captured at Sebastopol during the Crimean War.' He pointed to the next two medals, his voice more relaxed. 'The next one along is the Distinguished Service Order and then the Military Cross. He won his MC at Loos in the

September of 1915 and the DSO on the Somme in the July of the following year.'

Chelwood shuffled along the display cases pointing to the illuminated scrolls and identifying his distant cousin in photographs as a pupil at Wellington College, then as a student at Pembroke College, Cambridge. He casually pointed to other photographs of his relation, one during officer training at Sandhurst; another in a dug-out at Pozieres with other officers, all in mufflers and smoking their pipes; and a further photograph of a group of officers standing on the bank of the Yser Canal.

DCI Yin looked down upon the last display case at a variety of memorabilia ranging from a 1914 brass tobacco tin courtesy of the Princess Mary Christmas Fund; a pale purple Army Form 45 'Proceedings of a Medical Board' dated the 25th June, 1917, endorsed 'Fit for General Service' and some pencilled maps of trenches scribbled on torn pieces of note pad paper. But she noticed that in two of the cases there were some bare spaces and she asked: 'It appears that some items are missing, sir?'

'Yes, they are. Not stolen, of course, but I did lend a number of things to Fry.' He pointed to the empty spaces. 'Tatton's diaries, all four of 'em, and a couple of photographs. In fact, Fry came in here, tape recorder at the ready, cameras dangling around his neck – you know what these artists are like. You see, he wanted to know all the details, then he submitted some pencilled sketches to me and a Colonel Vaughan. The three of us had a meeting at the bank and we agreed which sketch best represented what Tatton had done to get the VC.'

'I'm sure I can look it up, sir, but could you tell me the circumstances?'

'Basically, he was leading his men over the top, but progress forward was held up by an enemy machine-gun and they were pinned down in No Man's Land, stuck in a series of water-filled shell craters. He called for two volunteers and they rushed the machine-gun, killing all three of the gunners. As a result they were able to advance again and reached their objective.' The 7th Earl was in his stride now, re-telling a story often told. 'The next day, he did the same bloody thing all over again, this time single-handed. He shot two of the German gunners dead with his revolver, wounded another and captured the gun, but in the process he had been wounded twice in the stomach. As the line of advancing troop swayed back and forth, he was left behind. Eventually the British were pushed back and he was left wounded out in No Man's Land. By all accounts, he was picked up by a stretcher party at nightfall and taken to a regimental aid post, then down to an advanced dressing station, but he died of his wounds the following day.'

DCI Yin had made a mental note of what she had seen and made a show of checking her wrist watch. 'Thank you, Lord Chelwood. You've given me enough of your time, sir. It was kind of you to take the trouble to show me around. Thank you.'

'It was a pleasure, Chief Inspector.'

They walked out of the room and along the landing to the top of the stairs. 'Other than the meeting with Colonel Vaughan, the only other time that you have met Mr Fry was during his one visit here?' she asked.

'Oh, yes, that's correct. Fry seemed to have everything he needed.' As they descended the stairs, the detective asked another question.

'Have you ever phoned him or contacted him in any other way?'

'No, although, I think he rang me on one occasion,' he replied, unsure of the direction of the question. 'I'm sure it was only once, rang me here asking me if I knew what service revolver Tatton had used. Wanted to get the detail right, I suppose, but I didn't have a clue. I assumed it would have been a standard issue Webley.' He stopped and chuckled and said, 'I think Fry was hoping that Tatton could have been depicted running about with a Mauser in his hand like Winston Churchill.'

'Oh, I see,' she said as they reached the bottom of the staircase. 'Thank you, sir. I don't think there's anything else.'

They returned to the study. Lady Chelwood was seated as Kay Yin had left her, although the son was now also seated.

'Miss Yin had only a few questions for me, my dear. I'm afraid I probably bored her with the family history.'

'Your husband certainly didn't bore me at all, Lady Chelwood. I'm grateful for your time. You must be very proud of your family.'

Lady Chelwood smiled in response to the compliment. For a fleeting second her eyes rested on her son. 'We are very proud, Chief Inspector.' Pride projected towards her only son, thought Kay Yin, or was it a protective gesture of a mother. Lady Chelwood spoke again, interrupting her thoughts. 'I hope you get your man, as they say, Chief Inspector,' she said charmingly, although her tone changed to one of mild impatience as she spoke to her son. 'Charles, see where Gribble is for the Chief Inspector's coat.'

They walked into the Wooden Hall through to the Stone Salon, followed by the butler and the son carrying her coat. Gribble went to the front door as Lord Charles Chelwood helped Kay with her coat. In so doing, the young man unashamedly caressed her shoulders. She felt as if she should shudder in anger but, she simply turned, her black coat draped over her delicate shoulders to shake hands with all three members of the family. Kay Yin thanked Gribble who had opened the door and she walked down the steps into the cold night air. She unlocked and stepped into her red Golf GTi, the butler silhouetted in the doorway behind her as she drove away along the tree-lined drive towards the gate house, across the road, to pull into the kerb alongside the old stables.

DCI Yin switched on the internal reading light and began to scribble a series of bullet-point notes in her little book. But she was distracted. She leaned back in the driver's seat and kept repeating to herself the same question. 'Why did Lady Chelwood and her son consider it necessary to wait in the study?'

Chapter 4

Friday, 9th March.

Bristol, England.

KAY YIN arrived at Mark Faraday's apartment at about 9.20pm, the first time that they had seen each other for more than three days. Since Monday she had been working more than fourteen hours a day, beginning at 7am and never finishing before 9pm, leading her team of fifty-three detectives, uniformed and civilian staff. As usual, the intensity and tempo of the murder enquiry was high and she felt exhausted.

Mark and Kay didn't eat, other than toast and decaffeinated coffee; they talked over fussy things of no consequence, then she showered, the bathroom filled with the scent of sandalwood and jasmine. When she emerged from the bathroom, she looked tired but utterly divine. Kay Yin's short, raven-black hair glistened in the hallway lights and her almond-coloured skin seemed to glow. She walked cat-like, confident in her surroundings yet vulnerable, her petite 5' 3" form accentuated by her loose-fitting, pure white *theong sam*.

'Let me tuck you in,' he said as he reached for her tiny hand.

Kay paused as she held his hand as tightly as he held hers. She looked up at him with her wide, brown fawn-like eyes. 'I'm so tired, Mark. I've been getting up at quarter to five and never into bed before twelve. The first night was OK, but I haven't slept properly for the last two nights.'

'Don't drive yourself too hard,' he said gently.

'I can't fail, Mark,' she said wearily.

'You won't fail.'

'I sometimes wonder whether I shall be up to it, Mark. You have such high expectations of me.'

'I don't have high expectations of you,' he replied lightly. 'In fact, I don't think about it too much, but you *are* good, Kay. Don't loose faith in yourself, I haven't.'

For a moment she seemed so fragile. 'I'm just afraid I'm going to fail, fail you, fail my father.'

'You'll never fail me, Kay, but we all stumble and your team will know that. Some will gloat, most won't, and if they know that you have the job and their interests at heart and not your own; if they know that you are decent and honest, you won't go far wrong.'

He had already dimmed her bed-side light and pulled down the duvet on her side. 'Come on,' he said, walking her towards their bedroom. They approached the queen-sized bed that seemed to envelope her as she let the *theong sam* slip from her naked shoulders and climbed into the bed and under the duvet.

'Just lie with me,' she said quietly, knowing that despite his powerful build, rugged good looks and infectious smile, her simple request would not be denied.

Mark turned off the light, knelt down at the side of the bed and kissed her gently on her exquisite mouth, then walked around the bed and lay beside her outside the covers, head propped up against the Chinese quilting of the headboard. He stayed there, happy to look at her perfect oriental profile, desperate to kiss her again, but wanting her to sleep.

'Thank you,' she said softly and within moments was asleep.

After about half an hour, and so as not to disturb her sleep, Mark quietly left the bedroom. He did not change out of his shirt and jeans but settled to sleep in the *Norton* recliner in the lounge, facing towards the French windows that gave views from the balcony towards the River Avon and Horseshoe Bend below.

***

At a little after three-thirty, Mark awoke, disturbed by Kay in the kitchen. 'Alright?' he asked as he stood in the doorway.

'Oh, Mark, I'm so sorry. I went off to sleep but I think it was too deep, I can't get back off at all now.'

'Do you want to talk,' he said, 'I could do with a cup?'

'Do you mind if I talk about the job?' she asked as she filled the *Krups* coffee machine.

'Of course not,' he replied, gathering some mugs from the cupboard. 'How is it going?'

They sat in the three-seat settee, Kay curled up besides him, both looking out at the early morning, sunrise just a few hours away. Kay described the actions of the 'First Officer Attending', what he had noticed, what he had done when he entered the victim's home, the access control with a *common approach path* and the scene protection he had capably established, and the careful notes he had made. She described the victim, Nicholas Fry, a tall man, apparently humorous with a ready smile, and absolutely committed to his work as a war artist. Forty-six years of age, he was a perfectionist who researched thoroughly every aspect of his commissions, the result being that he had established a remarkable reputation with the military. Some of his commissions commemorated past heroes and distinguished soldiers, others proud regiments recently disbanded or amalgamated. More recently, his commissions had vividly illustrated the actions of individuals or units in the Gulf wars, Kosovo, Bosnia, Sierra Leone and Afghanistan, all areas of conflict visited by the artist himself to such an extent that on a number of occasions he had himself come under fire, his only weapons a camera, pencil and sketchpad.

'Who reported the death?'

'A Geoffrey Rees, a retired airline pilot. They always met up on Saturday mornings at ten for coffee in the Avon Gorge Hotel. By eleven-thirty, he became concerned and called the police.'

'Checked out I suppose?'

'Yes. He's nearly eighty years of age with an impeccable RAF and civil airline record. He can throw no light on why the artist should have been murdered.'

'Last seen alive?'

'At about four-thirty on the Thursday at the local newsagents.'

'Is he married?'

'He was. Divorced about five years ago. No children, his next of kin is a sister living in Kent.'

'His ex-wife?'

'Karen lives in Bath with a boyfriend, Robert Ballantine. He's a few years younger than Karen, plenty of money, a property developer apparently, but with a conviction for theft of a few lorry loads of building materials about ten years ago. She has been interviewed as has Mr Ballantine, but still checking into both.'

'And the house?'

Kay Yin described Nicholas Fry's home in Royal York Crescent. 'It's large, five floors, three bathrooms, two toilets, three kitchens: sixteen rooms, altogether.'

'Split into apartments?' asked Faraday, visualising the crescent as he stared out into the early dawn.

'It had been at some stage, last tenants three years ago, but he now occupied the house alone.'

'Alone? Girlfriend, Boyfriend?'

'There is a woman, from one of the Clifton art galleries, they see each other about once a week. Elsa Chaudouet from St Egreve, France, but has lived in Clifton for about seven years.' She continued, anticipating his question. 'Their relationship seems to be more around mutual artistic interests than lovers, but she has been interviewed and a team is checking out her background and associates.'

'Was it a burglary?'

'It was in the sense that his attacker seems to have broken into the house, some sort of search was made and a few things seem to be missing.'

'How did the attacker get in?'

'There's a basement floor that leads out onto York Gardens. Someone had attempted to jemmy the basement door without success. A small pane of glass in the door was broken. That seems to be the entry point.'

'You said that things were missing?'

'Nicholas Fry carried a little black note book around with him all of the time. We have that, but not his diary, a *Filofax*-type, although we have four diaries lent to him by Lord Chelwood. On the second floor is clearly the suite of rooms occupied by Fry. The bedroom, bathroom, sitting room and kitchen on this floor are quite different from the remainder of the house. They are neat and tidy. On the forth floor is a study, also neat and tidy. However, all of these private rooms seemed to have been searched, drawers and cupboard doors pulled open. But, it's difficult to know if anything has been stolen.'

Sensing her theme, he asked: 'The rest of the house, the other rooms?'

'It's storage in the two rooms in the basement and the three small rooms on the top floor. On the ground floor is a sitting room filled with books, another room with books, unused canvases and boxes and a small kitchen at the rear. On the first floor at the front is his studio with a smaller room that has a computer and desk, with a toilet and shower room at the back. All the other rooms, corridors, stairways, even the other bathrooms, are crammed with paintings and canvases; boxes covered in dust and shelves upon shelves of books about one regiment or another; about jungles and deserts, trees and plants; mules and horses, weapons and armoured cars; uniforms and cap badges. In every room the floors are literally covered with hand written notes, little sketches and big sketches. Every surface is cluttered with tubes of paints, dozens of brushes and tea cups. It's a scenes of crime nightmare.'

'Locard wouldn't say so,' he said positively, referring to the French forensic pioneer Doctor Edmund Locard's dictum that 'every contact leaves a trace'.

'Yes, you're right, his attacker would have left some trace of his presence and taken away traces too, unique traces, but it's a large house and this will mean that there will be a considerable time delay before we get any forensic results.'

'Is it a mess?' he probed.

'Oh no. You quickly realised that the victim knew precisely where everything was, all the notes appear related to sketches, the sketches to reference books, but there must be literally thousands of pieces of paper on the floor, on shelves, stuffed in books and on tables. I've put DC Pau on to it – typically Chinese,' she said with a smile, 'he loves these sort of puzzles.' For the first time that morning she had smiled. Mark sensed this and turned to look at her, her smile that would brighten any day. It was good to talk, they both thought as they leaned into each other. 'I've been impressed with Samuel Pau,' she continued, 'he has been very forceful. Photographs have been taken and everything left in situ as he painstakingly examined and studied each piece of paper and each sketch.'

'In one sense that's good news,' said Faraday, always turning every hurdle into a positive. 'There will be a delay, and the examination of the scene can't be rushed. It can't be helped so at least it gives your action teams the opportunities to explore other avenues.'

'And there's a lot of those,' she said more positively. 'Fry had six commissions listed in his black book, all in various stages of completion.'

'And they were?' he asked as he looked again out through the French windows towards the light of the approaching dawn.

'There was one, nearly completed, of the Queen presenting new colours to a regiment. It was on one of his easels. It was remarkable how he was able to capture the different textures of the uniforms, the boots, leather gloves, the swords, that sort of thing. I have a DI in Edinburgh now with the 2nd Division following that up. There is another one of an Army Air Corp pilot winning the DFC in Afghanistan. A DS is in Colchester chasing that one up. Then there are two commissions regarding operations in Iraq, one was about a soldier in the desert rescuing a colleague from a light tank, a *Sabre*, I think it was called, used for reconnaissance work, and another about a medic. I have one of the DSs going down to Wilton for that. Another commission is a little tricky, all about some sort of top-secret incident, *Operation Iliad*. I'm up to Hereford this evening, staying over. The remaining work is a canvas portraying the heroics of a major in the First World War winning a VC.'

'Who are your contacts?'

'I've contacted the military units myself and this is what has been taking up a lot of my time, partly because all these guys are moving about all the time. In any case, you know the military, we won't get very far if a constable calls a colonel. But I've spoken to the colonels or lieutenant-colonels and, I have to say, they have been very helpful. It seems that the commissioning of any painting will always go through the man at the top, then it is left to a major or captain and the sergeant-major to liaise with the artist to arrange interviews, visits, technical details and schedules.'

'And you are going to Hereford?' without a hint of criticism.

'This *Operation Iliad* involved the SAS and is still classified. I've got a feeling that it involved an incursion into Syria. Whatever, it's classified, but they say that they will give me as much information as they can.'

'What about the VC?'

'That one is quite different. The painting has been commissioned by the bankers, Chelwood Kilbride, for their new offices at Temple Back East.'

'Why now after all these years?'

'A Major Lord Chelwood won the VC and they thought a painting would look impressive in their new boardroom.'

'And it was the Chelwoods you visited the other evening?'

'Yes, it seemed straight-forward enough.'

'I sense a "but" there?'

'I'm uncomfortable with the Chelwoods.'

'Why?'

Kay Yin described her visit to Chelwood House, the 7th Earl, Lady Cecelia and their son, Lord Charles Chelwood. She spoke of Lord Tatton Chelwood's bedroom and the displays of family memorabilia. 'What's bugging me is why Lady Chelwood and their son made an appearance.'

'Go on,' he encouraged.

'They just didn't contribute anything of importance. Maybe they were simply intrigued about the death of Nicholas Fry, but when I returned to the study, they were just seated there. They were just waiting. But waiting for what? Maybe they were waiting to go in for dinner, but surely they would have occupied their time with a pre-dinner drink. But they had no drinks, they weren't reading a book or a daily paper or a magazine. They seemed to be just waiting.'

'Waiting for what?'

'Waiting to see the outcome of my time with the 7th Earl, I assume, but why?'

'Are the Chelwoods your only contact?' Mark speculated.

'No, one of the team has liaised with the regimental museum's curator and we are ploughing through the victim's telephone records and his computer. He seemed to conduct most of his business over the phone or by e-mail.'

'Do you have any other worries?'

'Yes, lots,' she said, leaning over and squeezing this leg. 'We have to wait the PM report, but, I can't get out of my mind the ferocity of the attack.'

'The injuries were horrible?'

'Yes, but what's really on my mind is why was it necessary to hit Nicholas Fry so many times in the head.'

'You say he's not a slight man, maybe he challenged the burglar?' he suggested.

'He was a well-built man, but his wife says he wouldn't say boo to a goose.'

'Time of death?' asked Faraday, his mind attempting to discover the course of events.
'The heating was on and so, taking that into account, between 7 and 9pm, probably nearer nine.'

He tried to visualise Royal York Crescent at that time of the evening, made a mental note of the time and moved on. 'Any help from CCTV?'

'Nothing as yet.'

'Other burglaries in the area?'

'Yes, there appeared to be an attempt to jemmy a basement door of another house in Royal York Crescent and there was a report of a man lurking about in Oxford Place the previous evening where some residents of the Crescent park their cars. Awaiting forensics on the jemmied door, but nothing useful forthcoming from Oxford Place.'

'Dogs?'

'That was much more promising.' Kay uncurled her slender legs and walked into the study, her dainty feet hardly leaving a footprint in the plush pile carpet. She returned with an 'A to Z' map of the city, knelt down beside Mark and turned to page 66. 'Our dog handler was able to track from Fry's hallway out through the front door in Royal York Crescent to Sion Hill, along Princess Victoria Street,' she said, her beautiful finger tracing a course on the map, 'right into Regent Street, another right into Goldney Avenue, then left into Goldney Road and then another left into Goldney Avenue again.'

'Around in a circle, so he could have parked a car anywhere in that Goldney area.'

'I've got a team checking the owners of cars that normally park there; it should be mostly residents and their visitors. They might have noticed a strange car. But why did our suspect walk along Princess Victoria Street?'

'My guess would be that the attacker hoped to put off any police dog by walking past the pubs and restaurants which would have multiple pedestrian use and distracting smells.'

'You're guessing again?'

'Maybe. But what do we have? We might know *what* happened, but not absolutely sure. We might know *how* it happened, but also not completely sure. We don't know at this stage *why* it happened and we haven't a clue *who* did it.'

'It's going to be a long grind.'

'I'm sure it will be, but you're complying with the *ACPO Murder Investigation Manual* and all the appropriate avenues are being followed. Keep to the fundamentals and, as usual, trust no one and suspect everyone.' Kay raised an eyebrow, encouraging him to continue, knowing that he wanted to say more. Faraday continued with a series of rhetorical questions. 'There's the ex-wife, is she happy? Her boyfriend might appear to be well-off, but is his? Then there's Fry's girlfriend, what was her name?' he asked.

'Elsa Chaudouet.'

'Yes, Elsa. Statistically, many more men murder their lovers than the other way around. Nevertheless, what is her status and circumstances? Then there's Fry himself. His home must be worth two million. How has he managed to afford that sort of property? If nothing else, he is an attractive target for a thief or blackmailer. Then there's the top secret mission and the amorous Lord Charles Chelwood.'

'I don't think you like him, Mr Faraday,' she said seductively and provocatively.

For a moment, Mark Faraday remained silent. He wondered how Lord Chelwood viewed Kay. Did he see her as beautiful and alluring woman, but a professional officer, or just an easy lay. For another moment he felt anger, but dismissed the thought. 'Follow the evidence, but also trust your instincts.'

'Instincts?'

'Instincts aren't acceptable to the courts but they are to any enquiry. Already you are unhappy about the severity of the attack. I would be too. You have some unease about Ballantine and you are also uncomfortable with the Chelwoods.'

'And?'

'Pursue your instincts.'

'That will put the cat amongst the pigeons. The ACC won't like me interviewing prominent businessmen and members of the House of Lords.'

'That may be so, but Ballantine was a thief. It wasn't a spontaneous theft, it was no doubt calculated. He had to think about it, and I bet thoughts of a short-cut here and the quick buck there, still linger in his mind even now that he is a *respectable* property developer.' He thought for a few more moments. Kay didn't interrupt his thoughts as he looked out towards the sun rise and she looked up at him. 'Was this burglary spontaneous?' he asked rhetorically. 'I don't think so. The killer took with him a jemmy, he then took a complicated, well thought-out route back to a vehicle – well, we think he did. It's also interesting', he added, 'that the Chelwood's commission is the most recent. The other commissions were placed, what, between five months and twenty-two months ago. Yet, only six weeks after the most recent, that is after the Chelwood's commission was placed, the artist is murdered.' He looked down at her, seated at the side of the settee, and kissed her on the forehead. 'There are a lot of avenues worth pursuing.'

***

They made their separate ways to their work, Detective Chief Inspector Kay Yin to the District HQ at The Grove and Superintendent Mark Faraday to Force HQ and Ops Planning.

Faraday arrived at 8.35am, much later than usual, his arrival greeted by a barely disguised glance of disapproval from Inspector

Silvia Glass. Inspector Trench had a mischievous smirk on his face, which immediately vanished as he asked: 'Is everything alright, sir?'

'Yes, thank you Gordon,' he replied as he quickly tried to settle into his routine. He looked around the office, his eyes resting upon Constable Phillipa Blanchard. He had read her personnel file and now made up his mind.

'Morning Prayers' were at 09.30 as usual and followed their normal pattern at the round planning table. Faraday diaried-in specific appointments for his staff, the first of which was with Inspector Trench.

Gordon Trench followed Faraday to his desk where the inspector outlined the draft operation order for the Badminton Horse Trial, an international event attracting over one hundred and fifty entries. Both officers checked the schedule, the horse inspections taking place on the 2nd July, followed by two days of dressage, the cross-country stage on the Saturday and the jumping and presentations on the Sunday. But when Faraday quizzed Trench on timings, he was less certain.

'You will need to check when the estate is actually open to the public on a daily basis, Gordon.'

'But the cross-country starts at eleven and finishes up at four-thirty. So I've tagged on an hour each end.'

'Yes, that day's events start at 11am, but, if I recall, the cross-country opens early at seven. Likewise,' he continued, scribbling a note on the draft plan, 'the jumping on the Sunday starts at nine, but is open from 8am. Just "tagging on" an hour each end is not precise enough at all, Gordon. It's all about accommodating the thousands of visitors, particularly on the Saturday. The cross-country attracts literally herds of people wandering around and gathering at the thirty-odd jumps on the course. We need to be prepared.'

'But, sir, the organisers have this all in-hand.'

'And we have to have it in-hand, too, Gordon. Some of these organisers have been doing this since they were kids. Many of them are ex-military and are very well versed in what to do but, if they decide that the route of the course is to be changed this year we must ensure that this links in with our arrangements for escorting the royals. If the organisers decide to relocate the helicopter landing area or the field hospital, we may have to alter our external arrangements.'

'But I'm not a medic, sir.'

'Nor am I, Gordon, but that's what liaison is all about.' Faraday scribbled another note, partly to ensure that his annoyance didn't degenerate into anger. Neither Glass nor Trench, reflected Faraday, seemed to be able to grasp any of the important implications of the planning necessary for these sort of events. He and Chief Inspector Fowler had tried to coach them both, but he knew that he would have to let them go, albeit that Silvia Glass had been ill. When that moment came, Glass would play an equality card as she had done many times before and Trench would be protected again by Wynne-Thomas. Any attempt to move either would be dysfunctional and unpleasant, but they would both have to go. He finished his note making and asked: 'When are you making your next visit?'

'Next Wednesday.'

'Morning or afternoon?'

'09.30.'

'Excellent. I'm at Fairford on Wednesday for one o'clock. If you make your own way and I will link up with you at the Memorial Hall at Badminton at 09.15.'

'Right, sir, if you think that best.'

Faraday ignored the sourness in his voice. 'It will give me an opportunity to get some exercise,' he said, adding in a lighter note, 'and don't forget your boots, Gordon, and clear our visit with the estate steward.'

Trench returned to his desk and resumed his seat in peevish silence, with furtive looks to see if his lame performance had been noted by others. If it had not been noted by others, it had been noted by Faraday who scribbled in his diary in green ink. As Chief Inspector Fowler approached his desk, Faraday looked up at the ceiling-mounted display, smiled an acknowledgment to Fowler's perfect time-keeping. He said nothing to his deputy, simply selecting two files from his desk, one his Fairford file, the other a file from HQ Personnel and walked with Fowler towards the door. As he passed the desk of the two constables he spoke to Constable Phillipa Blanchard.

'If you have a few moments, Pippa?'

'Do I need anything, sir?'

'Just your Fairford file, a note pad and pen.'

Faraday opened the door for the PC and let her walk through. Trench's eyes followed them out through the door. He stood up and wandered over to the two clerks, a manoeuvre which allowed him to see Faraday, Fowler and Blanchard descend the staircase. Trench watched the dark-haired, trim Miss Blanchard in her tight-fitting uniform trousers and equally body-hugging white service blouse. He leaned sideways as his eyes traced the trio's movements, but more particularly to leer at the young policewomen's rear. He had noted, as did most men, Pippa's ice-blue eyes, eyes that were not in any way cold but sparkled with a remarkable intensity, a young woman who looked so similar to the model in the *Allure* perfume advertisement. When they were out of sight he returned to his desk. As he did so he exchanged conspiratorial glances with Inspector Glass.

In the staff restaurant, Mark Faraday, Geoff Fowler and Pippa Blanchard drank coffee.

'You seem to have plenty of work to do, Pippa?'

'Plenty to do, sir, but I prefer it that way.'

'And you always hold your own during "Morning Prayers". Well done.' He picked up and opened the buff-coloured Royal International Air Tattoo file. 'You've done a nice job with the file, Pippa.'

'There's still quite a lot to do, sir. I didn't realise how big the air show was until I started the research.'

'And what's our one biggest worry do you think?'

'I think there are two worries, sir,' she said hesitantly.

'Go on.'

'There are thousands of visitors, with more than three-hundred static or flying aircraft on show. This makes it a very attractive terrorist target. And, secondly, there's always the potential for an accident. I understand that one year, some Russian aircraft came in and were virtually un-airworthy and with the air displays, there's always the possibility of a mid-air crash.'

'Do you think that's likely?' Faraday deliberately probed.
'Yes, sir.'

'Why?'

'Two Russian *MiGs* collided in 1993 and, a few years ago, there was a mid-air crash involving the Jordanian *Falcons* in France,' she frowned as she searched her memory, 'or it might have been Belgium, but it was just before our air show.'

'I'm going up to RAF Fairford on the 14th. You're my bagman on this one so you had better come up with me. I've a meeting there at one, but I'm meeting up with Inspector Trench in the morning at Badminton and so we had better leave here at 08.15.'

She beamed, pleased to be included, her blue eyes sparkling with enthusiasm. Faraday made a note in the file before closing it. He pulled out and opened her HQ Personnel file, fingering a number of pages.

'You are twenty-five,' he read. 'You initially attended a secretarial college but later gained an honours degree in psychology from the UWE, although after uni you were employed as a secretary. Is that right?'

'Yes, sir, for about eighteen months.'

'Shorthand?'

'Ninety words per minute, sir.'

'OK,' he said impressed but hesitating, considering how much he needed to divulge to her. 'I need some help, Pippa, and I think you are the person to help me. As you know the department doesn't rate a secretary, but I am finding it increasingly difficult without one. I know that you're busy, but I would like you to help me from time to time, well, probably every day, with some secretarial duties, making sure that I am on top of my diary and commitments, helping me at meetings, that sort of thing. Would that be a problem for you?'

'No, sir.'

'A good starting point, and a suitable smoke-screen, would be for you to take minutes of our "Morning Prayers", just bullet-points with actions.'

'That's fine, sir.'

'Good. Have you a boyfriend?'

'Sir!' she said, surprised at the question.

'Don't get all pc with me, Pippa,' said Faraday, his slight frustration showing. 'It's simply that your work load will increase. I may wish you to accompany me to some meetings, that sort of thing. If you have a boyfriend, I don't want to disrupt your private and social life unnecessarily.'

'There's no one at the moment, sir,' she replied, although there was a tinge of sadness in her voice, an expression that had not gone unnoticed by Faraday.

'OK. Let's begin tomorrow. I will explain to everyone tomorrow that you will be the note-taker and, as soon as the meeting finishes, report to my desk and I can brief you on what I will require. The deal is that you tell me if I'm overburdening you. OK?'

'Absolutely, sir.'

'But,' he said, considering his next comment before continuing. 'There is no need for anyone to know that your duties may be more than simply note-taking.'

Pippa Blanchard fixed Faraday with her sparkling blue eyes, eyes so similar to those of Anna, Anna Manin in Venice. 'I understand, sir.'

As the trio returned to Ops Planning, Mark Faraday wondered whether she did.

Chapter 5

Saturday, 10th March.

Bristol, England.

HIS SONS left the little private room that they had been able to secure for him in the hospital. As they walked through the main hospital ward, they didn't speak, they were too shocked for that but averted their eyes from the stares of the other visitors gathered around the neat rows of beds. Curtains were drawn around some of the cancer patients' beds whilst other patients were surrounded by flowers and hopeful-looking friends, either sat there holding the patient's hand or busying themselves with meaningless little tasks.

There seemed to be constant movement in the ward, with nurses bustling about in their smart uniforms, the colours of which denoted their grades. Some pushed wheelchairs or studied charts, others walking with concerned relatives or huddled around their work station. Visiting children seemed to be either noisy or bored, this providing some of their elders with an opportunity to slip away. William Harding's two sons slipped away.

Bill Harding wasn't in pain and wasn't really too sad. He had suspected for some time that he was in trouble and the exploratory operation the previous day had confirmed how advanced the cancer was. Death was close, he knew that, but death had always been close. Bristol born and bred, his mother had died when he was young and his father had cleared off to Manchester with the neighbour's elder daughter, leaving young Bill to be raised by his grandmother, but she soon died. His schooling could only be described as rudimentary and ever since he had lived on the margins, virtually the whole of his fifty-four years of life being occupied with scams, cons, wheezes and rip-offs. He had seven convictions, mostly for theft, and had spent a total of four years and ten months in prison. Although never a major player, he had always been on the periphery. The main players tolerated him. When Bill over-stepped the mark and showed disrespect, they broke his nose and cut off his left thumb, but, he was rehabilitated and had since been useful to them from time to time. In any case, it was just business with no hard feelings and his toadying-up served to amuse them. Of course, his association with them provided Bill with some status and a certain measure of protection, which allowed him to survive in his shabby world of pawnbroker shops and doss houses, ill-lit archways and grimy corridors littered with burst bin bags and stale vomit.

But there was a smile on his wasted, weasel-like face. He had taken the call earlier that morning and immediately recognised the anonymous voice. What he also recognised was that the caller's network of informants was as efficient as ever and that what was on offer seemed too good a final opportunity. He smiled again. Revenge, he thought, casts a very, very long shadow.

***

Death was much closer for Moses 'The Prophet' Morrison. He was a nasty piece of work. Originally from Lower Gray, a few miles east of Bridgetown, Barbados, he ran three girls, two white, one black, in the red light district of Bristol. There were no days off for his 'working girls', just a short mid-morning break, their hours dictated by the punters. Essentially, prostitution was afternoon and evening work, seven days a week. Like any business, reasoned Morrison, the workforce had to be productive and, like any business, laziness or misconduct was subject to a formal disciplinary procedure. There was a difference, of course. Within Morrison's enterprise there was no system of appeal and the penalty was always the same. Any of Morrison's girls who were not sufficiently productive or stole from him or tried to be entrepreneurial and branch out were punished. Morrison's punishment of choice was to slash the girl's Achilles tendons – at both ankles. The result was that these poor girls walked stiffly and flat-footed. Like the victims of an IRA's knee-capping, Morrison's victims were a constant reminder to others of the necessity to obey and conform.

Dolores always possessed a non-conformist streak and wanted to branch out, branch out with Rafael, another pimp who had promised that she would be 'his woman' and her life would, as a consequence, be different.

The consequence for Morrison was that he needed to be removed, which would allow Rafael to fill the business vacuum. In Dolores, Rafael had the perfect instrument to fulfil his expansionist ambitions.

At seven, as every evening, Morrison mounted the five steps to his front door and entered the dreary, narrow hallway. He swaggered along his hallway, passed the doors to the front room and back room, all soon to be occupied by punters, following the spicy aroma of goat curry bubbling on the kitchen hob.

'Dolores,' he bellowed, angry that she was not there in the kitchen, waiting.

He stretched up above the freezer compartment, wrenched open the fridge door towards him and grabbed an ice-cold can of *Red Stripe*. But Dolores had been waiting, waiting in the back room. As Morrison shut the fridge door, Dolores plunged the ten inches of glistening Sheffield steel under his right arm and deep into his chest. Morrison staggered, but only for a moment, the black handle of the knife sticking out like another stunted limb. He fell backwards against the wooden kitchen table with a look of total bewilderment to almost immediately collapse onto the floor, face down.

He was still conscious as Dolores took this last opportunity to speak. 'You piece of gutter shit trash. You will *never* burn my daughter again.'

But Dolores was bright and she wasted little time on reminding Morrison of his cruelty towards her little daughter. She smeared Morrison's blood on the hallway wall and on the front door, returned to the kitchen and removed her yellow-coloured *Marigold* kitchen gloves, rolling them into a ball. She went to the kitchen door and threw them over the wall to Rafael, who caught the ball just like a wicket-keeper. Then, using her mobile, she called '999'. Only moments passed before the operator answered.

'I need an ambulance. I need an ambulance … and the police. Please, please hurry,' she wailed in her most theatrical voice. 'Some one stabbed my man.'

The medics and the police officers who arrived at the scene had quickly realised that Moses 'The Prophet' Morrison was dead, nevertheless, he was rushed to the A&E at the Bristol Royal Infirmary to be pronounced 'dead on arrival'.

Prophets are traditionally considered to be the revealers and interpreters of God's will. Rafael and Dolores felt that they knew differently. Certain it was that, unlike a true prophet, Moses Morrison had not foreseen events.

Chapter 6

Tuesday, 13ᵗʰ March.

Police Headquarters, Bristol, England.

DETECTIVE CHIEF Inspector Kay Yin drove her red-coloured VW Golf GTi up the sweeping road, through the security gates, towards the main car park of police headquarters, turning off to her right to park amongst the trees and shrubs. She didn't get out immediately, prudently content to view the shambolic scene as a group of about twenty jostled around the Assistant Chief Constable (Ops) and the Detective Chief Superintendent, some stumbling backwards to step onto the plants and scramble through shrubs, others to balance precariously upon aluminium step-ladders, encumbered with their microphones and cameras.

The police press officer did well to control the press pack's eagerness for answers although the owl-like ACC, in full uniform, looked increasingly irritated as he attempted to close the interview on a positive note. But the questions kept coming.

'Isn't it the case, Mr Wynne-Thomas,' asked one reporter, 'that this is the third murder this year in the red light district of the city?'   But, before the ACC(Ops) could reply, another question was shouted.

'Why isn't this murder seen as a priority?'

And another: 'Are the same resources being directed at this murder as they would be if the murder had been committed in the affluent Stoke Bishop area?'

'What I can tell you … ' began Wynne-Thomas, but his reply, as with his previous responses, lacked the authority and the conviction necessary to satisfy the press. They knew that he was already on his back foot.

'Isn't it the case,' asked another, 'that these knife crimes are all drug related?'

Detective Chief Superintendent Robert Perrin stepped forward. He was about 5'7", thin faced and clean shaven, tanned with jet black hair slicked down. He wore a beautifully cut, light grey, double-breasted suit and looked more like a wealthy Italian restaurant owner than the force's most senior detective. He held his hands out in front of himself, palms towards the press pack, like a thinner version of the Italian politician, Silvio Berlusconi, consequently he was often referred to as 'Roberto'.

'What *I* can assure all of you is this,' he said, pausing for effect, to continue pedantically. 'In *my* book … a murder … is a murder.' He paused again lowering his hands, a very slight but confident smile creasing his face, then added. 'The public expect me to arrest murderers. And that is precisely what *I* intend to do, but *I* can't do this alone. We have set up a confidential hotline and I am asking the public to use it. I am *not* interested,' he continued, palms towards the press again, 'I am *not* interested in whether the caller is a pimp, a prostitute or a punter. What I am interested in is what the caller can tell me. True, I don't know who the murderer is, although undoubtedly known to the victim. What I *do* know is that someone out there does and, before someone else is stabbed to death, I need someone to make that call. Thank you.'

He turned on his heels and walked through the doors of the headquarters, followed by the ACC.

DCI Yin stepped out of her car and, avoiding the press, walked to a side entrance, making her way up to the executive suite, where she waited for about fifteen minutes outside the ACC's office. Raised voices could be heard from within his office, although Kay and the secretary pretended not to notice. At 4.20pm, Detective Chief Superintendent Perrin emerged. There was anger in his eyes, otherwise he remained immaculate and apparently unruffled. The DCI stood as Perrin passed. He looked straight towards the door leading out of the executive suite, his pace not faltering but, as he neared Kay Yin, he simply said: 'Ring me tomorrow.'

'Miss Yin,' bellowed the ACC from the safety of his office. The DCI entered an office filled with residual tension. 'Give me a Crime Scene Assessment, Miss Yin,' said the ACC, now seated behind his desk, his uniform cap unnecessarily placed in front of him, a confirmation of his rank and status. 'How is the investigation going regarding the artist?' he asked, gesturing for the detective to sit in a chair.

DCI Yin detailed the post-mortem she had attended and the content of the pathologist's report. ACC John Wynne-Thomas sat behind his desk like an inanimate totem pole as she explained how Nicolas Fry had been killed as the result of severe blunt force trauma to his head. 'There were three blows, almost certainly delivered by a right-handed assailant. Undoubtedly, the first blow to the side of the head stunned the victim who fell sideways over a settee and face down. It seems that he was then struck twice in the back of the head. It was these two blows that killed him.'

'The weapon?'

'The weapon was probably the jemmy used in the attempt to force the basement door. There were some minute wood splinters found in the wounds. I believe they may have come from the basement door. I am awaiting confirmation from forensics.'

'Was anything stolen?'

'Apparently not, although his diary is missing and an untidy search was made of some of the victim's domestic rooms.'

'Interrupted in some way then?'

'I can't be sure.'

'Where there any other attempted burglaries in the area?' he asked with the slightest change in tone revealing that he had clearly read the reports.

'Yes, sir, there was. Three doors along, it appears that the same jemmy was used to attempt to break into another house via a basement door. Again we're awaiting forensics.'

'There we are then,' decided the ACC. 'My view is that this was always, and remains, a murder committed by an opportunist burglar'.

'I'm not sure that's the case, sir,' interrupted DCI Yin, an interruption clearly not welcomed by Wynne-Thomas. 'The attack was unnecessarily violent in my view. There is little doubt that the victim was unconscious after the first blow. There is no evidence of any sort of struggle; no bruising about the face, shoulders or arms; there are no traces of foreign skin or blood under his fingernails.'

The ACC's response was loaded with derision. 'You keep using phrases such as "there is little doubt", "the weapon was probably", "undoubtedly", "it seems", "I can't be sure" and "in my view". *My view is that it's all about hard choices in a cost-conscious world, Kay.* I think we need to scale this enquiry down to a Category B. It's all about the best use of resources. I need you to scale your team back to twelve, no more. The force can then re-focus on the murder of Morrison.'

'I have to say that I don't agree, sir,' persisted the DCI. 'Nothing was stolen from the victim's home; the attack was violent; there were plenty of other houses in the immediate vicinity that would have potentially yielded much better pickings for a thief and there is the evasive route taken by the killer.'

'But that argument could equally apply to the murder of Morrison. Nothing was stolen and the attack upon him was violent. Wouldn't you agree?'

'But Morrison was a cheap, nasty little pimp who had plenty of enemies. There appears to be no motive for the artist's death.'

'You're not suggesting,' said the ACC with a patronising grimace as if scoring a key point, 'that because Morrison was black and had previous convictions, that we should pursue his case less vigorously than that of a well-to-do artist, are you?'

'No, of course, I'm not,' she replied, anger beginning to determine the set of her jaw. 'But there are many avenues to explore with Morrison, I am merely concerned that the trail could go cold with the murder of Fry.'

'But it has already gone cold, Kay. I have to say,' he continued as if disappointed with the conduct of a newly appointed school prefect, 'that I believe the case could have been pursued more vigorously.'

'We have been extremely vigorous,' she countered as she bridled at the accusation, 'but Fry's house is large and the forensic examination has had to be thorough. The blood pattern analysis in particular. You would expect no less.'

'My view is that vital time was lost and is being lost with fruitless enquires.'

'I'm sorry, what do you mean, fruitless enquiries?' she challenged.

'What *I* mean,' he replied tersely, 'is that you have been wasting your time with interviews with the Earl and Countess Chelwood. Not satisfied with his helpful account, you have now been making enquiries with regimental officers and, apparently, a clergyman! Holding the rank of Detective Chief Inspector, albeit temporarily, is all about judgement, priorities and best use of resources. It is against these benchmarks that your performance will be measured, Kay. I believe that you need to look at these matters more … strategically. My earlier press interview was not about an artist it was about gun crime, knife crime and drug-related crime in the inner city. That is all the public and our political masters are concerned about.'

He leant forward and picked up the latest edition of the *Bristol Evening Post*. 'Here we are,' he said thumbing through the paper. 'The death of the artist is on page five; doesn't even justify having his photograph.' He closed the paper and held it up to present the front page to her, like an exhibit. 'The murder of Morrison is front page news and, I am told, Morrison's murder will feature on *News at 10* tonight.' He flung the paper forward as if it contained overwhelming evidence in support of what he said. 'Because this Morrison had the nickname "Moses", he has become newsworthy and something of a celebrity. All nonsense, of course, but this is the real world we live in, Kay.' Then added, as if presenting her with a consolation prize that could so very easily be snatched back – and would be: 'I will leave you, Kay, to decide who you keep on the enquiry, but scale it down to twelve, no more. That's all. Carry on.'

Detective Chief Inspector Yin left the ACC's office and entered the empty conference room and, using the internal phone, placed her call. The phone was immediately answered by Inspector Trench.

'Hullo, Gordon, is Superintendent Faraday there please?' she asked as formally as possible.

'Who is that calling?' he asked, knowing full well who the caller was.

'DCI Yin.'

There was a pause as Trench attracted Faraday's attention, 'Detective Chief Inspector Yin on Line One, sir.'

He waited until Trench had replaced his receiver then answered disinterestedly: 'Superintendent Faraday.'

'Can we meet at eight tonight, Mark, at Sion Hill with Caledonian Place?'

'Let me just see what I have in my diary,' he said, making a pretence of checking his commitments. 'I'm pretty well tucked-up this week and next week, but that time and date should be fine.'

Mark had parked in Caledonian Place and Kay in Sion Hill. She had arrived early and remained in her car until she saw him at the junction a few minutes before eight. They were formal when the met and talked as they walked, Kay explaining her meeting with the ACC and the most recent developments in the case. They were soon outside the front door of the artist's home, the crime scene investigator's aluminium powder still visible on the blue paint-work.

Kay handed Mark her buff-coloured file and began to open the front door with a key. Once inside the wide hallway she closed the door. They could hear the silence in the darkness but, undaunted, she turned, held the lapels of his trench-coat and pulled herself up to kiss him on the lips. He felt her delicate body melt into his, the scent of her *Amor Amor* perfume as intoxicating as the taste of her mouth.

They each reluctantly broke free, for a few more moments simply holding hands as he kissed her head.

'It's good to see you,' he said. Then they laughed in the darkness, maybe from relief or to break the tension. He switched on the lights. 'And it's really good to see you now,' he said and they kissed again, a lingering kiss.

'Come on, *sir*, there's work to do,' she said in mock rebuke.

In the hallway was evidence of the thorough forensic search. Faraday briefly accustomed himself before they entered the first room on their left, the murder room. The settee was heavily stained with crimson blood and little yellow, numbered markers indicated the medium-velocity blood pattern across the wall-mounted book shelves and even onto the ceiling, indicating the cast-off marks as the weapon swept upwards trailing the victim's blood, downwards again, then up once more with even more blood.

'Have we been able to reasonably determine the killer's height?' Faraday asked.

'Yes, from the analysis of the width and length of the drops of blood, CSI determined the angle of impact and convergence. They estimated the attacker's height to be between 5'9" and 5'11".'

'Almost certainly a male, then.'

'72% chance.'

'Fingerprints?'

'None.'

He looked about the wooden floor, partly covered in a large rug and books and papers. 'What about transfer patterns and footprints?'

'We know what shoes the victim was wearing and what he had in his wardrobe. There were some sole prints here where the killer most likely stood. CSI used "ELSA" and "ESDA",' she said, indicating two techniques for the electrostatic lifting of sole prints caused by dust deposits or the faintest indentations on paper. 'There are no patterns, so trainers are certainly ruled out, but they believe the sole impressions are from smooth leather soles, probably expensive leather shoes, size, probably 9 or 10. These smooth impressions have also been found in the studio upstairs.'

'Give me a minute,' he asked. They stood silently, surveying the scene, imagining the room once as part of someone's home, then the room as the scene of the occupier's murder. Faraday spoke first. 'Is that a kitchen through there?'

'Yes.'

'Can we sit down and just go through the reports, see what we have?'

They went into the kitchen, sat at a little table and poured over the reports of the First Office Attending, his actions, his recollection of which lights were on, his immediate impressions and lack of witnesses; the pathologist's report describing the injuries and actual cause of death; the technicians describing the comparisons of indentations in the victim's head and on the basement doors; the chemists describing the uniqueness of the glass fragments from the basement door. Then they turned their attention to the photographs.

'You say that a phone call was made to the house at about 08.30.'

'Yes, from the kiosk at Merchants Road, ten minutes walk away.'

Faraday pointed to one of the photographs showing two mugs. 'He was expecting a visitor,' suggested Faraday, 'either during the evening or the following morning.'

'We've checked. It wouldn't have been his girlfriend. We have confirmed that Elsa Chaudouet was at a reception at the Tate Modern.'

He looked towards Kay as he put the photograph down. 'Was the water in the kettle analysed?'

'Yes, and forensics confirm that the sodium and potassium sulphates and chlorides had been boiled out. I think it can be assumed that Mr Fry put on the kettle a short time prior to his murder.'

'OK. Can I have a look down stairs?' he asked.

Both officers descended into the basement, along a little corridor to the back door, the top half of which had glazed panels, now boarded over. 'You said you were concerned about this door?'

'If I lived here, and someone had once lived in this basement when it was a one-bed garden flat, I would have had bolts at the top and bottom as well as the key.'

'I agree,' concluded Faraday. 'The burglar or killer broke the glass at the top of the door where there was a very convenient bolt and also broke the glass mid-way where the key was very conveniently in the lock. If there had been a sturdy bolt at the bottom he would have had to make a hell of a din and break the door.'

'I don't like this at all,' she said. 'It's just too neat.'

'If the killer did come this way, would Mr Fry have heard the glass being broken?' Mark said, still focusing his attention upon the door.

'Unlikely,' she replied. 'We tested that and broke some glass here but, with the doors shut, we couldn't hear it upstairs at all, although,' she paused and looked at Faraday, 'the killer wouldn't know that.'

'No, he wouldn't would he. And the glass?'

'Forensics have the refractive index and also the chemical composition. These doors are original and fitted when the crescent was built between 1791 and 1820. The glass came with the door.'

'Right. Shall we try upstairs,' suggested Faraday.

Faraday followed Kay Yin up the stairs, avoiding the books and papers to one side of the stairs. He asked about the swipe patterns, those were the blood smears on the banister and identified by yellow numbered forensics tags. At the top of this flight of stairs they turned left and into a large room overlooking the city to the south, a room that provided the perfect lighting for an artist. The room had three large windows and was cluttered with canvases and paints, papers and books. Faraday quietly occupied a wooden chair clutching the file. He leant back against the chair absorbing the essence of the room, a room that represented a life-time's work; of the exploration and recording of people's adventures and hardships, lives and deaths. Faraday looked toward the painting of soldiers receiving a flag from their queen, resting on a three-legged studio easel by the furthest window and another partially finished canvas on a sturdy, gallery easel in front of the nearest. He checked the photographs taken by the crime scene officers, then looked around the room again.

'How tall did you say the artist was?' he asked.

'He was six foot.'

Faraday stood and picked up a long handled *Filbert* brush, approached the nearest 30" x 20" canvas as if to paint. He had to stoop.

'Look, the artist appears to have been working on the lower part this canvas,' he suggested, pointing to the painting of a desert road near a well. 'This can't have been the picture he was working on. If it was, he would have to have been kneeling down.'

Faraday examined the painting and, as he did so, walked around the back of the gallery easel and fingered a piece of card stapled to the picture frame.

'This is interesting,' he said.   They both examined the card containing neat columns segmented by rows filled with dates followed by figures. Above this matrix was written the title of the painting and the word 'hours'.

'It seems the last time the artist did any work on this painting,' observed Kay, 'was on the 27th February.'

'Might be nothing, but I'm curious to know what painting he had been working on last.'

They began to check the canvases leaning against the walls. Most were blank, some started but seemingly abandoned.

'Mark,' asked Kay as she pulled two canvases apart. 'How long does oil paint take to dry?'

He walked across to her at the fireplace. Propped at the side of the fireplace were two larger, 50" x 40" canvases facing into the chimney breast. 'This one,' she said, 'was stuck to the back of this one.'

Faraday pulled the canvas out into the room. He didn't turn it over but examined a card stapled to the canvas stretchers. 'It's dated "2/March – 2 hrs".'

'Nicholas Fry was murdered on the evening of the 2nd March,' she said as Faraday lifted the large painting up and turned the canvas towards them. The painting was in the early stages of depicting grey-brown churned-up earth and drifting blue-grey smoke with the pencilled outline of soldiers, some falling, others running towards the enemy, and an open-mouthed officer urging his men forward across 'No Man's Land'. Faraday carried the canvas towards the heavy gallery easel as Kay removed the smaller painting. He lowered the larger painting onto the hardwood shelf. She stood back.

'He was working on the officer,' she said and, looking at Faraday standing closer to the canvas, added: 'He would have been at just the right height and I should have noticed this.'

'It has been noticed,' he replied abruptly, 'and the reason why it has been noticed is because *you* asked someone else, not burdened down with a thousand pieces of information, to look the scene over with you.' He looked at her protectively, adding gently: 'Look, the important question now is why was the painting moved? I can't believe the artist would have done so. These blobs of paint here at the bottom were still wet. They're not part of the painting. It's as if he used that area as a pallet.'

Mark Faraday looked at her, his brow in a frown of deep thought. 'The artist must have known they would still be wet, so why should anyone want to move it?'

'To distract us, Mark,' she said.

Chapter 7

Wednesday, 14th March.

South Gloucestershire and Bristol, England.

SUPERINTENDENT FARADAY and Constable Blanchard were able to make up time after the delays at the Almondsbury interchange, leaving the M4 motorway at junction 18 at eight forty-five to join the A46 before branching off onto the Old Bath Road towards Tormarton.

Pippa Blanchard was easy to talk with, constantly showing an interest in the day's programme of their scheduled meetings at Badminton and RAF Fairford. They spoke about Badminton House, built in 1682 for the 1st Duke of Beaufort, and the venue since 1949 of Britain's most prestigious equestrian event. To some extent this was understandable. PC Blanchard had once owned her own pony and her father was with the military, recently returned from active service in Afghanistan.

They spoke as Faraday drove briskly along the narrow, winding road that cut through rich brown fields yielding to the ploughs, the tractors pursued by squawking flocks of birds.

'I think it's the next on the left, Pippa?' suggested Faraday, ignoring the Audi's integral navigation system.

'Yes, sir,' she said, her eyes darting from the *AA* map in her lap and the road ahead. She pointed into the distance. 'It must be there, sir, just where the men are working.'

Faraday reduced his speed to a crawl as he negotiated carefully around the two men, their backs to the road, working on the dry-stone wall. He turned left, the *Multitronic* automatic transmission coping smoothly with the change of speed and gradient as they drove up over the rise between trees and a row of pretty Cotswold stone cottages with thatched roofs and diamond-pane windows. At The Straights, they could have turned left again into The Limes and driven directly towards the gated entrance to Badminton House, but Faraday drove straight ahead towards The Hayes and the village memorial hall.

Faraday reversed the Audi in front of the building and checked the dashboard clock. It was twelve minutes past nine. Other than a farmer's Land Rover and a small Ford Fiesta Ghia, the car park was empty. Faraday and Blanchard got out of the car, Faraday wearing a green and brown Raglan field-coat with brown corduroy trousers and Blanchard in a green *Barbour Eventer* jacket and denim jeans. They went to the boot of the car and pulled on green *Hunter* Wellington boots to await the arrival of Inspector Gordon Trench. One of the doors to the hall was ajar and so Faraday walked up the four steps to the front of the memorial hall and wandered in. There inside, Mrs Dupe was attending to a series of displays on trestle tables.

'Hullo,' he said brightly. 'My name's Faraday. Nothing to worry about, but I'm with the local police,' he said, producing his warrant card from an inside pocket. 'I'm waiting for a colleague. Will it be alright if I leave my car outside for a couple of hours, it's the silver-grey one?'

An equally silver-grey haired and rather refined Mrs Dupe said nothing. Her eyes quickly assessed the policeman then bustled towards the door, peered out into the car park and, apparently satisfied that the car was of a worthy standard, smiled very sweetly. 'Of course, Mr Faraday.' And, not missing the opportunity to boost sales, added: 'Maybe you would care to support our charity today and be the first to purchase a cup of tea?'

'I think I can do better than that. Could I have three teas and,' looking towards Pippa Blanchard standing in the doorway, 'and three of those shortbread biscuits, please?'

'Let me just re-boil the kettle and it will be ready in a jiffy,' she replied, then bustled off towards the kitchens.

As Faraday waited he noticed the two brass plaques on the walls either side of the main doors. The one on the left listed those men of Badminton village who had died in the Second World War; the one on the right listing a larger number who had fallen in the Great War. All those named seemed so young, thought Faraday, the oldest being only twenty-five years of age.

PC Blanchard, clipboard under her arm and ever alert, interrupted her superintendent's thoughts. 'Mr Trench has just arrived, sir.'

Faraday walked through the doors to the top of the steps as Trench got out of the police Land Rover and adjusted his cap, looking around himself with a self-satisfied grin as if he had just arrived in the Garden of Eden. He looked ridiculous, not because he was wearing uniform but because he was wearing his stab-proof vest. Before Faraday could speak, Trench spoke.

'Bit delayed, sir, sorry about that.'

'Never mind Gordon, there's a cup of tea for us inside. However, he added lightly, please take off that vest. I doubt very much that His Grace the Duke of Beaufort will attack any of us today.'

Trench didn't argue but unclipped his protective vest and placed it into the back of his vehicle, mounted the steps and joined the others inside the hall. They drank their teas and ate their biscuits before clambering into the police Land Rover and driving off towards the entrance gates to Great Park, the stone pillars of which supported two very large ornate lamps. But, at the gate, no one had anticipated their visit, Trench excusing himself by saying that he had instructed PC Haverlock to contact the estate stewards.

Apologies were made and accepted and, after a short phone call to the estate office, Trench drove up the drive to leave the police vehicle near the front of the house and then begin their two-hour walk around the course. The vast majority of the thirty jumps were formidable, in particular *Keeper's Brush* with its water jump and fences; *The Lake* and the *Beaufort Staircase* with its obstacle of logs and demanding descent plus narrow fences, followed by a long gallop towards Badminton House itself. Faraday was satisfied with the location of the police command unit next to the Red Cross and close to the media centre just behind the dressage arena, but when Faraday raised any queries with Trench, the inspector didn't really have a firm grip on what was to take place in April or what actions he still needed to make, in particular, clarifying the emergency evacuation route from the undulating grass air strip situated between The Staits car park and hamlet of Little Badminton.

By 11.30 they had returned to the Land Rover and Inspector Trench drove Faraday and Blanchard away from Badminton House, the flag flying from its roof-top denoting that His Grace was in residence. At the memorial hall car park, Faraday confirmed with Trench what actions remained to be dealt with – and there were many – before Faraday and Blanchard changed out of their

Hunters and drove towards Didmarton and the A433 to Cirencester and RAF Fairford, the home of the US 420th Air Force.

The buffet lunch at Fairford was relaxed and Faraday was able to meet up with the district commander, Superintendent Newton. Roger Newton's district included Badminton as well as Fairford and so both superintendents were able to discuss the horse trial's operational order and clarify details, Pippa Blanchard at Faraday's side with his draft order on her clipboard and notepad at the ready.

The three-hour RIAT table-top exercise with over one hundred participants was, by contrast, intense as would be expected for an event involving over three hundred aircraft ranging from *Stealth* bombers to tankers, including nine-hours of air displays. Described as the greatest air show on earth, it seemed to Faraday that the Royal International Air Tattoo also represented the greatest terrorist opportunity on earth. But Faraday and Blanchard were on top of the planning and the liaison, well prepared for the next exercise in May and the event itself mid-July.

As Faraday drove down the M5 towards police headquarters, he quizzed Blanchard. 'Your father is a colonel in the Royal Electrical and Mechanical Engineers isn't he?'

'A lieutenant-colonel, sir.'

'If I wished to make enquiries about a regiment, any regiment, who should I approach do you think?'

'Probably the best person would be the colonel … if it was an official police matter. If it was a general enquiry, then the adjutant would help'.

'What if it was an enquiry concerning the Boer War or the First World War for example?'

'Oh,' she replied with a knowing smile, 'the regimental museum would have most of the answers.'

'What, most of them?'

'Probably. You see, what's on show in the museums is really for the entertainment of visitors, you know, medals, uniforms, swords, equipment, that sort of thing, but most of the regimental documentation and records would be stored there but out of sight. The curators are usually former regimental officers and love to hoard stuff.'

'You seem to be very knowledgeable, Pippa.'

'Not really, but I did work in the REME museum's coffee shop during my uni summer holidays.'

'Are you just talking about the REME or are you saying that all military museums are pretty much the same?'

'They all seem to be similar to me. Records of the most recent conflicts wouldn't be in the museum, some would still be classified, but those of the First and Second World Wars would be there.'

Black clouds had gathered, warning of the change in the weather; spots of rain first followed by a sudden torrent lashing against the windscreen. Faraday switched on the headlights as the 3.2 litre engine responded to gentle pressure on the pedal, accelerating them out of danger, sweeping the Audi past and through the sprayed water of the articulated lorries labouring up the gradient.

Unperturbed by the road conditions, Faraday continued. 'And how comprehensive would, say, the records of the First World War be, do you know?'

'I've always assumed that they were very comprehensive. Regimental histories were often written by a retired colonel, someone like that, and then published in the mid-twenties. Regiments were very proud of their service and I think all regiments published something, usually great leather-bound books with photographs, maps, that sort of thing.'

'And this would be the sole reference?'

'No, there would usually be the battalion war diaries or books written about specific battles and then these would always be memoirs.'

'Of course,' replied Faraday, realising that he should have worked this out for himself, 'of course there would be. What about records of casualties?'

Pippa Blanchard thought for a moment. 'There should be included in the soldier's service record. I had never come across any myself but I always had the impression that that sort of thing was stored in The National Archives.'

'And what about the details of those killed?' Faraday asked as he mentally ticked off another question on his list.

'Ah,' she replied, more confident of her answer. 'That would be the Commonwealth War Graves Commission.'

'OK. What about gallantry awards and medals?'

'I'm sure that The National Archives would have that, but I think there's also a unit near Gloucester or Cheltenham that keeps comprehensive records of awards, but I can check that for you,' she said helpfully.

'Could you do that for me?'

'Of course I can, sir,' she replied as if the task was simple and of no trouble at all.

Faraday's tone changed. For a moment it was harsher. 'I only require a contact name and number, but on no account do you say that you are a police officer.' He hesitated before continuing. 'The enquiries I am making are unofficial at this stage but I believe that one man has been murdered already making similar enquiries and I don't want another murder, certainly not you.'

They drove on in silence until they crossed the Avon Bridge when Faraday spoke again.

'You have been very helpful, Pippa, but I need to get a focus on this.' His mind flitted from one aspect of the murder of the war artist to another, commenting almost absent-mindedly. 'I think I need to sit down and discuss this with an army officer so as to get a real feel of an army regiment and where best to make enquiries. The REME museum, where is that?'

'Arborfield,' she replied and, seeing his questioning frown, added: 'Berkshire, sir.'

'And would it be a problem if I called the curator?'

'Oh no. He's a very helpful man, a Major Hutchings.'

Bill Harding was slipping away rapidly. He ate and drank little, in fact, he ate virtually nothing at all and only drank sips from the brandy bottle in his bed-side cabinet. When his sons had asked the doctor if he could be allowed a little brandy, the doctor had nodded his unspoken consent, commenting: 'It can't do him any harm now.' His 'boys', both in their thirties, had been shocked at how quickly their father had deteriorated He had said to them both that he needed to let go, that he wanted a dignified passing without nurses having to attend his every need.

He had told them that an operation would have been useless and that the hospital could only now offer palliative care as the cancer invaded every part of his body, seeking out and consuming the remaining enclaves of healthy tissue. Even so, Bill could still smile at the paradox. He had never quite understood the meaning of the word, but what he did understand was that, like the cancer in his body that would eventually destroy itself, the actions of the anonymous man with the familiar voice would result in that man's self-destruction.

The anonymous man had arrived in his private little room just after his sons had departed, wearing a black trilby hat and black cashmere coat, carrying in his hand two small brown paper bags, the fuller of the two marked 'Central Fruit Market, Corn Street'. The visitor had changed little, thought Bill, although greying around the temples, but still possessing the wise-crack smile of the man who had always had the upper hand.

'Are you up to doing a little writing, Bill?'

Bill feigned weariness, propping himself up in the bed-side arm chair. 'I can manage it,' he said, then coughed as if his illness was troubling him but, of course, he wasn't troubled at all. 'As long as the money's still good.'

'Here it is Bill, just as we agreed.' The man removed his trilby hat and Bill could see that he had aged a little under his continental tan. The man opened the larger brown paper bag and removed a bunch of green grapes. He placed these on Bill's side table, then proffered the bag held in his gloved hands so as to allow Bill to peer inside. Bill could see, but also smell, the crisp Bank of England notes. 'Ten grand, in two bundles. Five grand for each of your boys.'

Satisfied, Bill leaned back into his chair, pointing with his left, thumb-less hand towards a sports bag in a chair near the window. 'Can you put it in the sports bag under the clothes and zip it up tight like?'

'I can do that for you, Bill, all neat and tidy,' he replied as he walked around to the chair and thrust the brown paper bag inside the sports holdall. 'Where shall I put it, Bill. In here?' he asked, looking towards the locker.

'Could you put it on top there so I can see it and know it be safe.'

The man placed the sports holdall where he was asked and smiled down at Bill Harding as if looking at a dear old friend. He then returned to the dying man at the same time pushing the meal table towards and in front of Bill, the little wheels squeaking as he did so. 'I'll tilt it up, Bill, so as to make it easier for you to write.' He adjusted the large bevelled knob and secured the table at the appropriate angle. 'Shall I help you to sit up, Bill?'

'Yes, I could do with some help.'

The man supported Bill's body forward and pumped up a pillow behind his back. Satisfied with these arrangements, the visitor produced a cheap pad of lined writing paper from the other brown bag, folded back its red cover and placed it neatly in front of Bill Harding. He then dragged a little metal, tubular chair alongside the bed and sat down, at the same time producing a *Bic* ballpoint pen from the bag and removed the cap.

He handed the pen to the dying man. 'Now, Bill, write just what I say and you take your time.'

Chapter 8

Thursday, 15th March.

Bristol, England.

HER ALARM clock sounded at 5.40am. They both turned to face each other, Kay curling up towards him to be embraced in his arms – their early morning routine - just five minutes quietly together until his alarm sounded their final wake-up call. They showered together, the steam misting the *Huppe* glass screen as the *Little Dreamer* CD by Beth Rowley played in the background.

Breakfast in their bath robes was as easy as the music, just granary toast and pure orange. After they had dressed they drank coffee on the balcony, accepting the panoramic views as part of their escape from an uncertain and often violent world.

'Today will be good,' Kay said positively. 'We should be able to finalise a number of actions today. There will be referrals of course but my first meeting will be with the guys who came back last night from Edinburgh, Wilton and Colchester. And,' she added on another positive note, 'the detailed reports from the pathologist and from forensics have been promised for ten.' She looked at her lover as he stared out towards the incoming tide. 'But you are not happy with this case are you?'

'Nor are you,' he replied, turning to her adding with a grin, 'and that's good to know.' They leaned forward on the wooden railing deep in thought and remained silent for a few minutes. 'Let's go inside,' he said. They walked into the lounge and he closed the French doors shut. 'It's a pity that we haven't had anything so far from the Goldney area house-to-house enquiries and it appears that the break-in through the basement was the prelim to the murder, but I'm unhappy about that.'

'Why, because of the locks?' she asked leaning back against the breakfast bar.

'Absolutely. If the basement door had been secured by a stout bolt at the bottom, how would the burglar have got in, otherwise than by making a hell of a din.'

'A noise that could have been easily heard in York Gardens, if not upstairs by Nicholas Fry.'

'Then there are the blood smears on the victim's computer and that call from a phone box to Fry a short while before his death. What was that all about?'

'And?' she asked, knowing his moods and perception.

'Lord Tatton's bedroom.'

'Go on.'

'It may not be connected at all but, let's just speculate for a second. Lord Tatton was a distant cousin of the present earl. If he hadn't died so heroically, Lord Miles Chelwood wouldn't be the 7th Earl at all.'

'You aren't suggesting that our hero was murdered are you?' asked Kay incredulously.

'No, not at all. But, if he hadn't have died in 1917, the whole hereditary pack of cards would have been re-shuffled and would look quite different today. At the most he would probably now be just "The Honourable" Miles Chelwood or just plain "Mister" without any significant financial inheritance.'

'Do you want to pursue that?'

'You are uncomfortable with the Chelwoods, it may be worthwhile to look into their family. I've already asked Pippa Blanchard, her father's a colonel, to find out the best route to pursue enquiries about regimental histories, service records and awards,' adding reassuringly, 'nothing more than that at this stage, but you and your depleted team are snowed-under. As I'm away for *Exercise Corporate*, do you mind if she pokes about a little?'

She pulled him closer as she thought of his absence for three days. Kay Yin looked up at Mark Faraday, both hating the thought of their separation. 'I can certainly do with all the help I can get,' she said, then added more firmly, 'but I don't want her interviewing or alerting anyone. If it is just discreet information gathering, then let her loose.'

***

After 'Morning Prayers', Mark Faraday had a meeting regarding the Glastonbury Festival at the round planning table with Chief Inspector Fowler and Sergeant Purchell. The festival, the largest green field music and performing arts festival in the world, was scheduled for the weekend of the 22nd, 23rd and 24th of June and would consist of a tented town covering nine-hundred acres containing a population twice the size of the city of Bath. Because of the various planning and licensing applications involved, meetings had already been held with residents' associations from surrounding villages and hamlets; the Mendip district councillors; with representatives of the hospital, ambulance, fire and highway authorities; and the health and safety executive. Temporary police offices would be established in the villages of Pilton, Pylle and West Pennard with a police command centre at the Royal Bath and West Showground. Geoff Fowler and 'PP' Purcell had done an excellent job, the result of their pains-taking preparation and hours of planning.

At eleven o'clock, Faraday had a further meeting with Sergeant Max Weber who was responsible for the International Balloon Fiesta. The planning for this three-day event, to be held at Ashton Court on the outskirts of the city of Bristol, was primarily the responsibility of the local district commander. With over one-hundred and twenty hot air balloon launches every day, the event attracted thousands of spectators and created traffic congestion, but Max Weber was in front of the liaison.

'You are keeping comprehensive notes?' Faraday asked.

'Yes, sir.'

'And e-mailing confirmations?' he asked reluctantly as he noticed PC Blanchard talking outside their office into her mobile phone.

'Yes, sir, just as you asked. After every meeting I send an e-mail confirming what has been agreed and who is taking responsibility for what.'

'You know I hate this watching-our-backs business. We should be able to rely upon minutes, but last year the traffic congestion on the last day was a fiasco and I don't want to be left without a chair when the music stops.'

After discussing a few remaining issues, Max Weber rose from the table as Faraday glanced at the electronic display, checking the time. He looked across to Pippa Blanchard. She had returned to her desk, sat with files and note pad at the ready, looking directly towards Faraday, so Anna Manin-like with her 1920s *femme fatale* hair style and those intense ice-blue eyes. 'Thank you, Max. Good to see that you are on top of this.'

Faraday stood up and walked across to PC Blanchard's desk, collecting the RIAT file and his diary as he went. 'I'm suffering from caffeine deficiency, Pippa. Let's walk to the restaurant.'

Over coffee, Faraday and Blanchard quickly dealt with the minutes for 'Morning Prayers', then discussed the arrangements for establishing the police casualty bureau for the air tattoo. The term 'casualty bureau' was something of a misnomer. Casualties themselves were not dealt with by the bureau but the thousands of enquiries regarding casualties were. The bureau, centred upon the force's training college, received information from scenes of disasters, casualty clearing centres and hospitals which were then held and matched with enquiries from relatives and friends using the telephone number given out by the media. Because of the volume of calls from the public, these enquiries were actually received by four or five completely separate police forces and fed into the casualty bureau.

Faraday scrutinised her file. 'You've done an excellent job here, Pippa. Thank you.'

'Thank you, sir, but I was lucky, well not lucky I suppose, to have been called in to man one of the desks when the gay cinema was petrol bombed.'

'And what did you learn from that experience?'

'How many calls that sort of incident generates. The cinema only seated three-hundred, but the bureau received over twelve-thousand calls.'

'And what do we learn from that fact?'

'That most people don't know what their partners are up to.'

'Precisely. Anyway, Pippa, nice progress.' Faraday sipped his coffee as he changed the topic. 'You probably haven't had time but were you able to find anything out about gallantry awards?'

'Oh, yes. The Imperial War Museum has all the files concerning awards of the Victoria Cross and the MOD Medal Office at RAF Innsworth have details of all medals awarded since 1914.' Pippa Blanchard removed a typed note from her file and pushed it across to Faraday. 'These are the phone numbers and internet details, but I can do it for you if you wish.'

Faraday thought for moment but didn't respond directly. 'And what about the REME museum?'

'I called Major Robert Hutchings. You have an open invitation to go up to Arborfield at any time you wish.' PC Blanchard passed another typed note across to Faraday. 'This is his number, sir.'

'That's good. I will ring Major Hutchings. I'm away as you know Monday through to mid-day Wednesday. I could call in on Major Hutchings Wednesday afternoon en route back from Bramshill.' Faraday scribbled a note on the piece of paper Pippa Blanchard had given him. 'Meanwhile I want you to research for me the background of another major, a Major Lord Tatton Chelwood.' Miss Blanchard had already opened her note pad and was recording the instruction in swiftly written short-hand. 'Chelwood won the VC, the DSO and MC in the Great War. And, if you have a moment in the next five minutes.' He smiled and began to chuckle. 'OK, the next five or six days, you could research the Chelwoods for me from, say, 1990 to the present day.'

'Right, sir.'

'Pippa,' said Faraday, raising his index finger as his father always did when no argument would be acceptable, 'these must only be website trawls, no direct internet enquiries or phone calls. Do we understand?'

'Absolutely, sir.'

Faraday sipped the remainder of his coffee and replaced the cup gently in the saucer. 'Thank you for calling Major Hutchings for me, Pippa.' But her smile suddenly disappeared as he spoke again. 'Was that the person you were calling on your mobile outside the office?'

The question took Pippa Blanchard by surprise. She fixed Faraday with those intense blue eyes as if to read his mind. 'No, sir.'

'Who were you chatting to?'

She hesitated for a moment before replying. 'My father, sir.'

'And what were you talking about?'

PC Blanchard did not answer immediately, but bit her upper lip. 'It was private, sir.'

'Private certainly but I think it was police-related, Pippa?'

'Why do you say that, sir?' she asked evasively.

'You could have easily used the phone at your desk to speak to your father.'

'I suppose so.'

'And your behaviour when you were speaking was … furtive might be too strong a word … careful would be a better description.' They sat in silence, a silence broken only by Faraday. 'Since we have been here, drinking our coffee, your behaviour has subtly fluctuated. Eager when answering work-related questions and providing me with information and up-dates, but when I've been speaking, I detect a little anxiety. Do you want me to go on?'

'Yes, sir … please.'

'When I said that you could have used your desk phone, you could have replied that you were discussing the enquiries that I had asked you to make which you assumed were confidential or simply that staff are not supposed to use the office phones for personal calls. But you didn't.' Faraday collected up his papers. 'Is there a problem that you should be telling me about, Pippa?'

Constable Blanchard decided that further prevarication was pointless. 'I asked my father for advice and he said … he said that I should be loyal to you.'

'Then there must be a conflict for you, a conflict of loyalties maybe?'

'Yes.' The young constable relaxed slightly into her chair, relieved to inform her superintendent of her concerns. 'I came over here earlier to pick up some fruit, the best fruit goes quickly you see, and I heard Mr Trench and Miss Glass talking.' Constable Blanchard cleared her throat. 'Inspector Trench was saying that you are always finding fault with his work and that you deliberately humiliated him yesterday when you told him to remove his stab-proof vest.'

'And how did Miss Glass respond?' he asked as he reached for his pager. He read the little screen – a message from Kay. Pippa Blanchard waited until she had Faraday's attention. Faraday returned his pager to his belt and looked at her again.

'Miss Glass said that you are always criticising her work too and that … that you have your favourites.'

'And what do you think?'

'I don't think you would knowingly let anyone down and you think that people won't let you down.'

'And why should I think that?'

'Because you are honest and straight-forward,' she answered. Faraday, both elbows on the arms of his chair and with his chin on his clasped hands, looked down at his papers in silence, then looked up at her, his left eyebrow raised as if questioning the validity of her answer. Pippa Blanchard spoke again. 'You need to think that people won't let you down because you need to rely on others … rely on others more than most, sir, and those people you do rely upon might be seen as your favourites.'

Faraday picked up his papers but didn't look towards the young officer. 'If I recall you have a degree in psychology?' he said.

'Yes, sir.'

'Well, I'm going to have to be very cautious with you, Miss Blanchard-with-a-degree-in-psychology.'

Pippa Blanchard fixed Mark Faraday with her intense blue eyes. 'You would never have to be cautious with me, sir.'

***

Faraday had already prepared a fork salad supper with eggs and pasta, green beans, celery, apple and sliced chicken for them both. Kay had called to say that she had had a good day and would be at Mark's apartment by 8.45pm and so the coffee machine was primed and the orange juice chilled. Mark knew that she would want to talk and had up-dated the white magnetic dry-wipe board in the corner of the lounge that he had brought from Ops Planning.

The white board was placed to the left of a floor-to-ceiling bookcase and in front of a low coffee table together with another small table set against the right-hand wall. As Assistant Chief Constable Wynne-Thomas had determined to reduce the enquiry team and deny Kay the facility of a crime analyst or profiler, they were both equally determined to compensate for this.

A murder enquiry requires a logical approach. The process begins with formulating hypotheses and then testing these against the information that is available. If more information becomes available the hypotheses will be tested again and again, guiding the investigative approach, an approach that will be driven by fact, evidence and sound theory.

The board contained the five crime scene assessment headings: 'LOCATION', 'VICTIM', 'OFFENDER', 'SCENE FORENSICS' and 'POST MORTEM'. Under each heading were lists of between eight and fourteen sub-headings. Under 'LOCATION' Mark Faraday and Kay Yin had highlighted 'selection', 'escape routes', 'the encounter' and 'relationships'. Under the 'VICTIM' only 'relationships' was highlighted, whilst under the 'OFFENDER' heading, 'motive', 'planning', 'escape routes', 'travel mode' and 'approach to scene' had been highlighted, as had 'forensic awareness' and 'physical material' under the heading 'SCENE FORENSICS'.

At 08.40 he switched on the coffee machine and the orange and red lights glowed before walking down the hall, past their bedroom, to the front door of the apartment. Standing on the communal landing provided Mark with a commanding view over the gardens and the entrance driveway to the exclusive Avon View Court. He had not to wait long. At 08.50 Kay drove her red GTi through the entrance and followed the winding brick-paved driveway towards his double garage. She activated the remote control from inside her car and the garage door rose as Mark walked to the head of the sweeping staircase. As he looked back towards the garden he saw the Vauxhall Cavalier in Julian Road slow and stop opposite the entrance only to drive quickly away. In the darkness, Faraday could not make out the driver nor the precise colour of the blue, green or maroon-coloured car with a roof rack but, if it was blue it was very likely to be that of Inspector Gordon Trench.

Faraday returned his attention to Kay Yin. He smiled at the sight of her, a woman who could even make carrying a heavy brief case look elegant as she strutted along the path like a cat-walk model, the low-level garden lighting intermittently illuminating her beauty. She entered the lobby and they met on the top of the stairs; they kissed and he took her case.

Inside the apartment, they drank coffee. He was patient with her, as she was with him. He waited as she unburdened herself in rambling chatter, a chatter that continued as she showered. He helped her dry, kneeling in front of her, kissing her lithe body just below her ribs, firstly on one side then the other. He pulled her down towards him only to be interrupted by the kitchen timer.

'Later,' she purred.

After supper they stacked the dishwasher then pulled two chairs around the low table in front of the white board and began to discuss the murder of Nicholas Fry. Kay removed a file from her *Samsonite* brief case and stood to the side of the board.

'The PM confirms that there is no evidence at all of defence wounds nor is there anything useful from under his fingernails. From this we can reasonably assume that the victim was taken completely by surprise.' She drew two lines, one from 'relationships' under the heading 'LOCATION' and another from 'relationships' under the heading 'VICTIM'. 'If not completely by surprise then we can further hypothesise that the victim knew his victim or was at least comfortable in his presence. I think that the possibility that the killer crept silently about the house is possible but very unlikely.'

'And the two cups and boiled kettle suggest that he had been waiting for someone whom he would know or at least have had some contact with before,' said Faraday.

'And the mysterious call from a phone box, what, one-hundred yards away may indicate an appointment.'

'Or the killer checking if his victim was at home,' suggested Faraday.

'I think that that these are all reasonable assumptions,' she agreed and, where the two lines joined in a v-point under the two headings she wrote the words: 'visitor/friend?'

'And planning?' suggested Faraday pointing to the board.

'There was a degree of planning suggested by the phone call, but certainly by possession of the jemmy and the complicated escape route, although this could easily have been the actions of a cool offender who thought quickly on his feet and undertook a route deliberately designed to confuse us. Are we agreed that we should keep 'escape routes', 'the encounter' and 'relationships' as areas of concern?'

'Agreed!'

'I've had the CSI reports back. There were fingerprints but these have been eliminated. We discovered a bundle of invoices and as a result have been able to eliminate a delivery man's prints found in the hallway. He checks out. He was delivering a supply of *Herston Flax* canvas and there were also a plumber's prints - there was a problem with one of the toilets - he checks out too. There were, however, marks on the banisters and the door knobs both sides of the front door. These were probably made with latex gloves.'

'Forensically aware?' Faraday asked. Kay moved to the board and underlined these words in unspoken agreement under the heading 'SCENE FORENSICS'. 'And the blood smears on the computer?'

'Yes. It's difficult to say when, but the sides of the computer had been tampered with and the hard-drive removed or replaced at some stage. Whichever, there is no data on the hard-drive.'

'How come?'

'The technicians say that there could be a variety of explanations, but some of the circuitry was burnt-out, so they think it may have been put into a micro-wave for a minute or two.'

'And Fry had a micro-wave in his kitchen,' Faraday remembered. 'Any blood traces on that?'

'No.'

'Any DNA?'

'That's were we have had some luck from serology,' she replied. 'On the back of the settee there was a lot of blood from the victim, but we also found some of the victim's blood together with salivary amylase present - spittle that is not the victim's.'

'And your hypotheses?'

'Blood splattered onto the attacker's face and he spat the blood away.'

Faraday fixed his eyes on a nondescript point on the wall, his mind trying to make sense of the kaleidoscope of dyslexic thought patterns in his mind. 'None of this leads me to believe that this murder was spontaneous.' Kay nodded in agreement, waiting for him to continue. 'An aspect that does concern me, although I haven't worked out why it should be, is that the entry was apparently made via a short, discreet, dark entrance way under Royal York Crescent from the relative seclusion of York Gardens, yet the exit appears to have been made via the front door onto the well-lit Crescent.'

'It doesn't make sense.'

'But it must have made sense to the killer.' He closed his eyes before speaking again. 'I don't think the entry was made by way of the basement. If the killer phoned, as we think he did, he is unlikely then to have broken in through a basement door that could have been securely bolted.'

'But you don't know that it was the killer who phoned.'

'True, but why leave via the front door? You would only leave via the front door if to do so would *look* quite normal.'

'But we don't know that either.'

'OK, but what would you have done if you were the killer?' he asked rhetorically. 'If you had gone to all the trouble to break in through the basement, would you not slide out through the same door into the security of the shadows of the night? I'm not convinced that the offender did enter through the basement door.'

'I think that you are right, but there's a problem. The small splinters of wood found in the victim's head came from the basement door which would suggest that he broke in first then killed the artist.'

'I accept that, but from the information we have, do you really get the feeling that this was an opportunistic bungled burglary?'

'The ACC thinks so,' she teased.

'I wouldn't employ the ACC as a cloakroom clerk,' Faraday replied with a laugh, relaxing back in to his chair.

'Do I get the impression that you don't rate him very highly?' she said, dissolving into laughter with him.

'He's an idiot.'

'We know forensically,' she said, laughing again, 'that that is an irrefutable fact.' For a few minutes Kay tried to regain her composure. After pouring more coffee, she continued. 'Returning to the murder, where has this all got us so far?'

'You told me when you were showering, although you will understand that I wasn't concentrating fully on what you were saying,' he said as they exchanged provocative glances, 'that all enquiries with the military indicate that the victim's contacts with the units have been entirely business-like without any sort of animosity, and whilst Fry had previously completed another commission for the Army Air Corp, his contacts with the other units were new. But, didn't you say that he had been abroad with military units?'

'Yes, to Afghanistan, Iraq, Bosnia and Sierra Leone.'

'Had he been involved in any operations, you know, maybe compromised an operation, witnessed inappropriate behaviour by our troops or got a soldier killed, something like that?'

'We explored that. Every unit we visited we've crossed-checked with press reports, the army's SIB and the UN. There is no suggestion that any of these units have been involved in anything like that. He was a fully accredited and respected war artist visiting areas where fighting was still going on. On at least two occasions the military helicopter in which he was flying was fired upon. By all accounts he was respected and popular, very much one of the lads. They all, officers and troops, seem to have thought highly of him.'

'Are we monitoring?'

'Oh yes. If we get the slightest hint of any untoward incident or scandal involving these units or their personnel, then we will review.'

'OK, shall we move on to the question of motive?'

Kay listed the standard motivators on the board, speaking as she wrote. 'I would think that we could reasonably disregard ideological conviction, lust and gain, and I just don't see that thrill or hate would fit.'

'But you think that the motive could be jealousy, revenge or elimination?' Faraday asked.

'I'm sure some artists are pre-Madonnas but I haven't a clue how many war artists there are, or whether they are a very competitive bunch desperate for another commission to keep the bailiffs from the door.'

'Or just professionally and personally competitive?' Faraday speculated. He looked along the shelves of his books with their red, blue, green and orange spines embossed with black, gold and white titles and authors. His eyes lingered on two titles: '*Management and Machiavelli*' by Peter Jay and '*The Venetian Empire*' by Jan Morris, both of which prompted his thoughts. 'During the Renaissance, Italian artists and their patrons were killing off their rivals all the time. It could be that I suppose.'

'Or simply jealousy,' she suggested. 'Inadequates are often jealous, a jealousy that will rear its ugly head from time to time throughout their lives.'

'Unfortunately that is true. Jealousy is very much like revenge. Both are strong motivators and often linger for years never ever to be fully satisfied. Jealousy and revenge are always possibilities, but elimination?'

Their eyes scanned the board, Mark and Kay considering the possibilities and options in silence. Both knew that the term 'elimination' in the ACPO manual referred to a murder committed in order to escape, to silence a witness or to protect the identity of the offender.

'I'm not sure that we can completely ignore gain,' offered Faraday eventually. 'Maybe the killer was looking for something which he found or did not find.'

'You think we must keep gain, jealousy and revenge as possible motivators?'

'Yes,' he replied without too much conviction as he leant sideways and massaged his forehead with his right hand. Kay let Mark unscramble his thoughts until he spoke again. 'Yes, they are definitely prime motivators but, maybe, we should keep in mind the prospect of elimination.'

'Why do you say that?'

'Well, the victim may have unwittingly been the witness to a crime. He might have knowledge of an offender and not realise it at all. There was the case on the south coast last year when a holiday maker was killed after he had, by chance, bumped into a man in a holiday apartment who was wanted for murdering his wife.'

'And the victim didn't realise that he was wanted, but the killer thought he had been clocked,' she said as she endorsed the white board with the word 'elimination'. Kay resumed her seat adding: 'You think that the violence of the attack could indicate the possibility of the motive being elimination?'

'Yes, it's another possibility.   For whatever reason, whether personal gain, jealousy, revenge or hate, the killer was determined to silence the victim.'

Their debate and speculation had helped them both focus on key issues, but she sensed that they needed to finish. She scribbled some final notes, returning her pad and papers to her case, securing the *Samsonite* closed, then curled her beautiful legs under her in the chair but lowered her head slightly and looked at Mark with her large brown, fawn-like eyes. 'Unfinished business do you think?' she asked sensuously.

Mark smiled as he rose from his chair and, as he walked behind her he kissed her exposed neck. 'I'm going to quickly shower,' he said.

'And I am going to slowly get our drinks and undress.'

'You get the drinks but,' he said kissing her neck again, 'you could leave the undressing to me if you like.'

She turned uncurling her legs and knelt in her chair. She reached up, her hands pulling his head towards her mouth. She kissed him, a long passionate kiss, their eyes closed shutting out their other world. 'I like,' she said.

Chapter 9

Friday, 16th March.

Chepstow, Wales, and Washington, USA.

AS FARADAY, dressed in civilian blazer and grey trousers, approached the toll booth, he touched the button and his driver's door window slid slowly open. He stopped and handed the crested piece of paper to the attendant who quickly glanced at the notation: *'the driver of this vehicle is on official police business travelling from Police Headquarters, Bristol to the Army Apprentice College, Chepstow'*. The attendant did not reply to Faraday's 'Good Morning' but just waved him forward at the same time as raising the barrier.

Faraday crossed the Severn Estuary, the currents swirling angrily around the massive supports of the Severn Bridge below, the Audi sweeping along the elevated six-lane section of the motorway, passing over the Wye inlet and the college below to his right.

Security was tight, as at all military and government establishments, but the delays were minimal and Faraday soon found himself ushered efficiently into Colonel Andrew Vaughan's office. The colonel was charming as he poured Faraday a cup of tea, then settled back into an easy chair near the windows overlooking the parade ground. Vaughan, in his early fifties, appeared typically military, well groomed even in short-sleeve order, seemingly proud to wear the coloured stable belt of his corp. His voice was crisp like his neat but wavy hair and trim moustache.

'Always willing to assist the police, of course, particularly in the case of the death of Fry, but can't quite see how I can help you further.' He sipped his tea, his eyes bright above the cup.

For a moment, Faraday had been tempted to say that the murder of Nicholas Fry had been the result of a bungled opportunist burglary and that he was merely tying up some loose ends, but he quickly dismissed that idea. Instead he chose to make no explanation but pulled a clear forensic envelope out of his briefcase containing four pencilled sketches. 'I understand that Nicholas Fry produced these sketches at the meeting he had with you and Lord Chelwood?'

'That's right,' he said, placing the cup into the saucer and peering at the sketches Faraday laid upon the table. 'Those are his, of course, Fry's that is.'

'Why do you say that?' queried Faraday although he knew that the sketches he produced were the originals discovered by DC Samual Pau at Royal York Crescent.

'Fry sent Lord Chelwood and I photocopies by post prior to our meeting. Those are Fry's,' the colonel said pointing to some pencilled notes in the margins of the one depicting an officer in No-Man's Land urging his troops forward. 'He scribbled those notes, or at least some of them, during our meeting and also made some little supporting sketches. He was a very clever chap, he lapped-up all the detail we were able to provide and converted this information into those little supplementary sketches as we spoke.'

Faraday moved the sketches about, placing one on top of all the others. 'And what about this one, colonel?' he asked referring to the sketch depicting a montage of seven pencilled scenes.

'Lord Chelwood wouldn't hear of it. He didn't like this one at all.'

'Why not?' asked Faraday casually as he picked up his cup and saucer.

'Buggered if I know,' he replied shaking his head, not dismissively but as if completely mystified. 'You see, Fry has a very impressive website and I knew that he had produced a number of really marvellous paintings, some of which were montages of the history of a regiment or a battle or campaign, and so I thought the montage approach was a very attractive idea. Anyway, Fry suggested to Lord Chelwood that a montage would be just the thing considering that the VC was really won over two days of action. I said that I thought that a montage would be a very good way of providing a clear portrayal of the young officer's bravery, but Chelwood wasn't keen.'

Faraday replaced his cup and saucer on the table and changed tact. 'Can you help me with these names scribbled here, colonel,' asked Faraday pointing to the sketched figures with names printed near each figure, little pencilled arrows indicating the names of the individuals. 'These two men here named Taylor and Rosser?'

'These two scenes on the left illustrate the action on the first day when young Chelwood attacked the German machine gun with two volunteers, Corporal Taylor and Private Rosser.'

'And I assume that the third scene illustrates the action on the second day when Major Chelwood attacked another machine gun, but this time single-handed?'

'Yes, that's right.'

'And this,' asked Faraday pointing to another pencilled scene, 'must be the stretcher party of four going out at dusk to find the major?'

'That's it. Morly, Palmer, O'Neill and Wakely with the chaplain, Patterson.'

'I see that Patterson features in two further sketches here and here?' commented Faraday as he indicated the pencilled figures.

'That's right, the little sketch there is of the dying Chelwood and Patterson at the advanced dressing station. The sixth sketch is of a group of soldiers at Chelwood's burial, gathered around a make-shift cross with Chaplain David Patterson presiding over the whole affair.'

'And the central head and shoulder's sketch is of young Chelwood's himself?'

'Yes, that's right.'

'But Lord Chelwood didn't like this montage idea at all?' continued Faraday.

'No,' said the colonel at a loss to reply otherwise.

'Why not, it would seem ideal?' asked Faraday, apparently bemused.

'Can't understand it really.'

'You seem mystified, colonel. Why can't you understand it?' probed Faraday gently.

'Because I would have thought Lord Chelwood would have liked Patterson to have been included. You see, David Patterson was the Chelwood's family priest.'

***

The British Airways' flight from London Heathrow to Washington's Dulles International had been smooth and arrived on schedule, although passengers had been asked by the captain to remain in their seats whilst 'immigration officials' boarded the aircraft. The 'immigration official' was actually an immaculate and charming, but alert, Special Agent Gene Brandeis of the US Diplomatic Security Service. He entered the aircraft as its doors swung open and quickly identified his charges, escorting Lord and Lady Chelwood swiftly towards immigration where officials of Homeland Security stood mute but intrigued as they passed through, gathering another three special agents as they walked towards the exit and the awaiting Rolls-Royce.

The chauffeur stood at the rear off-side door awaiting Miles Chelwood as a Third Secretary opened the rear near-side door for his wife. There was no luggage - other than the small cabin bag carried by Lady Chelwood – their luggage would be brought up later to Massachusetts Avenue by embassy car. The air outside the airport was hot; the Union flag hanging limp from the neat bonnet-mounted chrome pole. As Lord and Lady Chelwood made themselves comfortable, doors were closed silently and air conditioning cooled the interior as the V12 engine gracefully took the silver limousine on its twenty-six mile journey to The Great House, the name of the official residence of Her Britannic Majesty's Ambassador to the United States of America.

The residency is impressive, as it was always intended to be, situated in four acres just below the Observatory. Built in 1928 by the great British architect Sir Edwin Lutyens of red brick with limestone dressings, the high roofs and tall chimneys give the impression of a Queen Anne English country house.

They knew each other well, both Lord Chelwood and the ambassador, Sir James Whitmarsh, had been pupils together at Shrewsbury before going up to Cambridge. The Chelwood's had been guests at the residency before, but it was not simply their familiarity with The Great House that engendered a relaxed atmosphere, it was the general ambiance exuded from its very English-feeling; the black and white diamonds of marble of the entrance hall, so reminiscent of Chelwood House; and the paintings adorning the walls of the twin staircases leading up to the reception rooms, of familiar street scenes of Cheltenham and of Bath. They were shown to their bedroom, the *Dean and Inverchapel* suite, with its painting of *Eldon Place* by Roger de Gray – typical attention to detail displayed by the ever-attentive Sir James and Lady Whitmarsh who selected this particular suite knowing that a distant cousin of Miles Chelwood had once owned a house in Eldon Place.

Later, the two men and their wives took afternoon tea on the terrace overlooking the gardens, a terrace upon which Winston Churchill had stood during the Second World War as he addressed the embassy and military staff.

At eight o'clock, dinner was taken in the intimacy of The Morning Room where these old friends were joined by the Chairman of the Federal Reserve and Mrs Miriam Rossi. Their meal began with paupiettes of smoked salmon with sevruga caviar and mixed salad with herbs. The atmosphere was warm and congenial but Vernon Rossi was, as always, jovial but, at the same time, thoughtful and astute, with his own nation's interest always paramount in his thoughts. There were similar focused considerations for Sir James.

His primary role was to promote the United Kingdom; to influence opinion within, and create access to, the key institutions of the only super-power in the world.

The main course was of pan-roasted fillets of beef with duck liver foie gras served with a fricassee of girolles and truffle sauce. As they ate, they laughed at jokes, spoke of their children and past and forthcoming holidays. They also discussed the 'World Economic Outlook', published the previous month by the IMF, and spoke of the performance of American-based companies that were British-owned as well as the level of investment by American companies in the UK. They commented upon the proposed UN aid to Zimbabwe and considered the impact of the lower growth in China and Asia reported during the last quarter.

As midnight approached Mr and Mrs Rossi took their leave and Miles and Cecelia Chelwood retired to their suite. Both were tired after their nine-hour flight but, nevertheless, Lord Chelwood checked through his briefing papers whilst sat up in bed. He knew that the next day would be hectic, his wife insisting that he accompanying her back to Dulles International for her flight, then travelling to Reagan National for his short internal flight to New York's La Guardia Airport and on to the United Nations. For Lord Chelwood the diversion to Dulles would be an inconvenience, for Cecelia Chelwood the presence of her husband the following day would be key to her plans. She valued highly her status as the wife of a British banker and diplomat but, tomorrow, his presence would be a useful distraction of particular value.

For Miles Chelwood the thoughts of the diversion to Dulles did not occupy his mind as he read his papers and made his notes, but his concentration was erratic and when he did turn off the bedside light his sleep was fitful. He turned one way in the bed then the other, eventually sitting up in the darkness. One thought was persistent. He tried to dismiss this thought as a mere coincidence, but it persisted nevertheless. The thought that so occupied his mind was the simple fact that Sir Edwin Lutyen not only designed The Great House and over three-hundred other houses and buildings, but also the Cenotaph in Whitehall, that empty tomb commemorating all those young soldiers who were killed during the First World War. Chelwood knew that one of those young soldiers was family whilst others were merely known of, one of whom whose manner of death would continue to haunt him.

Chapter 10

Monday, 19th March.

The Police Staff College, Hampshire and Police Headquarters, Bristol, England.

HIS MOBILE rang. Mark Faraday wasn't expecting the call. He instinctively checked the clock: 09:54, as he pulled the Audi into the lay-by on the A33. Faraday switched off the engine, removed the mobile from the holder and checked the number of the caller. It was not a number he knew. He held the mobile to his ear.

'Hello?'

'It's PC Blanchard, sir,' she said as if a thousand miles away.

'Hi, Pippa. Go ahead,' said Faraday, listening intently whilst checking the time again, realising that the departmental 'Morning Prayers' had obviously concluded early.

'I have been able to research the Imperial War Museum records over the weekend. They have all the complete records of VC awards. I have crossed-checked these with the National Archives. They have a comprehensive register of all VCs, together with details of the recipients and the circumstances of the awards of DSOs and MCs. These records confirm Lord Chelwood's awards. I am wondering what else I can do for you, sir?'

Faraday wondered why Pippa Blanchard was calling him on her mobile and with information which wasn't in any way startling. He let that thought linger for another moment. 'Are you able to go back over these records?'

'Yes, I have all the reference numbers.'

'OK. I want you to check the records again and see if any mention is made of an army chaplain called Patterson.'

'I can do that today for you, if you wish, sir.'

'This is not official, Pippa, and so I would prefer it if you could do it at home, if that's not too much of an imposition?'

'I … well … I should be able to do it some time during today.'

Faraday picked up the cue but let it pass. 'OK. If you could also see if there is any connection between Patterson and the Chelwood family prior to and after the First World War. Would that be a problem?'

'No problem, no problem, sir,' she replied with the slightest hesitancy.

'And so why have you called me on your mobile, Pippa?' Faraday asked.

There was a pause before PC Blanchard answered. 'I need to tell you, sir. It may be nothing at all but Mr Trench and Miss Glass have gone over to the ACC's office together.'

'Were they called or was their meeting pre-arranged?' he asked.

'It was mentioned during "Morning Prayers" but I don't think that there was a call from the ACC. It seemed to have been pre-arranged.'

'OK. Not to worry,' replied Faraday, pre-occupied with his part in the forthcoming *Exercise Corporate*. For someone invariably acutely perceptive when dealing with operational or non-personal matters, Faraday was so often oblivious to, or dismissive of, the disloyalty of others. 'Thank you for the call, Pippa. If you could e-mail my car with any information you have regarding the Chelwoods' and Patterson, I would be grateful. I'll give you the address.'

His private e-mail details given to PC Blanchard, Faraday resumed his journey along the A33, turning at the Wellington Monument and through the woods of Heckfield Heath onto the B3011. A short distance later he turned left into the tree-lined drive and under the red brick, crenulated gateway, descending through Deer Park and across the stone bridge towards Bramshill House on the hill above, the seventeenth century ancestral home of Lord Zouche of Harringworth, one of Elizabeth Tudor's ministers and a lawyer appointed as part of the commission for the trial of Mary Queen of Scots.

Bramshill House, considered one of the finest examples of Jacobean architecture in England, had been the home of the Police Staff College since 1953, and would be the venue for the three-day *Exercise Corporate*. Faraday parked on the gravel drive-way at the south-west front of the house and mounted the stone steps to the entrance porch, and walked through the oak doors and into the panelled Tudor reception hall.
Assistant Chief Constable Wynne-Thomas had arranged coffee for his two visitors who sat, with their ACC, in his large office around a coffee table in easy chairs.

'I am always eager to keep my finger on the operational pulse,' said the ACC to both Inspector Trench and Inspector Glass as he placed two thick manila files on the carpeted floor at the side of his chair. 'It is so very easy for me to become detached from the harsh realities of policing that I need to rely upon staff to keep me fully abreast of developments.' He leaned forward in his chair and attempted an engaging smile, although this attempt gave the appearance of an owl suffering from a stroke. Trench and Glass had no regard whatsoever for the ACC, other than that he could serve a purpose for them both and so, they were patient. Whilst the motive of Wynne-Thomas was to cripple Faraday, the motives of the two inspectors were to save or maybe enhance their careers.

The ACC's questions were light enough. He asked about the planning for the Badminton Horse Trials and the St Paul's Carnival, accepting their superficial responses. They relaxed as Wynne-Thomas poured a further cup of coffee for them both as he asked about their career aspirations. Having baited their aspirational hooks, he then asked them about the performance of Constable Haverlock and Sergeant Weber whom he knew worked specifically to Trench and Glass respectively. Apparently satisfied, the ACC made ponderous reference to the work loads of Operational Planning and acknowledged the burdens upon all the staff, including Chief Inspector Fowler, Inspector Hogkiss and Sergeant Purcell. In so doing, it became even clearer to Trench and Glass that they had little to fear from this interview with their assistant chief constable.

John Wynne-Thomas thought himself much cleverer than most. Although this was untrue, he was certainly devious. He knew full well that Faraday could be a hard task master and these two inspectors with whom he shared coffee were not the brightest candles on the cake. He remained silent as he retrieved the two files from the floor and made the pretence of studying both inspectors' personal files, nodding knowingly as he turned each page. Then he spoke again.

'I would always be willing to support you both in achieving your aspirations for advancement.' He paused so as to allow the significance of this remark to register with them before continuing. 'You both have excellent records,' he said, although this was far from accurate. He placed the files on the arm of his chair, tapping them with his right hand as if pondering their content. 'I value experience, ability and commitment, but, above all else, the chief constable and I value loyalty,' his words given added authority by reference to the chief constable. 'Loyalty is not always easy to divine, but, would you both not agree that your first loyalty is always to your chief constable and the police service?'

Both inspectors shifted in their chairs, looked at each other and replied in unison. 'Of course.'

Wynne-Thomas feigned a reluctance to continue as if weighing in the balance the decision to trust these inspectors with a confidence. 'May I share something with you both?' he asked, knowing that each would be more comfortable if they were both equally implicated. The inspectors nodded their agreement. 'This is a delicate matter but I need to place my confidence in those whom I can trust, those whom I know I can rely upon for their *discretion*, for their complete *loyalty*.' The inspectors didn't need to look at each other now, but spontaneously nodded their agreement and commitment to the ACC. 'I have some concerns, lingering concerns, regarding Superintendent Faraday. I am sure that you will understand as I share these confidences with you,' he said as he continued to weave his mischievous tapestry. The inspectors nodded solemnly like cardinals seated before their Holy Father. 'It is one thing for Mr Faraday to be demanding, another for him to be a … shall I say, a bully.' He paused again as if reluctant to go on. 'Can I ask you this: would it not be reasonable for someone to perceive Superintendent Faraday's conduct, on occasions, as bullying? I'm sure that bullying would not be his intention, oh no, but a man under strain.' He allowed these words to linger in their minds before he pressed on. 'Maybe, behaviour completely unintended by Mr Faraday, could quite reasonably be viewed by others as bullying. Would you not agree?'

This invitation was like opening the flood gates. Silvia Glass, with a reputation as a serial complainer, needed no further encouragement as she spoke of what she considered Faraday's unreasonable criticisms of her work; his childish reference to the planning table as 'King Arthur's Round Table', his 'worry board' and the fact that Faraday had taken a magnetic dry-wipe board from their office and was seen to placed it into his private car.

In equally vitriolic turn, Gordon Trench, who had earlier that morning spread poison about Mark amongst the higher echelons of the force, referred to Faraday's criticisms of his work. Trench referred to his superintendent's inappropriate description of visitors to the Horse Trials as 'herds' and claimed that Faraday had made the preposterous suggestion that His Grace The Duke of Beaufort would be capable of attacking a police officer. Trench also spoke of his humiliation in front of a subordinate, PC Blanchard, when he had been told by his superintendent to remove an official and authorised piece of equipment, namely his stab-proof vest.

'I am grateful to you for your candour and I know that this must be difficult for you but, Gordon, you mentioned Miss Blanchard,' said the ACC reasonably. Again, he paused as if hesitant to involve them even more deeply, but he continued in the knowledge that scandal can be a tool of the envious to bring an innocent man down. 'It is one thing, of course, for a superintendent to be *protective* toward his staff. I think you will agree that it is quite another to be *too* close, maybe even *intimate*. Have either of you harboured the mildest suspicion that Mr Faraday could sometimes be *too* close to *some* members of his staff, particularly *female* staff?'

Chapter 11

Tuesday, 20th March.

The Police Staff College, Hampshire, England and off Castries, St Lucia, the Caribbean.

EXERCISE CORPORATE had started well and Superintendent Mark Faraday's twenty-minute presentation the previous day outlining Bristol's Civil Contingency Emergency Plan was well received. This morning, Faraday's syndicate had made much better progress than the other syndicates when they had to respond to the total communications break-down injected into the exercise scenario. Faraday's imaginative suggestion to utilise over fifty bikers at a nearby Hell's Angel's chapter as dispatch riders was met with derision by other syndicates but applauded by the Directing Staff.

Now at lunch time, Faraday could be found alone in the Great Drawing Room awaiting her call. This was one of the grandest rooms in Bramshill House with an elaborate plaster pendant ceiling and containing an imposing fireplace of dull red, pink and white marble. But what was the most striking feature of the room were the set of Rubens tapestries depicting Decius Mus and The Third Samnite War of 279 BC.

At precisely 1.30pm, Faraday's mobile phone rang. 'Hi, Pippa. What do you have for me?'

'Good news, sir. Although a lot of the records were destroyed during a bombing raid in 1940 and a disastrous fire in 1975, eighty-six percent of officers' records were saved and as chaplains were commissioned officers we have his records. The Army List confirms that Patterson was a chaplain from 1914 until 1921.'

'As late as 1921?'

'Yes, sir. He volunteered at the end of hostilities to remain in France and Belgium to assist the war graves people.'

'Oh, I see,' acknowledged Faraday although this fact raised a question in his mind.

'We were talking the other day about the police casualty bureau,' continued Constable Blanchard, 'and that made me think of the casualty clearing stations and field hospitals during the war. I've searched through the records and it shows that Chaplain Patterson was with Major Lord Chelwood when he died.'

Pippa Blanchard was on a roll and Faraday resisted the temptation to say that he was aware of that fact.

'I also checked with the National Army Museum. The museum has amazingly comprehensive records, even including the records of a deceased's personal effects and their disposal. Some of Chelwood's personal effects were shared out amongst his fellow officers — it was customary to do this, socks, cigarettes, food hampers from home, mittens, that sort of thing — but his uniforms and service kit, letters and diaries are listed as being given to Patterson.'

'That's excellent, Pippa. Can you e-mail what you have?'

'Sent to your car this morning, sir. But there's more,' she said enthusiastically.

'Go on,' urged Faraday, although little encouragement was needed.

'Patterson's father was the Chelwood's family priest from 1893 until 1910. Strictly speaking, he was actually the rector of St Matthew's church but the church was part of the Chelwood estate and so he was effectively the family's personal priest. Then Patterson became the rector of St Matthew's from 1910 until 1922.'

'But you said that he was in France from 1914 until 1921?'

'Yes, but a locum, well, two of them, were temporarily looking after the parish whilst he was on war service. The first, Philip Downes, for less than a year; the second, Leonard Stower until 1921.'

'What happened to Patterson after 1921, do you know?'

'Oh, yes,' she replied, pleased that she had anticipated his requirements. 'He was appointed a canon at Tewksbury Abbey in July 1922, then the dean in October 1925. Rapid promotion, huh?'

'I'm not sure what to make of this,' said Faraday now deep in thought.

'You asked me to research the Chelwood family from 1990 onwards', PC Blanchard said, 'I can start on that or I can just keep digging for you if you wish, sir.'

Pippa Blanchard was proving an invaluable confidant but Faraday's dyslexic mind was now cluttered with information and he needed to sit in his bedroom and quietly consider what he had been told.

For want of anything else to say he said: 'I need to think this through, Pippa. You are on a roll so just keep digging. Background on Lord and Lady Chelwood and their son would be useful, but, website trawls only and no personal contact with anyone.'

***

Lady Cecelia Chelwood stood at the starboard rail on the upper sun deck as Captain Frederik Jelstrup guided the one-hundred and ninety-foot, 1,300 tonne *Odyssey* along the west coast towards Soufriere and the port of St Castries. As they passed Gros Piton and Petit Piton, the spectacular volcanic peaks of St Lucia that rise sheer out of the sea and surrounded at their base by rain forest, Lady Cecelia was joined by her hosts, the multi-millionaire senator from the 'Prairie State' of Illinois, Jim Turner and his wife, Kathy. With the other guests, commodities broker Bill Kaufman and his wife, Shelly, they pointed energetically towards colourful fishing villages and secluded beaches as these came into view.

At 11:43 local time, the *Odyssey* was made fast alongside the quay and the gangway rigged.

Chapter 12

Wednesday, 21st March.

REME Museum, Arborfield, Berkshire, England.

MAJOR HUTCHINGS was a rather short, rotund man with strangely sad eyes set in a round, otherwise smiling face, who clearly relished his retirement role as the museum's curator and custodian of his corps' history. He delighted in showing Faraday the collection of medals, including Victoria Crosses, and historic equipment, although his mood changed a little when he pointed out to Mark one of Nicholas Fry's painting. When the 'tour' of the museum was completed, they walk along corridors, passed innumerable plaques and framed photographs, stopping from time to time as the major provided his visitor with an interesting explanation or comment, until they came to his office.

Robert Hutchings brewed a little pot of tea, all the while talking as he did so about regimental histories, war-time magazines and the plethora of records available to search.

'Well, Mark, has that been useful so far?' he asked as he sat behind his desk, Faraday seated to the side on a comfortable chair.

'Yes, it has. I didn't realise how many sources of information there were, it's like a huge jig-saw puzzle and a complicated maze put together.'

'It is I suppose, but when you have spent all your adult life in the army you live and breathe it, you see,' adding modestly, 'It all very much fits into place gradually over time,' concluding mischievously, 'but you still need to ferret about a bit.'

'Well, I'm ferreting about at the moment, Bob. On the face of it, the murder of Nicholas Fry was a straight-forward burglary that went tragically wrong.'

'But you're not so sure that that is the explanation?'

'What I am sure about is that the violence used against Nicholas Fry was not necessary to facilitate a burglary. The murder was unnecessarily violent, if that makes sense.' Major Hutchings nodded his head in agreement whilst, at the same time, munching his biscuit. 'And then there are other things I don't quite understand. They are probably not important but I would like to clear them out of the way. Part of the reason for my unease is that I just don't know enough about the army.'

'You think the army is involved?' he asked with a concerned frown.

'I doubt it very much,' Faraday replied, pausing before he went on as if checking off the facts in his mind once again. 'Always a possibility, but I doubt it very much,' adding with a smile, 'I'm just left with a few little nagging questions. But, there again, the little questions might be nothing at all. What might seem a little quirky or odd to an outsider might be very reasonable and understandable to you. Can I talk just talk through a number of these little nagging questions?'

'Of course, fire away,' he said, now more relaxed.

Faraday pulled Nicholas Fry's sketches from his briefcase and selected the one with the montage of sketches. 'This is one of Nicholas Fry's sketches,' he said as he handed the A4 piece of paper to the major. 'You will see that one of the little sketches is of his burial with a wooden cross in the background. That cross, well I'm pretty sure it's that one, is now in Chelwood House, but the young man doesn't have a grave stone apparently, although I'm told that his name would be carved on a memorial. Why no grave stone?'

'Oh,' replied Bob Hutchings as if disappointed that the query was so easy to answer, 'not unusual at all. Tens of thousands have no known grave. Many were just not buried at all. Some were of course, like young Chelwood, then reburied properly so to speak later on, only for the grave to be lost. This was particularly so at Ypres. Bloody dreadful business.'

'Why particularly at the Battle of Ypres?'

'You see, Ypres wasn't just one battle. There was First Ypres during October and November, 1914, then Second Ypres the following April and May. Third Ypres, known as Passchendaele, commenced at the very end of July, 1917 and went on until the November. These battles, and there were various phases or smaller battles within each of these major engagements, just moved back and forth over relatively short distances throughout the war, churning everything up as they went. In fact, whole villages and small towns just ceased to exist. Some have not even been rebuilt, completely lost, lost … ,' there was a moment of contemplation before he added: 'along with a lot of good men.'

Faraday sensed a personal hurt and thought it better to move straight on. 'Right, I see. So Major Lord Chelwood's body could have been brought home?'

'Oh, good God, no. Bad for public morale and logistically difficult. No one was ever brought home, other than the Unknown Warrior that is.'

'No one at all?'

'Not a soul.'

'But,' Faraday questioned, 'what about the Portland Stone headstones in English church yards, many of those date from the First War?'

'So they might, but those would have been of sailors washed up on the shore, British aircrew shot down and soldiers brought over from the Western Front to hospitals in the UK, but then died here of their injuries. Oh, no, only one soldier was brought back and he's buried in Westminster Abbey amongst the kings, and all down to an army chaplain.'

'A chaplain?'

'Yes. His name was David Railton. He had seen so many soldiers killed and whose identities were unknown, that he came up with the idea that an unknown soldier should be buried, a soldier that would represent all the war dead.'

'But Lord Chelwood was buried wasn't he?' he persisted.

'Let me check,' said Hutchings helpfully and pressed a series of keys on his desk-top computer, 'won't be a minute.' It was less than a minute.

'Yes, here we are, his name appears on the Tyne Cot Memorial to the Missing, in our cemetery just outside of Passchendaele near Zonnebeke.'

'Not buried then?'

'Well, he could have been, of course. The Tyne Cote cemetery contains over twelve-thousand graves, the largest Commonwealth cemetery in the world. But,' he said with a shake of the head, 'over eight thousand are unnamed and more than a hundred are completely unknown.' He scrutinised the screen as he pressed further keys. 'Yes, here we are. Chelwood's name is engraved on the memorial.'

'It's not important, but I thought that all the names of the missing were inscribed on the Menin Gate?' queried Faraday.

'Too small old chap. That was the original intention but just not enough room for them all. They decided on a cut-off date, August something or other, 1917. As Chelwood was killed in the November, his name appears with the other thirty-four thousand at Tyne Cot.'

'Thirty-four thousand! The numbers are staggering, Bob.'

'Yes, and that's only Belgium. But the good news is that records were collated and it's pretty certain now that the very vast majority would have a grave or memorial on the field somewhere – and all down to a Bristol man you know.'

'A Bristolian. In what way?'

'All down to the determination of Fabian Ware. Interesting chap. Born in Bristol, became a teacher, then an editor, I think. Tried to join up in 1914 but was far too old so he became an ambulance driver with the French army. He quickly realised that they was no proper system for recording the graves of soldiers or informing their families. He complained to the War Office, so they gave him the rank of major and told him to sort it out. By the end of the war he had laid the foundations for the War Graves Commission, was a major-general and picked up a knighthood for his marvellous work.'

'And virtually everyone accounted for?'

'Virtually, there are many thousands of graves simply marked: "A Soldier of the Great War" and of course there are those who gave false names, were under age, that sort of thing, or were attached temporarily to other regiments and units and the records got a bit jumbled up, but, the vast majority are accounted for somewhere, even those who were executed.'

'Executed?' asked a startled Faraday.

'Sir Fabian Ware was insistent that all headstones should be the same, irrespective of rank, race and creed. The headstones would display a national or regimental badge, together with the name, rank, date of death, age and religious emblem, if they were known, of course.   The names of executed men appear on memorials along with their comrades and some actually lie alongside their comrades too,' adding in a softer tone: 'and it's as it should be.'

'You don't share the view of some that they were cowards and disgraced the uniform?'

'There were a few who committed murder, but for the rest, the disgrace was the manner of their conviction and death.' There was silence again as if Major Hutchings wasn't comfortable to continue. He took another sip of tea, then replaced the cup pedantically on to his saucer. 'Did you know, two young constables enlisted, into the Bradford Pals if I recall, both executed for desertion.   No evidence at all. Absolute bloody disgrace. Anyway enough of that. Let me pour you another cup.' He poured the tea and Faraday added just the slightest hint of milk and two sugars. 'What you can be assured of, Mark, is that the civil police can be very proud indeed of their contribution in both World Wars. In fact,' he said thoughtfully, 'a Somerset constable, Wilfred Fuller, was a VC and his chief constable won the DSO twice. And then there was the chief constable of Gloucestershire, a Colonel Chester-Master, another DSO, but killed in action. Good people, Mark ... *all* good people.'

Faraday detected an underlying sadness and so changed tact. 'Well, you've cleared up the question I had regarding Major Chelwood's grave, or the lack of one, but you mentioned army chaplains a while back, Bob, can I talk about them?'

'Of course.'

'I am interested in one particular chaplain who for some reason served throughout the First War and on until 1921. Was it usual to serve beyond hostilities?'

'Did he have a war-time commission or was he with the Chaplaincy before 1914?'

'He was a parish priest of some sort before joining up in 1914'.

'The Chaplaincy has been around for over two-hundred years and the BEF took with them about a hundred commissioned chaplains although, by the end of the war, I think there were over three thousand of them. Is that the one?' he said pointing to the sketch. 'Yes, a man called Patterson.'

'I can look him up for you,' he offered.

Faraday glanced at his watch. 'It's getting late, Bob, and I've taken up a great deal of your time. But, if you could later on and e-mail me with any details you have.'

'I can do that for you, Mark. The chaplains are good people, too,' his tone again tinged with sadness or weariness, Mark wasn't sure which, maybe both he thought.

Faraday handed the major one of his personal cards containing his home e-mail address.

Bob Hutchings took the card and read the details. 'Not to your official e-mail then?'

Faraday wasn't absolutely sure and so didn't answer the question directly but looked at the photograph in a polished wooden frame placed at an angle alongside the computer screen. 'Your son was a very handsome young officer, Bob.'

'Yes, yes he was,' he replied, confirming Mark's thoughts. 'Taller than me of course,' he continued, trying to make light of his comments, but painful memories easily flooded back. 'And much more hair. Just like his mother. But it did for her, his death in action. Afghanistan, 27th of this month, you know. But you have to just get on with it, don't you.' He moved his right hand in an arc as if to include the museum. 'This is my family now, Mark.' He fixed Faraday with those sad eyes as if to challenge him.

'Bob,' said Faraday answering the unasked question, 'you know that I *have* to follow the evidence. If this murder is anything to do with the army, I will try desperately not to embarrass your family and keep it in-house.'

Major Hutchings bit his lip as he thought of his son, a son who had gone back to encourage his troops forward. A son who would never, never consider his men to have been cowardly. Confused, disorientated, unsure maybe, but never cowards. And if that was good enough for his son it was certainly good enough for him. He studied Faraday for a moment and saw something of his own son in this policeman.

'I think I know that, Superintendent,' he replied formally as if to apologise for questioning Faraday's integrity. But he needed to say more. 'Pippa said that you're a good man. She seems so sure that you would try your level best not to damage us.'

Chapter 13

Thursday, 22nd March.

Antigua, the Caribbean and Police Headquarters, Bristol, England.

LADY CECELIA Chelwood enjoyed the visit to Antigua, an island shaped like a heart and boasting a gleaming pink-white sandy beach for every day of the year. She had taken photographs of the magnificent views from high up on Fort Shirley and had walked the cobbled streets of Nelson's Dockyard in English Harbour with Kathy Turner and Shelly Kaufman, the attentive and alert Shane Ward always just a few paces away.

'You could have almost imagined Horatio Nelson in the officers' quarters, checking progress in the engineer's office and speaking with the quarter-masters in the lumber stores,' she said to Kathy and Shelly as *Odyssey* prepared to go to sea.

'Was Horatio really here?' Shelly asked as if discussing a personal acquaintance and an event that had occurred during the previous few weeks.

'Oh, yes. In the 1780s, I think,' she replied adjusting her large pink hat so as to protect her pale complexion from the sun.

'And with that dreadful woman, his lover?' Shelly asked relishing any talk of scandal. 'What was her name, Kathy?'

'Lady Emma Hamilton, isn't that so, Cecelia?'

'You are always so precise, Kathy, when it comes to indiscrete behaviour,' complimented Cecelia, conveniently ignoring the fact that the young Captain Nelson did not even know Lady Hamilton when he was on the West Indies station.

'There you are,' said Shelly with a laugh, 'if you want to know all the gossip, just look to Kathy.'

The three ladies clinked glasses as Jim Turner guided his $50,000,000 boat passed Fort Berkley under the ever watchful, and slightly anxious, eye of Captain Jelstrup.

***

Mark Faraday and Kay Yin had talked until the early hours over a bottle of *Saint Benoit*. He had updated her on his visit to the REME museum and she had talked about the forensics; the enquiries into Nicholas Fry's girl friend, Elsa Chaudouet; Fry's ex-wife and the businessman Robert Ballantine; the inquest, opened, then adjourned; and the follow-up enquiries as a result of the operation throughout the 16th and 17th, exactly two weeks after the murder.

Whilst any vehicle used by the killer had not been identified, a talkative teenage courting couple, Peter Weaver and Sandra Bennett, did report a man leaving Nicholas Fry's home by the front door at about 9.40pm, dressed in a dark-coloured raincoat, wearing a dark, possibly black, trilby hat and carrying one, maybe, two cardboard-type tubes. A similar sighting was reported about ten or fifteen minutes later at Princess Victoria Street. But nothing could have prepared Kay Yin for the revelation at mid-day.

Nurse Chloe Marsh had discovered the letter the previous evening when the body of Bill Harding was being prepared for removal to the hospital's mortuary. In accordance with routine instruction, she did not open the letter addressed to the coroner. The staff nurse took the letter to sister. Sister handed the letter unopened to night staff who, in turn handed it on to early morning staff. The letter was taken to the court in Backfields and given to the Coroner's Officer by a grey-suited NHS manager.

'Ask DCI Yin to step in,' the assistant chief constable told his secretary. Kay Yin tapped on the door to be greeted by a stern-faced ACC seated behind his large desk, hands steeped, Detective Chief Superintendent 'Roberto' Perrin standing at his side. Perrin gave the young officer the slightest of winks, a gesture of support or caution, she did not know.

The ACC didn't ask the young detective to sit.

'How much do you know of the 7th Earl Chelwood and his family?' he asked with an all-knowing sneer as if talking to a simpleton.

She knew a great deal or, at least, as much as Mark Faraday had e-mailed to her and discussed the previous evening, but she was not allowed to answer.

'Do you know,' he continued as he leaned forward on his desk, 'that William Chelwood came to prominence during the reign of Henry VIII and was knighted?' It was a rhetorical question as were the others that followed. 'Did you know that Sir William's son, another William, was created Baron Chelwood for his service to Elizabeth Tudor, in particular as a result of his intelligence activities with Lord Howard of Effingham? During the Civil War, the Chelwoods supported the king and fled to Holland when he was executed, returning to England at the Restoration. One of his ancestors fought alongside the Duke of Cambridge during the Crimean War, another was an ADC to a king and his grand-mother was a lady-in-waiting to the Queen Mother.' The assistant chief constable fell back into his chair as if impatient with the need to explain such obvious facts to a subordinate.

'This family's lineage and history can only be described as distinguished. The present earl's grand-father played a significant part in the financing of the engineering feat that joined the Great Lakes to Montreal as well as laying the foundations for the creation of Avonmouth Docks. During the First World War, young Lord Chelwood was killed in heroic circumstances and during the Second World War, the earl's father worked closely with Lord Beaverbrook in the Ministries of Aircraft Production and Supply. Indeed, he was confidant of Sir Winston Churchill.' He sat upright again in his chair, anger tingeing his tone.

'I instructed *you* specifically,' he turned towards Perrin and repeated: 'specifically … that you, *Miss* Yin, were not to pursue your half-baked enquiries of the Chelwoods. Are you out of your mind?'

Detective Chief Superintendent Perrin glared at Kay Yin and shook his head gently from side to side – a warning, a warning that she reluctantly heeded. 'No, sir.'

'Yet *you* persisted. *You* have made further enquiries with Dean Paul Patterson. For God's sake,' he said in total exasperation, 'he is shortly to be appointed the Bishop of Lincoln and that means he gets a seat in the House of Lords alongside Chelwood. Chelwood is the Lord Lieutenant, the Queen's *chosen* representative, the person upon whom Her Majesty relies. What is it with you?' he said, genuinely perplexed. 'Chelwood is a respected banker, has links with the intelligence services and holds diplomatic status with the UN. Do you have any idea at all what all of this means?' This comment was not intended to encourage a response. 'What it means is that you do not *mess* with these people.' Kay was about to speak, but a withering glare from Perrin stilled her comments.

'Fortunately, I have been able to placate the dean,' he said, pleased with himself as if only an officer of his gifted abilities would have been able to accomplish such a delicate task. 'I have assured the dean that there will be no further enquiries of him. I have been able to reassure him of this as a result of information that came in to my possession early this morning.'

His last comment was made in a tone suggesting that he, and he alone, would naturally be privy to significant information. He pulled towards him a dark-blue folder embossed with the crest of the *Association of Chief Police Officers*. He opened it slowly. The folder contained two pieces of paper. He placed his hands at each side of the leather folder as if ministering to a holy relic on an altar.

'This is a copy of course,' he said as he removed the hand-written note, 'a scrawled letter in a common hand, each line riddled with grammatical and spelling errors, nevertheless, its contents *are* significant and I shall read it to you.'

Assistant Chief Constable Wynne-Thomas read the letter painfully as if it was a distasteful chore to have to read such a poorly constructed letter.

'To Her Magerstis coronor. Iv done a lot of bad things but for the ferst time in me life i feels giltey like cause i aint got much time. Nows i knows that i was in truble. I thaught it were indergestion then i had to go to the hospiall and thaught id have one last go to get me boys somit befor i goes to me Maker. Id thaught that therd be rich pickins in Clifton but i paniked and keped hittin the artist bloke. i didnt meen to kill him but i was pissed with him cus ther was nottin ther worth havin
Bill Harding'

'William Harding,' remarked the ACC as he picked up and read a type-written form, 'is, in contrast to Lord Chelwood, a thief, and not a very successful one. Fifty-four years of age with seven previous convictions, including burglary, for which he spent four and a half years of his useless life in prison.'

He replaced the note in the file and closed the leather cover shut. 'He died in hospital yesterday of cancer and the note was found by a nurse who was both *diligent* as well as *competent*.' He leaned back into his chair, allowing the comparison between the nurse and the detective to hit home. 'We have had the writing analysed, of course – there's enough of it in his bulky file. The note has been authenticated as that written by William Harding, albeit in a shaky hand. As a consequence, the case of the tragic murder of Nicholas Fry is now closed. All *you* have to do is close down your operation and endorse the file with William Harding's name. Do we understand each other?'

'Absolutely, sir.'

There was a malevolent and ominous pause before the ACC continued. 'I hope you do, Miss Yin. One more foul-up by you and your career will be as dead as Harding. Carry on.'

DCI Yin left the office, collecting her brief case and rain coat from the secretary's office. She was shaken and bewildered, her mind in a whirl as she walked down the corridor towards the front entrance of headquarters. As she reached the top of the stairs, Perrin called after her.

'Miss Yin.' She stopped and turned outside the conference room, holding onto the stair rail for support.

'Sir.'

'Here's a copy of Harding's note. Check it out for me.'

'Right, sir.' She turned, only to turn back. 'You helped me in there, sir. Thank you. I'm sorry if I've let you down.'

As she turned to walk down the stairs, the detective chief superintendent touched her on the elbow and said quietly. 'You haven't let me down, Kay. I smell a rat here, as you do. Check it out, and dig deep.'

Chapter 14

Friday, 23rd March.

Police Headquarters, Bristol, England.

'MORNING PRAYERS' lasted longer than the normal fifteen minutes. Inspector Trench talked of his meetings with the event managers and outlined the admissions and signage arrangements as well as his liaison with the security contractors, although dismissive of the arrival of irrigation equipment on site the previous day.

'It's not vital for today, Gordon, but you might like to check the security arrangements for this equipment with the event managers. I'm sure it's in hand but we don't want animal rights activists sabotaging any of the equipment.'

Inspector Trench made a note sullenly, resentful at what he perceived as another example of unwarranted criticism, a resentment exacerbated by Faraday's insistence that the superintendent would also be meeting with Special Branch, the Lord Lieutenancy, and representatives of the Metropolitan Police and the Foreign and Commonwealth Office, to discuss the presence of the King of Spain at the Trials.

Chief Inspector Fowler updated the meeting on the key performers scheduled for the Glastonbury festival and PC Blanchard confirmed the suspension of highway maintenance work on red, blue and green routes during the air tattoo. At the end of their meeting, Faraday discussed with Fowler his participation in the forthcoming round of promotion boards and spoke with one of the clerks, Jade Hancock, about her university studies, then walked over to the restaurant with Pippa Blanchard.

Minutes agreed, Pippa Blanchard pulled off some sheets of paper from her clipboard and passed them to Faraday, finishing her coffee as Faraday read the two pages of typed notes that she had prepared.

Faraday did not notice others as they entered or left the restaurant. He tried to make sense of what he was reading. He was sure he knew what it all meant, yet he hoped to see feasible alternative explanations. He absent-mindedly looked away from the papers, fingering the side of his mouth, then, as if he had snapped out of a deep sleep, he acknowledged colleagues. He spoke briefly to Superintendent 'Dusty' Miller and Chief Inspector Richard Davis as they walked past to sit with other district colleagues. Following Faraday's lead, PC Blanchard made no effort to cover the papers and thereby draw attention to their content. He glanced around the restaurant again and there were more smiles of acknowledgment. Satisfied that they would not be overheard, he spoke again.

'This is dynamite, Pippa. Are you sure that this is correct?'

'Yes, sir.'

'No doubt at all?' pressed Faraday.

'No doubt at all,' she replied as she fixed Faraday with her intense crystal-blue eyes. 'I just kept cross-checking and cross-checking. Chaplain Patterson was present at the execution of a Private Edward Haynes on the 23rd November 1914.'

He noted the precision of her answer but continued to press her. 'And you are sure that Haynes was an estate worker?'

'Absolutely.'

'There are no absolutes, Pippa,' he said reasonably. 'Major Hutchings only told me the other day that records did get muddled and hundreds of soldiers gave incorrect names and dates of birth for all manner of reasons. You could be mistaken, surely?'

'I could be, but I'm sure I'm not, sir,' she replied with a certainty that he had not really seen before. 'Edward Haynes was employed as a groom on the Chelwood estate. His name is inscribed on the Menin Gate.'

'Haynes would not have been an unusual name. I would guess that there are a number of Haynes on the memorial?'

'But only one Edward Haynes who appears on the village memorial, the memorial that contains the names of Major Lord Chelwood VC and other estate workers.'

'And you say that young Haynes enlisted and went over to France as Lord Chelwood's manservant?'

'Yes, this,' she said producing a photograph, 'is a collection of young volunteers, including Haynes, outside the recruiting office in Bristol.'

'That's the museum, isn't it?'

'Yes, well, it was the art gallery then,' she corrected. 'The recruiting office was next door, where the Wills' university tower now stands.'

'And what's this?' asked Faraday pointing to her notes.

'These details confirm that Private Edward Haynes was billeted in the Colston Hall, then entrained from Temple Meads to Swindon.

There followed some weeks of initial infantry training before he moved on to Southampton and a paddle-steamer for the crossing to Le Havre. More rudimentary training took place in France before marching on to Cassel, a few miles from the front.' Pippa Blanchard said nothing as she withdrew another piece of paper from her clipboard and placed it in front of her superintendent.

'And this?' he asked.

'It's a copy of Form W3996. It's ....'

'It's alright, Pippa. I see what it is now.' There was silence as he re-read the words on the War Office form. 'When did you get this?'

'Major Hutchings faxed it through early this morning, sir.'

Faraday read the words again on top of the form in silence:

INSTRUCTIONS FOR THE GUIDANCE OF COURTS MARTIAL
WHERE A SENTENCE OF DEATH HAS BEEN PASSED

'It's in the name of Private Edward Haynes,' she said after a little time, 'and signed by the court's president: Captain Lord Chelwood.'

'And the execution took place at Boesinghe,' he asked, 'in the town square, I suppose?' Pippa Blanchard could not lie to him and so didn't answer. 'In the town square?' he asked again.

'In the abattoir, sir.'

Both remained utterly silent. Faraday fiddled with the handle of his cup, then pushed the cup and saucer to one side. He picked up the little bar of *Kit-Kat* chocolate. He didn't open or eat the bar but simply placed it into the empty cup, his eyes stinging with anger.

'We need the transcripts of the trial.'

She didn't answer immediately. He looked at her questioningly and she replied. 'There are very often no transcripts, sir. Do you want me to keep on with this?'

'What would you do, Pippa, if you were in my position?'
'Pursue it, sir.'

'Then get on with it, Pippa, but trawl, no personal contacts.'

***

'You wanted to see me Robert?' asked Deputy Chief Constable Mary Priestly. 'I can only give you five.'

'I'll get straight to the point then,' replied Detective Chief Superintendent Perrin. 'The murder of Nicholas Fry is back on the front burner.'

'On the front burner? John told us that the case was now closed, other than the formal inquest. Some local burglar, what was his name, William Harding, he admitted it, didn't he?'

'Well, it's now wide open again. Harding could not have committed the murder. At the time he was at the bingo hall in Winterstoke Road with his two sons and daughter-in-laws. He was a winner that night, not the main winner but he won enough to be called up on to the stage for a photograph with the compare,' adding unequivocally: 'Be assured that Harding could not have murdered Nicholas Fry.'

'Oh, shit.   Does this means we will have to interview Lord Chelwood?'

'It must be done.'

'Who's on this? DCI Yin isn't it?'

'Yes.'

'John doesn't value her ability very much.'

'He's incapable of judging the value of a door mat.' The DCC raised a disapproving eyebrow, but Perrin spoke rapidly with calm reassurance. 'DCI Yin is up to it, but I agree that this is a delicate matter and, in the interests of protocol, it makes sense for a superintendent-rank to be involved, not as SIO but just for the interviews of Lord Chelwood and the soon-to-be bishop, Dean Patterson.'

The DCC became distracted and irritated as her phone rang. Perrin took the opportunity to recommend a solution for her. 'I'll put an appropriate superintendent into the mix, ma'am.'

'Yes, yes. OK, Robert,' she replied impatiently, 'but keep me in the loop'.

Detective Chief Superintendent Perrin left the DCC's office, closing the door quietly and walked through her PA's office, already occupied with her next meeting. He made his way down the carpeted corridor, turned left and into his secretary's office.

'Come in you two,' he said to Superintendent Faraday and Chief Inspector Yin. He opened the door for them both. 'Take a seat.'

They both sat in two comfortable chairs as Perrin sat on the corner of his desk, carefully adjusting his double-breasted jacket and shirt cuffs. Satisfied with his sartorial appearance, he spoke again.

'I have spoken to the DCC and explained the significance of the letter. Written by Harding but its content is absolute nonsense, thanks to your enquiries, Kay. That means that the case is open and on-going.' He turned his attention to Mark Faraday. 'Kay tells me that your Phillipa Blanchard is something of an authority on the First World War.' Faraday was about to clarify the point but Perrin raised the palms of his hands. 'It suits my purposes that she is. The important aspect is that a connection has been discovered between a Private Haynes, the gallant Lord Chelwood and Chaplain Patterson. The Chelwoods and the Pattersons will need to be investigated and interviewed.' He shifted slightly on the corner of his desk and concentrated his charming attention on the young DCI. 'With no disrespect to you, Kay, but for appearance sake and so as not to upset the sensibilities of the nobility, we need someone of superintendent rank to head this up.' There was no objection from DCI Yin but, nevertheless, Perrin performed his Berlusconi palm gesture again. 'You will remain the SIO in this case, Kay, but when it comes to Chelwood and Patterson, I want Mark in the mix.'

'It will not be an issue, sir,' offered Kay Yin.

'And what about you, Mark, will this role create any professional difficulties for you?'

'None at all, we have worked together before, sir.'

'And will this new arrangement,' he asked softly, 'create any *domestic* issues for you both?'

'Do you believe it could, sir?' asked Mark Faraday carefully.

Perrin smiled at the answer. 'Look, you are both good people and single. What you do in your private lives is a matter for you … provided it does not impact upon the case or subsequent trial. We only have to look across the pond to the O. J. Simpson murder trial to see the problems that can occur,' he said, referring to the allegations that were made by the defence lawyers against the presiding judge and his wife who was also a police captain. 'I want to keep you two on this case and so I am relying upon you both to minimise the potential for any difficulties.'

'Your network seems to be very good, sir?' ventured Kay Yin, hoping to elicit more information. She wasn't disappointed.

'You, Kay, were seen to enter Mark's apartment on the 15th March by Inspector Trench. He telephoned giving me details and asked to see me. What an idiot he is – it gave me time to make some checks. I was able to access your private car log, Mark, and noted that you had visited Chepstow and a Colonel Vaughan, then I remembered that you were both involved in that military intelligence operation last year. It wasn't difficult to work it out. I thanked Trench, of course, and said that you were both working on a small but delicate matter for me.'

'And the ACC?'

'He's licking his wounds at the moment, so my advice to you both is to keep your heads down, but, have no doubt, his ego has been dented and he will be waiting for you to slip up.' He stood up and away from his desk. 'OK, off you both go.'

They moved to leave the office, Perrin looking admiringly at the young lady's cat-like walk. Faraday opened the door standing to one side so as to allow his lover to leave first.

'Kay, what is the main question in your mind at the moment?' Perrin asked, halting them both in their tracks. They turned and face the head of CID.

'There can only be one, sir,' she replied without a moments' thought. 'Why did William Harding write a letter that was so clearly untrue?'

'Good,' he said with an approving smile. 'If you can answer that question then, maybe, we will discover the identity of the killer and the reason for the murder of Mr Nicholas Fry.'

Chapter 15

Monday 26th March.

Police Headquarters, Bristol, England and SW of the Grand Cayman Islands, the Caribbean.

THE MURDER enquiry team had been hard at work since 7am. Superintendent Mark Faraday had been introduced to the team a little after eight o'clock and his role explained to them by Detective Chief Inspector Kay Yin, Faraday deliberately adopting a secondary role so as not to undermine her authority as the Senior Investigating Officer. There were no gasps of surprise as Kay spoke, the team, still restricted to twelve in number – a concession to the ACC - were just pleased that they were back on the case. They were also pleased, maybe relieved, for another reason too. They were aware of Faraday's reputation and understood the underlying implications for them of Faraday's presence – it meant that no one was off-limits.

Faraday spent over a half-hour listening to Kay's succinct briefing and the allocation of *actions*. In addition to the information gained from the reconstruction held on the evening of the 16th and the tedious on-going analysis of CCTV footage, specifically focused *actions* would target the Chelwood family and their business interests; the Patterson family; and William Harding's career, family and associates.

'Whilst the writing is shaky,' she said pointing to the copy on the screen, 'there is little doubt that the Harding letter was written by him. However, I am having the language patterns, grammar and spelling compared with the statements written by him that appear in his file. Meanwhile, Mr Faraday has on his staff an officer, Phillipa Blanchard, whose father serves in the army. As Pippa worked in a military museum, she will be digging into military records for me as far back as 1912.'

There were no questions from her teams and Kay did not offer any further information about the apparent link between the Chelwoods, the Pattersons and the execution of Edward Haynes. Whilst these links could provide motive, she preferred her teams to concentrate upon tangible specifics for at least the next few days.

Faraday arrived at Ops Planning a little later than usual, a fact not unnoticed by Trench and Glass, but in ample time to chair 'Morning Prayers'. He concluded the meeting by mentioning that he could be absent from the department from time to time because of a possible involvement in the investigation of the murder of Nicholas Fry, a comment that resulted in Trench and Glass raising their heads.

'I understand that some mistakes have been made, sir?' Trench speculated.

'No mistakes have been made, Gordon,' replied Faraday, his impatience showing through. 'A letter was received by the coroner suggesting that a named individual had committed the murder. This promising development was investigated by DCI Yin and was found to be some sort of hoax amongst many.'

'But I assume that you will now be taking overall charge of the investigation?' asked Trench mischievously.

'Certainly not,' replied Faraday sharply. 'My main responsibilities remain here?'

'Can I ask how you are involved, sir', persisted Trench. 'This is very intriguing, we are all eager to know?'

'Gordon, it's simply a matter of a small area of experience that I happen to have which could be of use from time to time during the enquiry.'

'Hidden talents, sir?'

'And they remain hidden, Gordon, but may be to be revealed at the end of the enquiry. OK, that's enough for one morning. Thank you, we are done here.'

Faraday spent a few minutes with Silvia Glass dealing with a query regarding road closures for the St Paul's Carnival, a discussion interrupted by Geoff Fowler gesturing with a rotating index finger. The chief inspector had just taken a call from the Princess Royal's Personal Protection Officer notifying the force of an impromptu visit by the princess to Gloucestershire General Hospital following a road traffic accident involving one of her staff. Last minute changes in plans involving the royal family were not infrequent occurrences and the department took the usual steps. Calls were exchanged with Special Branch, the Traffic Division and hospital, timings, routes and escorts confirmed and actions agreed.

'OK, Pippa, I'm suffering from caffeine deficiency again,' he said casually and PC Blanchard gathered up her papers. As they walked towards the door, Faraday stopped to speak to Miss Hancock. 'If you are free for twenty minutes, do you want to discuss your assignment over coffee?'

'That would be brilliant,' she said and pulled a large A4 envelope from her desk drawer and followed the superintendent out through the doors towards the restaurant.

Over coffee Jade Hancock outlined her progress with her latest assignment. She was making good progress, thought Faraday and he only made some very minor suggestions. They discussed referencing then Jade returned to the office, leaving Pippa Blanchard to up-date Faraday on the private research that she had carried out over the weekend.

'Major Hutchings obtained a copy of the regimental history as well as copies of some of Private Haynes' records, pension entitlement, the certificate of service, that sort of thing, but it's a bit of a bundle.'

'Can you bring it in? You could hand it over in the car park and I'll take it home.'

'But I'm on leave tomorrow.'

'Yes, I know that,' he said as if of no importance at all. 'It's not urgent; Wednesday would do, although you do live in Westbury-on-Trym, could you not drop it over to my apartment this evening?'

'I can do that, sir,' she replied willingly.

'But make it no later than seven.'

'Seven o'clock it is.'

***

Five time-zones away, the *Odyssey* had cruised over the Bartlett Deep, described on maritime maps as the Cayman Trough, the deepest part of the Caribbean Sea, and towards the Crown Colony of the Cayman Islands. Captain Jelstrup navigated *Odyssey* toward

Georgetown, the capital of Grand Cayman, on the south coast of this the largest of the Cayman Islands. Clearance having been granted by the port authorities, *Odyssey* gently approached her mooring and, once alongside, the crew made fast her lines.

The title of 'Third Officer' was a *nom de ruse* for ex-US Special Forces veteran Shane Ward, a holder of the Iraq *Coalition Service Citation*. His key role was to ensure the boat's security and to provide on-shore security when required. On-shore security would be required today.

The coral islands have a world-wide reputation for their beaches and superb diving opportunities. Grand Cayman also has over seven-hundred banks – more than New York City – and as a result is one of the best known financial centres in the world. Today, it would not be Seven Mile Beach or scuba diving that would attract Lady Cecelia Chelwood's attention but just one of those many banks.

Third Officer Ward provided reassurance as he escorted her ashore; the Stars and Stripes catching the breeze at *Odyssey's* stern impressed the admiring and the diplomatic baggage tag dangling from her leather *Mulberry* bag was sure to deter official scrutiny. She walked confidently along the waterfront of this charming town, safe in the knowledge that no questions would be asked of her about a modest deposit to be made into a numbered account. Lady Chelwood considered the sum of £200,000 a very small price to pay and smiled at the thought that these islands had long ago been a popular hiding place for pirates, including the infamous Anne Bonny and Mary Read, both of whom escaped justice as a result of their powerful connections and feminine appeal.

***

At ten to seven in the evening, Pippa Blanchard parked her Mazda MX5 in one of the visitor's bays at Avon View Court. She approached the glass doors and entered. At the reception desk, the night security officer, David Parkin, was anticipating her arrival.

'Mr Faraday's expecting you, miss. Straight up the stairs. It's number 16.'

Pippa Blanchard mounted the stairs with her heaped bundle of books and paper. At the door she pressed the bell. She waited. When the door opened she didn't know how to respond.

'It's Pippa, isn't it?' said Kay Yin with her huge smile. 'I'm Kay. Come on in and let me take those from you.' Kay relieved Pippa of her burden. 'We are straight through,' she said without a care in the world. 'Could you make sure the door is shut, please.'
Kay walked down the hall in bare feet, dressed in the slightest, pure-white *Jack Wills* shorts and a pink candy-striped blouse. They entered the large lounge with its panoramic views of the river and the setting sun.

'Pippa, you've bumped into Kay before, haven't you?' asked Faraday.

'Yes, sir. I've seen you around headquarters, ma'am.'

'Ground rules, Pippa,' said Faraday. 'It's Kay and Mark, please, or no supper for you.'

'Supper ... sir?' she replied uneasily.

'We thought you might like to have some company tonight,' said Kay as she separated a large, leather-bound book from the papers and placed them neatly by the dry-wipe board.

'Company?'

'Why don't you stay for supper, Pippa?' suggested Mark gently as if it would be the best thing to do.

'How did you know?' she enquired almost silently as Kay moved reassuringly to Mark's side, her crystal-blue eyes sparkling with moisture.

Mark took a few seconds before replying carefully. 'Major Hutchings mentioned to me his son.' He paused again then went on. 'When he said that he was sure my enquiries wouldn't damage "us", I had at first assumed that he was talking collectively about the army, but when you asked to have tomorrow off I checked your personnel file,' he said as Pippa nodded knowingly, ' ... I saw that you had been on sick leave for a few weeks after Paul's death.'

Pippa Blanchard sat down on the edge of one of the lounge chairs. For a moment she sat there, elbows on knees, deep in thought starring at the carpet in front of her. She cleared her throat. 'Paul had just been promoted captain. I had seen him a few times when he visited his father in the museum and we just started to go out together ... it seemed so natural at the time ... it was just for a few months ... only a few months, then he was posted. Silly really.'

'I hope we haven't presumed too much, Pippa,' asked Kay as she moved towards their young visitor. 'You're not angry are you?'
Pippa Blanchard stood up, those intense blue eyes brimming with tears. 'No,' she replied as she hugged Kay like the sister she didn't have. 'It was kind of you to think of me.'

They didn't talk about the First World War, there was no need. Pippa Blanchard had prepared a bullet-point briefing page and everything was tagged. As they ate, they spoke of holidays in Spain and Hong Kong, of Chinese and French cooking, of Golf GTis and Mazda MX5s, of *Jack Wills* and *French Connection*, of nothing and everything.

At eleven, Pippa prepared to leave. 'I have something for you,' said Kay. She went into their bedroom, returning with a little wooden box measuring about three inches by seven. She handed the box to Pippa who opened the lid. Inside was a white porcelain figure nestling amongst the purple satin.

'It's a statue of Kuan Yin, the great Chinese Goddess of Compassion,' explained Kay. 'Tradition tells us that when she had finished her ministry on Earth, she ascended into heaven to listen to the cries and to understand the anguish of the world.'

She turned the statue around in her hand. 'Do you believe that?'

'In the world that we inhabit, Pippa,' replied Kay, 'I'm not always sure what I should believe,' adding reasonably, 'but it can't possibly do any harm … can it?'

Once Pippa Blanchard had left, Mark and Kay cleared the plates and loaded the dishwasher.

***

Later they drifted off to sleep, the scent of the sandalwood and jasmine candles still filling their bedroom, the flickering light softly illuminating the outline of their naked bodies. When her back had arched and that most primitive part of their minds seemed to explode in unison, Mark had cried out and Kay had understood. She understood how much she relied upon her lover, but she also understood the power that she had over him, a power that she would never abuse.

Chapter 16

Wednesday, 28th March.

Police Headquarters, Bristol, England and at anchor, the Island of Cozumel, the Caribbean.

SUPERINTENDENT FARADAY and DCI Yin had decided not to involve Pippa Blanchard in their discussions surrounding the death of Edward Haynes. They sat around Kay's desk in the office down the corridor from the incident room as the afternoon began to give way to the evening. On a side table, neatly typed notes were laid out alongside notes scribbled in pencil; and copies of original documents lay alongside the four leather-bound diaries and a copy of the bulky regimental history.

'I've gone through Tatton Chelwood's diaries,' said Faraday, 'there is no reference, not even the slightest hint of Edward Haynes' offence, trial or execution, yet, in every other sense they are amazingly detailed. But there is a pattern. In the first month or so of the war, they read like a *Boy's Own* adventure comic with optimistic comments that "it will all be over by Christmas". Once in France and at the Front, they become more measured. From 1915 until his death, the text, whilst remaining detailed, becomes more and more - I'm not sure how to describe it - excitable? Maybe, theatrical would be a better description?' He fingered at the diaries, opening the pages at the yellow tags. 'The diaries are riddled with comments like "the men displayed pluck and fighting spirit", the attack was "pressed home with a desperate dash", the men "clapped heartily". It all seems so staged and artificial.'

She touched his hand, her fingers entwining with his. 'Isn't that how officers used to speak?' suggested Kay.

'You are probably right,' conceded Faraday knowing that his judgement was being impaired by his dislike for Tatton Chelwood.

Kay Yin pulled out a copy of one faded brown-coloured monthly magazine. 'This magazine: *Gallant Deeds of the War*, says on the front cover: *Everyone should read these stories of our brave heroes at the Front* and *Thrilling stories of luck on land and sea*'.

She looked at him with those beautifully dark, wide eyes. He smiled acknowledging how right she was.

'There's nothing in those magazines, I suppose?'
'Chelwood is mentioned twice. He's also mentioned in these,' she continued indicating three volumes of *The Great War - I Was There*. 'He is mentioned three times in the second volume, but nothing about Edward Haynes.'

Faraday's objectivity returned as he plucked at a red marker tags in the diaries. 'And no mention is made of the execution of Edward Haynes in the diaries. On the 23rd November 1914, his entries refer to a *hearty breakfast*, a problem with *scaling ladders*, the collapse of a stretch of *firing steps* and a visit to a *forward observation post* but nothing about this execution, although he does refer to an unexpected *Ferocious attack by the Boche* just after stand-to on the 19th and an *unpleasant disciplinary business* on the 21st.'

'You said *this* execution?' she asked.

'There was another execution that took place in 1916. Chelwood was not involved, other than being a witness to the execution. But he refers to it in his diary that evening.' Faraday ran his finger down the red protruding tags and opened at a page. 'He remarks that *I was frightful sick after the execution that was carried out in a steadfast manner. Out of sorts all day.'*

'But nothing about Haynes,' Kay reflected.

'Yes there was,' he said, fingering the green tags.

'The green tags,' she said, her brows furrowed, 'there are hundreds of them?'

'These all refer to letters Chelwood wrote to the wives or sweethearts or parents of soldiers killed in action. A note says: *Wrote letter to Private Haynes' mother – died of wounds.'*

'And these green tags are all about notifying the families of a death?'

'Not all. There are notation about letters to the War Office about temporary ranks and pension entitlements, that sort of thing.'

'He was attentive then?'

'Yes, he was. He also seemed keen to recommend individuals for awards or promotions. If any soldier was killed and held a temporary rank, he seemed to always make sure that the War Office and Pay Corp were aware of this so that the correct payments were made to relatives.'

'Any other details of correspondence about Private Haynes?'

'We have a copy here,' he said, selecting another photocopied piece of paper, 'of the official cause of Haynes' death which was recorded as *died of wounds.* We need to find out who the next of kin was.   I assume it was his parents I suppose, and what information they were given.'

'Shall we give that task to Pippa?' suggested Kay.

'I think it should be OK for her tomorrow, in any case, I don't think that she would want to be excluded.'

'What does the regimental history say?'

Faraday heaved the heavy book off the desk and opened the volume at a series of red tags. 'It refers to an attack on the 19th and the *steadiness* of the men, counter-attacks made with *great determination* later that day and the following day and that there had been *heavy casualties* but that the men had *done well*.'

'No casualties by name?'

'Yes, a Captain John Little, four lieutenants named Grigg, Skilton, Dunn and Westhouse and a Sergeant-Major Kershaw and forty-two "other ranks killed". In the index are listed every member of the regiment who were killed, missing or wounded. Haynes is listed under the heading *killed*.'

'And the execution in 1916, is that mentioned?'

'Oh, yes. The 30th May for *wilfully disobeying an order*. It's very detailed indeed. It lists the officers of the Field General Court Martial, the Medical Officer, those present at the execution, its exact time: 04:35.'

'Lord Chelwood wasn't that old,' observed Kay Yin referring back to the execution of Edward Haynes, 'and he was only an *acting* captain and inexperienced. There didn't seem to be any checks and balances so as to ensure fairness.'

'Major Hutchings says that the courts were much more formalised later in the war, but at the beginning …', his voice trailed off as he thought of what the major had told him. 'The real problem was that the presidents and members of these courts had to show themselves as being resolute and strong and invariably recommended a death sentence believing that those higher up and more experienced would recommend leniency, whilst those higher up thought that they should endorse their junior officers' decisions and support them in their difficult task.'

'Is that what you believe happened in the case of Edward Haynes?'

'No,' Faraday replied unequivocally.

'Why not, it would be reasonable to assume that Lord Chelwood would have been under the same pressures and assumptions as others?'

'Yes, he would have been, but there's more than a whiff of cover-up in the case of Private Edward Haynes.'

'Do you want to keep going with the military angle?' suggested Kay. 'My team is still snowed-under with exhibits and it's Bill Harding's funeral tomorrow at eleven at the South Bristol Crematorium. I'm told that the family and friends are all going to a pub on the A38 after the service, so I've got one of the team helping behind the bar.'

Faraday realised that such a move was risky and had the potential for adverse press publicity, but he supported her decision.

'Go for it,' he said casually, but Kay knew that in so doing he was providing her with insurance. She said nothing but their exchange of smiles acknowledged that they would always protect each other in equal measure.

'Can I also leave you and Pippa with the Pattersons,' she said.

'Yes. She's already got into Shrewsbury's Sixth Form records, all conveniently on their website, as well as his university's congregation records for the year he graduated. He certainly wasn't top of the class.'

She lowered her head slightly and narrowed her eyes. 'There's a little turn at the corner of your mouth.'

'Is there?' feigning surprise.

'What are you up to?' she asked.

'Let me talk hypothetically,' he replied. 'We know that Harding didn't kill Nicholas Fry. Let us assume for the moment that Patterson didn't kill him either. Let us speculate that at a time convenient to us the Chelwoods get wind of our enquiries concerning the dean, I'm just wondering what their reaction would be?'

'Darling, be careful.'

'It only has to be very reasonable *little* enquiries that would not alarm the innocent but would certainly worry the guilty.'

'You think we should set up an interview with the dean?'

'Oh, yes,' he replied lightly. 'It's quite reasonable for us to ask the dean the nature of the three phone calls that we now know Nicholas Fry made to him. What we really need to know is if the dean has any of the chaplain's diaries or records. But I would suggest we wait?'

'Why?'

'Because at the moment his elevation to a bishopric has not been confirmed. The date of any such appointments is the 8th April. I think a visit to him just before the scheduled announcement should catch him on the back foot.' He looked directly at Kay Yin and raised his chin just a little. 'I would be quite prepared to threaten him that, should he not cooperate with us, I would guarantee that his association with a scandal would become a press sensation and mean that he would never become a bishop.'

'Mark,' she said as if to protest, but she knew him too well. She knew that he was determined to bring to justice those responsible for the death of Nicholas Fry. And so simply asked: 'And the Chelwoods?'

'Ah, the Chelwoods... Major Hutchings was very helpful. I think a little visit by us to St Matthew's parish church would be enough to cause his lordship's heart to miss a beat.'

***

At 02:00 the boat's clocks were retarded by one hour to GMT-6, at which time *Odyssey* was some seventy nautical miles due east of the Mexican island of Cozumel, just off the Yucatan Peninsula. Captain Jelstrup reduced speed to eleven knots which he calculated would allow for *Odyssey* to reach her anchorage in the small bay as breakfast was about to be served on the upper sun deck to his wealthy employer and his guests.

With perfect timing, *Odyssey* dropped her port anchor into the crystal-clear turquoise sea just below the walls of the Temple of the Wind, the tower that had guarded this ancient Mayan city of Tulum for nearly seven-hundred years.

Bill Kaufman followed Jim Turner's lead and stood behind the yellow and white striped cushioned chairs and gallantly assisted Cecelia, Kathy and Shelly as they sat around the breakfast table decorated with exotic fruits and extravagant, sun-burst flowers. The ladies graciously acknowledged the Pilipino waiters as they helped them with their serviettes. As they ate, these wealthy ladies talked and laughed as they would at their exclusive tennis and golf clubs, all completely at ease as *Odyssey* rode gently at anchor.

Chapter 17

Thursday, 29th March.

Police Headquarters, Bristol, England.

THERE IS an ornate Victorian lamp post at the mouth of Caledonia Place at its junction with The Mall, Clifton. Five feet from the top of this lamp post is fixed a modern CCTV camera. The camera, number 169, judders a little as the rusted mechanism whirls and the wiper blade sweeps the rain from the lens as it pans 170° from Portland Street to its left and Princess Victoria Street and the *Zizzi* Italian restaurant to its right. As the camera transits The Mall, it scans the magnificent edifice of Number 22, the building designed by Frances Greenway in 1777 and later to become the exclusive *Clifton Club*.

Greenway was a gifted and clever man who was also convicted in 1813 of forgery and transported to Australia. There the governor of New South Wales, Lachlan Macquarie, appointed him Civil Architect and Assistant Engineer. Known as 'The Father of Australian Architecture', eleven buildings of Frances Greenway's design still stand in Sydney and a $10 Australian bank note bore his portrait. Nicholas Fry's killer was not so gifted or so clever.

DC Samuel Pau had been searching through the discs of dozens of CCTV cameras since Monday in the hope of seeing the man reported by the young courting couple, Peter Weaver and Sandra Bennett. As he searched through the CCTV discs from camera 169 for the evening of the 2nd March, he spotted a man wearing a dark-coloured coat and black trilby hat carrying, under his arm, what appeared to be long cardboard tubes, walking past the Italian restaurant. The time was 21:52.

Sam had shown the images to other members of the team and one of the longer serving detectives had recognised the man. Now he froze the picture again as the man in the hat looked up as he tried to avoid other pedestrians. Three further pictures showed the man's face, not perfectly, but sufficient to show an individual with a slightly pointed nose and clean-shaven.

Superintendent Mark Faraday craned over the detective constable's shoulders in the gloom, his face illuminated by the screen.

'It gets better, sir. I'll freeze it there,' he said then, adjusting the controls on a second disc player, another monitor glowed showing what appeared to be an identically dressed man walking through automatic doors in a corridor. 'As you can see,' he continued, pointing to the numerals in the corner of the screen, 'this image is at 18:11 on the 14th March, on the corridor leading to the ward where William Harding was a patient.'

'Well done, Sam,' said Faraday squeezing the officer's shoulder.
'One more, sir,' he said as he swivelled in his chair and pressed the keys on a third machine. Another screen illuminated to show the same man. 'And this is the same man leaving the hospital at 19:14 on the 14th.'

DCI Yin touched Faraday's elbow. He looked around as she opened an HQ personnel file at the first page. On this first page was a photograph. Faraday looked at the first screen and then back to the file. They were very similar, probably the same. He read the name on the front of the file:

Detective Chief Superintendent
George Donald Somers
Retired: 10th May 2001

Chapter 18

DETECTIVE CHIEF Superintendent Perrin would test her again as he knew he must, continuing to assess her, and those other detectives coming up through, and preparing those who would eventually take his place.

Kay Yin had done well. As soon as she had identified George Somers as a suspect, her first action was to declare William Harding's private room at the hospital a new *crime scene*. The hospital authorities were not happy, nor was the new occupant but, on her own initiative, she had arranged a room in the private BUPA hospital near-by with the costs, including those of a private ambulance, being met by the police. Perrin thought that Faraday may have played a part in this initiative – it would have been action typical of him – but Kay Yin had defended her decision, described by the Wynne-Thomas as cavalier, before the ACC and DCC. It was a heated meeting but she had stood her ground as her CSI team examined the hospital room.

Nothing of evidential value had as yet been discovered as Robert Perrin sat with Mark Faraday and Kay Yin in his office discussing ex-Chief Superintendent George Somers. He looked across to them both and saw their chemistry as they became more at ease in the privacy of his office. They both trusted him, he thought, although Faraday more so than Yin. That was one of Faraday's few faults, he mused. Faraday was probably too trusting with those near to him.

Perrin directed his attention towards Kay Yin. He had not noticed it before. She was beautiful and sensuous, but her dark oriental eyes never seemed to be at rest, constantly alert like those of a protective animal. True, he thought, Faraday had shot and killed a man and would do so again if he had to – driven by his acute sense of duty - but, Kay Yin was deadlier than the male, he had no doubt.

'Did you ever meet him?' Faraday asked interrupting his thoughts.

'I did once or twice when he was the head of CID in the Gloucestershire force. I was a superintendent then, but he retired when the forces amalgamated.'

'And your opinion of him?' he asked.

He wasted no time in thought. 'He was a rather sharp dresser with a charming manner but, underneath, he was a corrupt and arrogant shit.'

'And according to this,' Kay said, producing another paper prepared by Pippa Blanchard, 'he seems to have charmed his way into the position of an assistant director of security for Chelwood Kilbride.'

'That's an interesting coincidence, don't you think, Kay?'

'I didn't think you believed in coincidences, sir?' she replied.

'Did I say that, Kay? I'm going to have to be on my toes with you,' he said with a smile. 'You are right. There are always coincidences, but they needed to be treated with the utmost caution.'

'I see that the director of security is Sir Tim Metcalfe, a former deputy commissioner from the Met,' said Faraday, reading from his papers. 'Chelwood Kilbride list four assistant directors. One for IT and facilities, Somers for the UK, one for North America and Caribbean and the forth for Australasia.'

'And is there a significance, Mark?'

'There could be. If nothing else, it means that Somers is conveniently local for any little dirty jobs that might need to be taken care of.'

Faraday was as usual astute, thought Perrin, always grasping the operational essentials, identifying likely connections, noting the missing links. They made a good team concluded Perrin.

'And your next move?' asked Perrin as he stood up and looked out of his window that provided panoramic views over the Gordano Valley.

'The RAF may be able to enhance the CCTV sufficiently for us, but it is not evidence, as you know,' said Faraday referring to the rulings that the enhancement is actually a process that distorts the original image with no guarantee that the image presented to the court is accurate. 'We could arrest Somers, but for what? Carrying cardboard tubes? We could arrest him on suspicion of anything really, then we would be allowed to take his DNA.'

'And what would that achieve?' asked Perrin resuming his seat.

Kay answered. 'We would be able to put him at the scene but, as Mr Faraday said, so what? Somers is, no doubt, street-wise and he would have already prepared his story.'

'And what story do you think he would have concocted, Kay?' he asked, testing her ability.

'I suspect something along the lines that he called around to check on the progress of the painting and was utterly shocked to find that Nicholas Fry had been savagely murdered,' she said, her comments laced with drama. 'He will then recall that he did, indeed, cough at the scene, in fact, he thought he was going to vomit. But, in order to protect the bank's reputation during a time of volatile financial markets he foolishly, with hindsight, did not report the horrific scene that he had encountered and bitterly regrets having not done so.'

'Precisely. And so, the next move?' he asked them both.

'There's that turn at the corner of your mouth again, Mark,' said Kay, looking at her lover, then corrected herself. 'I'm sorry, sir. I thought Mr Faraday was about to contribute something of interest.' There followed just a few seconds of embarrassment.

'Thank you for that *intimate* insight, Miss Yin. Maybe you could answer the question, Mr Faraday,' he said, barely able to control his chuckling.

'Did he murder Fry?' posed Faraday rhetorically. 'Let us assume that the answer is yes. Then we can assume that any evidence has now gone.' Perrin raised an eyebrow as if to question this rash assumption, but Faraday continued. 'There have been a number of indications that the killer was forensically aware. Somers would be. He would almost certainly have cleaned his clothing, shoes and vehicle. If there is any evidence remaining, and there could be: blood on clothing, glass or wood fragments and so on, it will probably stay were it is now. It is significant that, searching through Bill Harding's files, we now know that Somers had arrested Harding on numerous occasions and had been an informant of his. The key question is: what induced him to kill Fry?'

'Go on?' he asked the superintendent.

'I do not think, however, that we should arrest him at this stage – he will present the sort of arguments outlined by Kay. I would recommend that we interview him on the pretext that we are at a complete loss and wonder if, in his capacity as a security director, he could possibly help us with any information he might have about company employees, visits that may have been made to or by Nicholas Fry.'

'And the objective of that approach?' Perrin probed.

'Two-fold, sir. Firstly it will put pressure on the Chelwoods to react.'

'What will that achieve?'

Faraday did not answer that question directly, his mind conjuring with thoughts. 'I would intend that we also interview Dean Patterson. There could be some interplay between them which we should be able to pick up during interview.'

'Go on?'

'Secondly, if nothing else, we will undoubtedly get a denial that Somers had ever visited Fry or that he has not had recent contact with Harding or both. We should be able to prove him a liar.'

'But liars are not necessarily convicted of murder.'

'No, but he doesn't know what we know, and so he may say something that would incriminate him or others.'

'It's not much, Mark?'

'I agree, but it is still early days. We must await the outcome of the examination of Harding's hospital room, meanwhile, we continue to dig into the backgrounds of the Chelwoods, the Pattersons and George Somers.'

'You are holding something back, Mark?'

'There is another avenue that we are exploring which could be fruitful. I will know with certainty when we visit St Matthew's church and I have received information being collated by PC Blanchard from the Registry of Births, Marriages and Deaths.'

Perrin simply nodded his acceptance. 'What order do you intend to interview them?'

'Somers, Patterson, then Chelwood.'

'Why Chelwood again?'

'To put pressure on them to squabble amongst themselves but, officially, it will be for the purpose of up-dating his lordship on the progress of our enquiries.'

'Who will interview Somers?'

'I haven't discussed that with Kay yet.'

'Discuss it with me now,' encouraged Perrin.

'I think that Kay should interview him, sir.'

'Do you? Why?' he questioned, glancing at Kay hoping for a reaction. But there was none, other than a nodding of agreement. But Kay Yin, like Robert Perrin, waited for the answer.

'Because Somers is likely to be cocky and drop his guard.'

'And why should he do that?' he asked, but he already knew that answer.

'I've read his personal file which contains reports of a number of complaints made by female officers during his service,' he said, glancing towards Kay Yin before continuing his answer. 'He is very likely to be a chauvinistic ... shit, as you eloquently put it, sir.'

'Any views, Kay?'

'I can play the inexperienced, little female detective,' she replied dropping her head and mimicking a precocious teenager, 'who is out of her depth in the presence of such an awesome figure as a former detective chief superintendent from whom I shall be so grateful to learn.' Kay smiled at Perrin mocking his rank, but he took no offence as she knew he wouldn't.

'Approved,' agreed Perrin with another grin.

'And your view on the connection between Somers and Harding?' asked Faraday.

'A very long time ago, Mark, I learnt a fundamental lesson. If you fit-up prisoners, it will come back to haunt you. Both of you are honest officers. Have you been the subject of resentment from criminals that you have had locked up?'

'Initially, perhaps,' replied Kay.

'Precisely, Kay. Initially. When the prisoner is taken down to the court cells after sentencing, he's angry, angry mostly at himself for being such a fool as to get caught. Yes, he will swear and curse you, the judge, the jury, his brief, in fact, everyone in the world. But, at the end of the day, he is angry with himself and he spends his time in prison thinking about how not to get caught again in the future. Fit a prisoner up, plant evidence, lie to the court, and that prisoner will spend his time in prison thinking of ways in which he can get back at you, the corrupt officer. I will bet you a pound to a pinch of salt that the letter to the coroner was a nice little bit of revenge by Harding against Somers.'

He stood up. 'Proceed as you have both determined: Somers, Patterson and Chelwood.'

Chapter 19

Saturday, 31ˢᵗ March.

Willemstad, the Netherlands Antilles and South Gloucestershire, England.

ODYSSEY PASSED between the Water Fort and Fort Amsterdam and waited on station for the 550 foot-long Queen Emma Bridge, consisting of fourteen floating pontoons linking Otrabanda and Punda, to chug open.

This wooden bridge spanning the mouth of St Anna Bay, pivots on Otrabanda and swings open by means of the propulsion of a diesel-driven propeller in the very last of the pontoons. As the bridge opens to allow the great tankers and merchant ships to sail onward to one of the largest oil refineries in the world, it undulates like a great snake. But, for the passengers of the *Odyssey*, oil refineries were far from their sight and their thoughts as Captain Jelstrup guided his vessel forward and berthed.

Once the lines were made fast, the ladies stepped ashore on the Handelskade with its gabled houses in the Dutch style, all pastel pinks, yellows, greens and blues. A table, in the most prominent position, had already been reserved for them under the quay-side restaurant's large parasol. Soon the ladies relaxed in the hot sun cooled by the favourable trade winds. For one, the relaxation was short-lived.

Lady Cecelia Chelwood pulled her mobile phone from her bag and looked at the screen. She read the caller's name: Somers.

'Reception is so poor here,' she said so as to excuse herself in order to answer the call in privacy. 'It's Charles. Boys will be boys,' she added gaily. 'Would you excuse me for a moment.' She left their table and walked along the quay for a few yards, turned and waved happily to her friends. Her smile was radiant but her Caligula-like eyes, hidden by her *Chanel* dark glasses, mirrored her annoyance.

'Yes, George?' she said curtly.

'Has the money been deposited?' he asked.

'Yes, of course,' she answered abruptly but carefully.

'That's bloody good then,' came his agitated reply.

Lady Chelwood was minded to curtail the conversation then but curiosity dictated that she ask George Somers a question.

'Why do you ask?'

'Because that little Chinese detective wants to interview me.'

'Have you been arrested?' she asked haughtily.

'No, but I don't like how this is developing.'

'The only thing I don't like is you calling me. You are an assistant director of security and an ex-policeman. Handle it,' she said and with her thumb curtailed the call.

She held the phone to her ear as if continuing the conversation and considered her options. As she did so the pontoon bridge swung open again to make its ponderous passage, its service to pedestrians being taken over by a ferry, darting back and forth, horn-hooting, as another cargo ship made its cautious progress into the heart of the island. For a moment, the bulk of this great ship blocked out the sun's rays and cast a cold shadow over Lady Cecilia, a formidable woman, who had already covered her tracks. She snapped the phone shut.

Mark parked his Audi a few hundred yards from the stone gate that gave access to St Matthew's church. He walked to the passenger door and opened it, allowing Kay Yin to step out. They walked to the entrance and pushed open the creaking wooden gate. The grass in the church yard was cut and the graves neatly tended, although some headstones leaned forward or sideways in accordance with their age. Most of the stones were modest, a type of stone that flaked with age or the newer black or white marble. But, to the right, on a slight rise in the ground, was a collection of marble graves that were more like monuments. These tombs were of the Chelwood family. Without a word, Kay handed Mark the papers, reading his mind. He scanned the names and dates that Pippa Blanchard had given him and compared them with the names inscribed upon the tombs. Her name was there.

Satisfied, they walked on around the church. At first the little grave could not be seen – although they were. The rector of St Matthew's had seen them from the porch way of his church, as they hoped he would.

Unperturbed, they searched each row and read every inscription, then discovered what they had been looking for. In a corner, under an English oak, was the little grave of Daniel, aged only four months, with the inscription:

'In short life loved
In death lamented'

Mark and Kay returned to the path and walked on behind the church and back around to the front and the war memorial. All the names were there of the men who had fought and died for their country in the First and Second World Wars, in Korea and The Gulf. Major Lord Tatton Chelwood VC, DSO, MC was listed along with the name of Private Edward Haynes.

They returned to the church and pushed open the porch door. Their steps were hollow as they walked to the far aisle. The wall of this aisle was filled with memorials and two tattered flags hung from above, each side of a stained-glass window. They examined the memorials, some in marble and some of brass.

'You are interested in the memorials?' he asked. They had heard him approach, of course, even in his rubber-soled shoes.
'Hullo,' said Faraday. 'We are, particularly in this one.'

'It was a thoughtful gesture of the Earl Chelwood,' said the Reverend Peter Webb. 'It commemorates all of those who lived and worked on the Chelwood estate and died in The Great War.'

'It's a magnificent piece of work,' he said as he examined the marble relief depicting the soft cap of an infantry man and the hardened manganese steel helmet that were not issued to our soldiers until 1916; the belts and buckles of the regiments; the folded rain cape and a Lee-Enfield Mk IV rifle. 'Family members as well as employees I see?' said Faraday as he ran his fingers down each side of the memorial. He found what he sought and made a mental note of the inscription.

'Yes. Major Lord Chelwood is there of course along with his cousin, but it was a remarkable gesture for the day, don't you think, for the names of an under-gardener, a footman, a stable boy and tenant farmers to be included along with this illustrious family's most famous son.'

'Yes,' replied Faraday thoughtfully. 'It does serve to remind us vividly of the great sacrifices made by every household, village and town. But isn't it strange, the words here?'

'I don't understand ah ... ?' he paused hoping for an introduction. This was as good a time as any, thought Faraday.

'I'm Superintendent Faraday and this is Chief Inspector Yin.'

'Oh, the police,' he said rather bemused, adding: 'The words you say?'

'Yes. The names are listed then the words *and others unknown* are added underneath. Isn't that significant?'

'Is it? I've never really thought of it.'

'Well, it *is* strange, Reverend. You see, on the war memorial outside is listed a young soldier, Private Edward Haynes, who I know was employed on the Chelwood estate as a groom. Yet his name doesn't appear here.'

'How very odd.'

'Yes,' Faraday replied slowly, 'it is odd, isn't it?'

The priest took a few seconds to reply. 'I suppose his name is included, as it were, under *and others unknown.*'

'Yes,' replied Faraday again in a manner that deliberately made it clear that he was not at all convinced by such an explanation. 'You see, my colleague and I have checked and no other person's name *is* missing from this memorial, only that of young Edward Haynes.' Faraday faced the rector who found his penetrating stare unnerving and the change of tone that followed uncompromising. 'Now, why should that be, I wonder?'

Chapter 20

Monday, 2nd April.

Police Headquarters and Central District Police Headquarters, Bristol, England.

SHE WORE a black trouser suit and her widest smile as she approached George Somers in the reception foyer of police headquarters at precisely 10.00.

'Hullo, sir,' Kay Yin said deferentially, acting more like an air stewardess greeting a First Class passenger on an *A380* than a senior detective meeting a suspect. She shook his hand and introduced herself before turning her attention to the receptionist.

'Thank you, Janice,' she said as she picked up the visitor's pass and careful inserted the piece of card into the plastic holder. She turned again and clipped the visitor's pass onto the breast pocket of his expensive suit jacket. As she did so she could smell the peppermints on his breath mixing with a heavy cologne. She noticed that his teeth were tobacco-stained. Maybe the peppermints were to disguise the tobacco, she thought, although much more likely to disguise the smell of whisky, if his reputation was anything to go by. 'There we are, sir. Thank you for coming in to help me.'

'No trouble, detective,' he said with a note of superiority in his voice. Perfect, she thought.

'Have you been here before, sir?'

'No, this place,' he said dismissively, 'was opened after I had retired.'

'Well, we can go this way, through the conference room if you like. It's where the chief holds court.'

They walked up the stairs and through the impressive conference room with its curved rows of plush seats and the force's coat of arms resplendent just above the largest of chair, the chair occupied by the Sir John Sinclair, the chief constable. Once in her office, Kay Yin invited Somers to sit in a comfortable arm chair as she occupied a seat behind her desk on which was laid-out symmetrically two brown folders and three pencils neatly to the side of a pristine note pad, arranged as if she were a student about to sit an examination – precisely the impression she wished to create. She adjusted the pencils and rearranged them in perfect line, one above the other just above the note pad as if nervous in the presence of the seasoned ex-detective.

'Well how can I help you, Miss?'

'I am struggling with my investigation into the murder of Nicholas Fry.'

'So you said on the phone.'

'You know that he was painting a commission for your bank?'

'Of course,' he replied, adding unnecessarily, 'it was going to be quite an expensive painting and the Earl Chelwood asked me about security, particularly as he was thinking that the VC and other medals could be displayed with it.'

She pretended great thought as if wrestling with an inner conflict. 'I think I can tell you, sir, that forensics have drawn a blank.'

'And what about house-to-house enquiries, any luck there?' he asked naturally, one detective to another. He balanced his right ankle on his left knee as if relaxed but, in reality, he was eager to gain the slightest indication of detection.

'Nothing at all and that was disappointing. We had officers on the ground two weeks after the murder and I would have thought someone would have provided a concrete lead. But no good. We have tried to check back through the artist's likely contacts. He had a lot of contacts apparently, but these were formal contacts, you know, people in the army, colleagues at the Royal West of England College of Art, those sorts of people, but he had very few friends.' Kay waited for him to query why she had used the words 'we have tried' and why 'apparently'. But of course he did not because he knew that the artist's diary had been stolen.

'And they check out?' Somers asked.

'Yes, they do. We are still trawling through his formal contacts, some of whom are now serving overseas.' She stood up. 'Tea or coffee?' she asked brightly.

'Oh, tea,' he said trying to assess her ability and her line of questioning.

Kay Yin, her back to Somers, fussed with the electric kettle and mugs on the top of the grey filing cabinet, placing a tea bag in each. 'I understand that Nicholas Fry visited Lord Chelwood at the bank … sugar?' she asked as she turned.

'Two.'

'Could any of the bank's staff, Lord Chelwood's PA or a driver or some other employee, have visited Nicholas Fry?'

He looked at her back as she poured the steaming water into the mugs, cautious with his answer. 'Why should they want to do that?' Wrong answer, thought Kay.

'I don't know,' she shrugged. 'To deliver some old photographs or mementoes that might help the artist ... milk?'

'As it comes, dear.'

'Do you know of anyone who might have visited the artist?' she asked, almost casually, as she handed him his mug of tea.

'No,' his sub-conscious mind replied distancing himself from the crime, then added, 'but I can check for you.'

'If you could, I would be grateful,' she said sitting back behind her desk. 'I do need your help, sir.' She fiddled with her note pad as if giving herself time to formulate her request. He sipped his tea waiting for her to explain her needs. 'There's probably some silly data protection rule, but ... could you possibly let me have a list of all employees at Chelwood Kilbride?'

He would agree but pretend to be reluctant to break the law, although for Somers, data protection issues were another aspect of legislation that he would easily brush aside as he had done so throughout his police career. 'But there must be ten-thousand employees around the world.'

'I was only thinking of those at your head office.'

'Well, that must be about seven-hundred,' he said in mock amazement.

'It's just a list, sir, just a piece of paper.'

Somers picked at some non-existent fluff on his knee before going on. 'Look, I'm not e-mailing or faxing anything,' he said as if his whole career could be in jeopardy if he did. 'I'll get a list up together for you, but you come to our reception and collect it. It will be in an envelope for you. Is that OK?'

'That would be brilliant. Thank you, sir,' she said gratefully and then added if shy to ask. 'Could I ask you something else?'

'Fire away,' he replied as he pretended to relax into his chair, but the cut of his chin and his predatory eyes showed that he was not relaxed at all. Although Somers had concluded that this young Chinese detective was completely out of her depth, he had assumed that she would have been aware of his connection with Harding and could not understand why the confession of this criminal had not already been raised by her.

'I am told that you have led the investigations into dozens of murder, sir.'

'Yes, I have.'

'What is likely to be the motive in this case would you think?'

Somers had not anticipated this question, but he quickly gave a standard response. 'Most murders are domestic. If they're not domestic then the victim is usually known to the killer. That should be the focus of your enquiries?'

'What if it was a burglary?'

He began to feel uncomfortable. 'Then it would be for money, valuables.'

'We had someone in the frame. A burglar you had arrested from time to time.'

He began to perspire, his response non-committal. 'I've arrested a lot of burglars too.'

'His name was William Harding.'

Somers could hardly reply that Harding was incapable of murder and so he showed no surprise. 'Bill Harding, I arrested him a few times and he was also an informant,' he replied placing his relationship with Harding onto a formal basis.

'William Harding confessed to the murder.'

'Confessed. I wish all my cases could have been wrapped up that easily.'

'Do you think that William Harding capable of murder?'

Somers had anticipated this question and his response was well prepared. 'He had convictions for theft and burglary,' he said. 'He was a bit of a scrapper, you know, boxed once or twice locally at bantam-weight, I think. He wouldn't pick a fight but would have a pop, if you know what I mean.'

'But could he deliberately have killed someone?'

Somers' sub-conscious thoughts became enmeshed with his reasoning. 'I suppose we could all kill someone in the right circumstances. And he's admitted it, you say?'

'Yes, he has.'

'Then that's it, isn't it?'

'No it can't be,' she said.

Somers took his leg off his knee and unbuttoned his jacket to relieve his discomfort and perspiration. 'Why not?' he asked.

'Because he's dead. Died late on the 21st.'

Somers knew that Harding's death alone could not be a valid reason and had to question the assumption. 'But that doesn't mean that he couldn't have murdered the artist, Miss.'

'No it doesn't, but I know that he was somewhere else at the time of the murder.'

He felt like shrieking 'bastard' at the top of his voice. He knew that she was waiting for his answer but he was confused, not sure whether to pretend to be shocked or unconcerned and his answer was far too slow in coming. 'Are you sure?'

'Yes. We have him at a crowded bingo hall at the critical time.'

'A bingo hall,' was all that he could say as his mind raced grappling with what he considered to be a betrayal by a worthless thief. 'A strange thing for him to do,' he said eventually, 'confess to a murder.'

'When did you last see Harding?'

Somers had anticipated this question but its timing had taken him by surprise.

'Haven't seen him in years, not officially. Saw him once or twice in the street, nothing more.'

'But you would know how Harding's mind would work, why do you think he should do such a silly thing as admit to a murder he could not have committed?' He didn't like her tone. He looked at her and for just a moment wondered why *he* had been so silly.

'To protect someone, I suppose.'

'Who? Do any names come to mind?'

Somers was off-guard again and replied quickly. 'He used to work for the Villiers gang. They ran tenant rackets and the launderettes and Harding did a few jobs for them.'

'A few jobs?' she asked as if impressed.

'Nothing like that,' he replied, his contempt and frustration seeping through. 'Harding was just an errand boy.'

'But the Villiers family you suggest. Anyone else?'

'No, not really.'

'Oh. Well, never mind. It was good of you to come in. I would be grateful for the list of employees, otherwise I seem to have wasted your time. I'm sorry about that. Let me take your mug and I'll walk you out.'

Once George Somers had left, DCI Yin met Superintendent Faraday in the conference room.

'How did that go?' he asked as they sat down. 'Well by the look of the smile on your face.'

'He's a chauvinistic liar.' They sat down on the blue-backed chairs facing each other. 'He says that he has never visited Nicholas Fry at Royal York Crescent. He didn't ask anything about how Fry was murdered, although I accept that the papers did refer to a "savage attack". When I asked why Harding should admit to killing someone he hadn't, he suggested that the confession was to protect someone else, but, the group of people he didn't suggest were members of Harding's family.'

'You are reasonably satisfied?' Faraday asked.
'Oh yes. We have his denials, not whilst under caution, but there again we have no firm evidence to suspect him of murder and nor has he been arrested.'

'Shoes?'

'Expensive and leather and Tailors Store have him still on record as being a size 9 and 5' 10'

'What next?' he asked.

'I bet he's now scurrying back to Chelwood to tell him that this murder has not been written-off and that we are back on the case. Somers has agreed to give me a full list of the bank's employees. They might be useful, but it was a smoke screen really and will allow me to call on Chelwood Kilbride and collect.' She smiled. 'And I will make sure the security and reception staff know who I am.'

'And?'

'Just in case Somers doesn't keep his masters informed, I want to make sure that Lord Chelwood is aware of our activities. You keep telling me, Mark, that the aristocracy are past masters at the art of survival. If the Chelwoods are behind this murder, they won't want to take the heat. Somers will be in the line of fire for this. That means that they will need to get him out of the way.'

'And how do you think they will do that?'

'Either they will manipulate events so as to ensure his conviction for the murder of Nicholas Fry, but that is risky and will implicate them. Or, more likely, they can buy Somers off or kill him.'

'OK,' concurred Faraday. 'But, meanwhile, we need to keep to the motivators we have identified as possibles: personal gain, to silence a witness or to protect the ID of an offender.'

Faraday fixed his eyes on the crest of his force above the chief constable's chair as he calmly processed what they knew but, more importantly, what he believed. Kay Yin didn't interrupt his thoughts. Then he spoke.

'Are we still agreed that, from what we now believe, the motive for this murder is very likely to be a combination of all three?'

'Yes.'

'Then a visit to Dean Patterson should be next on our list. What do you think?'

'Yes. Patterson next followed by Downes?'

'OK. And possibly, who was that other guy that followed him?'
'Stower.'

'Yes, Stower. Might not be needed but do we know where the Downes' family live now?'

'Pippa's on to them both. Meanwhile, I think we also need to look at Harding's sons a little more closely.'

'Are you going to do that?' he asked.

'No. I'll brief DS Williams.' She touched his knee. 'I think that you and I need to hear what Dean Patterson has to say for himself?'

'Ideally we should keep observations on Somers, but we don't have the resources and we wouldn't get the authority anyway, so Dean Patterson next, I think.'

'But Special Branch at the airport is alerted?'

'Oh, yes,' he replied.

Chapter 21

Tuesday, 3rd April.

Police Headquarters, Bristol and near Moreton Valence, Gloucestershire, England.

ASSISTANT CHIEF Constable Wynne-Thomas was virtually constipated with glee. He strode purposefully along the corridor towards the chief constable's suite, brushing aside the protests of secretaries and staff officers in his eagerness to relay his news. He had only just heard that, after the unnecessary disruption of the hospital's routine, the distress caused to a private patient and the exorbitant cost of transferring and relocating a patient, no forensic evidence whatsoever had been found in the private room once occupied by the late William Harding.

The ACC viewed the lack of forensic evidence as a clear sign of his superior professional judgement when compared with that of DCI Yin, whom he considered had been encouraged in her impetuous decision by that maverick superintendent, Mark Faraday, who, he had learned from Inspector Trench, was about to interview Dean Patterson.

Wynne-Thomas flounced into the chief's officer to break the news – but Sir John Sinclair had already been pre-warned by Robert Perrin.

***

Kay Yin drove Mark Faraday's Audi A5 coupe along the M5 towards the city of Gloucester. As they approached Junction 13 she reduced her speed to take up her position in the inside lane, indicating her intention to leave the motorway at the 300 yards 'count-down' marker. She turned onto the A419 for the half-mile until the A38 and the short distance to Moreton Valence. The interview with The Very Reverend Dean Paul Patterson was scheduled for eleven o'clock.

The Audi approached the Old Rectory along the gravelled drive, passed the coach house, to stop one hundred yards from the front entrance of the three-storey house built in 1909 of local stone with Cotswold quoins and mullion leaded light windows. Once described by an architect as 'a handsome rectory by Edmund Sedding', the seven bedroom house had been taken over for the dean's use whilst extensive renovations were being carried out to his official residence in Gloucester.

Mark Faraday and Kay Yin were deliberately ten minutes early and parked facing the house so as to appear, if not menacing, intriguing. Both officers discussed the approach that they would adopt to the interview. Mark and Kay were sure that Dean Patterson would not be fully co-operative, evidenced by his contact with Lord Chelwood following Kay's very routine telephone calls to him. They were also reasonably confident that, as Chaplain Patterson had had a distinguished war-time service and subsequent career, the Patterson family were very likely to have retained some or all of the chaplain's diaries or letters. Kay favoured a diplomatic approach, although acknowledging that this would probably fail, whilst Mark proposed what he described as a 'robust' approach. Their approach would now be a blend of the two, but not the 'hard cop-soft cop' approach so often ridiculously portrayed in the movies. Their approach would be careful and patient, professional and intelligent. Kay put her mobile on speed-dial as they saw Patterson, firstly at the curtains of the drawing room then, a few moments later, standing back from the window in his study.

At two minutes to eleven, Kay engaged *drive* and the Audi gently moved forward to the front of the house. As she gracefully stepped out of the car, her beautiful legs and confident movement was noticed by Dean Patterson who had been told by the Earl Chelwood, who had himself been unduly influenced by Somers, to expect a pretty, inexperienced and rather timid junior detective. The dean also attempted to assess her plain-clothes male colleague. Mark Faraday was an unknown quantity and someone he instinctively did not take to. Unsmiling with penetrating dark brown eyes, he seemed to be assessing everything he saw.

A maid, dressed in black and whites, answered the pull of the front door bell and invited them to step through the entrance lobby and into the hall, and from there into the drawing room. It was a bright room, capturing the mid-day sun, bathing the interior in a golden glow. Books were in abundance, family photographs and mementoes rested on the top of a grand piano, paintings adorned the walls, heavy curtains where drawn back and held in perfect position by silk sash ties. The two officers exchanged glances and determined where they would sit - to the side of the mullioned windows.

Dean Patterson entered, resplendent in dog-collar. There was an aloofness about him reminding Faraday of a slimmer and slightly older version of Trench.

'Thank you, Mavis,' he said dismissively to his maid and waited for the two officers to introduce themselves.

'I am Chief Inspector Yin and this is my superior, Superintendent Faraday,' she said deliberately so as to ensure no confusion. 'Thank you for seeing us today, Dean.'

The dean made no attempt to shake hands but waved them to some exquisitely upholstered chairs. Kay sank into hers which exposed more of her legs which she crossed at the ankles. She placed her brief case to her side and removed a bundle of papers.

'I had been led to believe that there would be no further enquiries of me, Superintendent?'

Faraday didn't answer but looked towards Kay Yin.

'Events change, Dean,' said DCI Yin, 'As you know, I am investigating the murder of a Mr Nicholas Fry. Mr Fry was an artist who …'

'I am aware of who Fry was,' interrupted Patterson. 'What I am not aware of is why it is necessary to question me. I thought that I had given you sufficient information over the phone. I have, have I not, already confirmed that my grand-father was present when Major Lord Chelwood died and cannot quite see what more I can say.'

He was being far too positive, thought Kay, as if he couldn't possibly have anything else to add. She began softly. 'The situation has changed, Dean. A local criminal admitted killing Nicholas Fry in a most savage fashion, but I am now able to prove that this individual could not possibly have been the killer.' She preferred to use the words 'killing' and 'killer' so as to emphasise the obscenity of the act of murder. 'And so the case is now wide open again. You see, Dean, Nicholas Fry was a simple artist. He was a pleasant, unassuming man with a limited circle of friends, although highly regarded by the military. Yet, for reasons completely unknown, he was brutally killed.' Kay removed Nicholas Fry's original pencilled sketches from her brief case and stood up, walked the few steps to the chair occupied by Dean Patterson and bent her knees at his side.

'These sketches are the originals made by the victim.' The dean began to feel uneasy at her nearness as she shuffled the sketches still contained within clear forensic envelopes. He noticed her beautiful hands, her perfume and her perfect oriental profile.

'This sketch,' continued Kay, determined to take Dean Patterson back in time to a credit-worthy period of his family's history, 'shows the stretcher party of Morely, Palmer, O'Neill and Wakely, recovering the badly injured Lord Chelwood, and there of course is your grand-father, out in No-Man's Land with these other brave men.' She placed another sketch on top of the collection of exhibits. 'This one depicts your grand-father at the regimental aid post, tending Lord Chelwood as he lies dying.'

Kay Yin stood up and returned to her chair leaving Dean Patterson with the evocative sketches on his lap. Faraday had been studying the reaction of the dean. Kay had not bothered to show him the sketch of the montage of scenes or the burial itself, but allowed the dean to bathe in the reflected and emotive glory of his grand-father – and he was. His demeanour, at one stage uneasy at the close presence of the beautiful Kay Yin, had changed from aloofness to smugness as if it was in the nature of things that he should continue his family's distinguished tradition and ascend to a bishop's throne.

'Your grand-father was commissioned as an army chaplain and served throughout the war.' She turned some papers over in her hand as if to read the content. 'I understand that he was awarded the Military Cross and stayed on until the end of 1921 assisting Sir Fabian Ware and the war graves commission,' Kay said.

Although the chaplain had only met Ware once, she rightly judged that the dean would be eager to link his family with Sir Fabian's achievements. 'Yes, that is so,' he said as if acknowledging a self-evident fact.

'Lord Chelwood was fortunate to have had the comfort of your grand-father at his side as he slipped away, a matter that is much appreciated by Earl Chelwood and recorded at The National Army Museum.'

'I'm not surprised, of course, although I didn't realise that the museum kept that sort of thing,' he said arrogantly oblivious to the trap so carefully laid by the two officers.

'Yes, the museum keeps some amazingly detailed records, Dean,' remarked Kay casually. 'These records interestingly include the disposal of the personal property of the dead.'
Dean Patterson looked at Kay Yin as he became nervously aware of the importance of this revelation. But it was Faraday that unnerved him, not only because of his unflinching stare but also because of what he then said.

'We know that your grand-father took possession of Lord Chelwood's uniform and service kit, his letters and diaries. We need to see any documents relating to him, Dean,' he said subtly blanketing letters and documents from both Major Lord Chelwood and Chaplain Patterson together. 'Would you care to get them for us please?'

'The records may show that he took possession of those items, not that he retained them,' he said evasively.

'We know that he retained them, Dean,' replied Faraday almost quietly. 'The uniforms on display at Chelwood House are those brought back to England by your grand-father.'

'There you are, Superintendent. The items you seek must be at Chelwood House,' he replied prevaricating.

'Not all of them, Dean,' Faraday said with a certainty that made Patterson doubt his own knowledge.

'We have nothing like that here,' he replied raking his brain for confirmation.

'I think you do,' said Faraday as if knowingly.

'I've told you that nothing, nothing at all, belonging to Major Chelwood is here.' Probably true concluded Faraday but the reply was made with renewed confidence and too much emphasis on Major Chelwood's belongings. Both officers now knew that they were on the right track.

'Dean, I understand that the See of Lincoln is one of the oldest in England?' observed Faraday.

'Yes,' he said, confused with the unexpected change in direction. 'That is so,' adding pompously, 'first founded in 1072 and the largest diocese in England.'

'I visited Lincoln Cathedral a few years ago, Dean,' remarked Faraday. 'It *is* magnificent, situated on the hill as it is.'

Dean Patterson, for a moment relieved at the more agreeable topic of discussion, began to imagine himself, as Faraday was certain he would, in procession through the cobbled streets of

Lincoln at his forthcoming enthronement. 'It is not only its situation,' observed the dean, 'but the building itself, taller that the largest pyramid and considered the finest Gothic cathedral in England.'

'And it is your … your *hope* … to be enthroned as the 73rd bishop,' continued Faraday.

There was a silence that was crushing. The dean's heart raced at the suggestion that his enthronement was simply a hope. 'It is not a hope, Superintendent. It has been approved by Her Majesty.'

'But not yet announced,' replied Faraday bluntly.

'It will be shortly,' he replied defensively.

'Quite a leap from dean to bishop when, ordinarily, it is a bishopric that would only be granted to an experienced junior bishop.'

'What are you suggesting?' he demanded in an agitated voice.

'What I am *suggesting*, as you put it, is very simple, Dean. Some would consider that the ecclesiastical authorities must be taking a considerable risk in appointing you, a risk to be confirmed when the details of your family's sordid association with the death of Edward Haynes become public knowledge.'

'He was a coward,' he replied angrily.

'And how do you know that?' Faraday asked slowly fixing him with an uncompromising stare.

'It … it was common talk,' blustered Patterson.

'No, no it wasn't, Dean. The War Office listed him as "died of wounds" and his regiment's official history makes no mention of his execution, although they mention other executions in detail. The history merely lists Edward Haynes as "killed" in the index.'

'It may have been discussed by family members, I can't recall.'

'Dean,' Faraday said in a tone that implied that it was now time for the deception to come to an end, 'your grand-father made meticulous records, we know that. What we now need to see is his diaries and letters.'

'I haven't read his diaries,' he replied. No straight-forward denial of the existence of diaries, thought Mark Faraday and Kay Yin.

'Edward Haynes was no coward, Dean,' continued Faraday as if reciting an official record. 'In any event, Her Majesty gave Her Royal Assent to an Act granting Edward Haynes, and the majority of those executed during the First World War, a pardon. I doubt whether, when the full facts are revealed regarding the execution of Edward in an filthy and obscene abattoir, that Her Majesty, as Supreme Head of the Church of England, would be prepared to give Her seal of approval to your appointment as one of Her bishops.'

Unseen by Dean Patterson, Kay Yin surreptitiously pressed the speed-dial button on her mobile phone. Moments later Faraday's phone rang.

'Faraday,' he answered to the non-existent caller. 'Wait one,' he said sharply and, turning to Kay Yin, he spoke again angrily. 'I will have to take this call. You can deal with this bloody nonsense.' He stood up and made his way to the door leading to the hall. 'You said there was common talk, Dean. The only forthcoming common talk I can envisage is about your family's involvement in this grotesque and unseemly affair.' Faraday stormed out through the hall and to the front of the Old Rectory. He walked around the gravelled driveway which surrounded the beautifully kept lawns, just in front of the drawing room windows, in full view of Dean Patterson - an ominous reminder of his presence.

'Dean,' said Kay Yin gently. 'No one intends to destroy your family or its well-deserved reputation, but there is an opportunity here for us to quietly and discreetly right a wrong. You must understand that I can't leave here until I have seen your grand-father's diaries and *all* of the correspondence.'

Chapter 22

Thursday, 5th April.

Police Headquarters, Bristol and Kewstoke, North Somerset, England.

CONSTABLE BLANCHARD had done a brilliant job. She had meticulously searched through innumerable records, including, Seymore's *Great Houses of Britain,* Davies' *Landowners of the British Isles,* Burke's *Landed Gentry* and Hone's *The Manor and Manorial Records.* As a result, Pippa had discovered the details of a niece of a parlour maid who had been employed at Chelwood House between 1912 and 1927, and who had been able to provide the address of a former servant, Minnie Rosa Sweet, aged 109, living in a residential home in North Somerset.

'And this matrix, sir,' said Pippa Blanchard to Mark Faraday, as they sat opposite each other across one of the conference room tables, 'contains the details from St Catherine's House and Somerset House of births, marriages and deaths connected with the Chelwood, Haynes, Patterson, Stower and Downes families.'

Faraday scrutinised the matrix that the young officer had prepared. The matrix acted as the frontispiece of the plastic folder behind which where the photocopies of the original documents. He ran his finger across the columns of information, noting the highlighted sections that corresponded with the coloured tags neatly protruding from the right-hand side of the file.

As Faraday appeared to finish reading the information, she produced another matrix, the information arranged in a similar way. 'These are the details of baptisms and burials from a variety of parish records.' She took the first file from Faraday's hand and placed it in front of him on the conference room table, then placed the second file alongside the first. She said nothing as Faraday compared the matrices. No words were necessary as Faraday easily identifying the connections highlighted in yellow, pink, pale green and pale blue.

'It's very telling, don't you think, Pippa?'

'And confirmed in these population censuses,' she said, producing another file, the single matrix frontispiece containing details from both the Public Records Office in London and County Record Offices in Bristol, Gloucestershire, Wiltshire and Kingston upon Hull.

Faraday smiled with admiration at her thorough work. 'You have done an excellent job, Pippa.'

'We were lucky with Minnie Sweet,' she said modestly.

'How so?'

'A census has been taken every ten years since 1801, with the exception of 1941. Minnie Sweet's name is on the 1911 census. If she had started her employment with the Chelwoods in last the few months of 1911, her name would probably not have been included on the list and we might have missed her.'

'There's always an element of luck, Pippa, but you have been commendably thorough. Well done.'

'There's just two other pieces of information, sir,' she said as she produced yet another matrix. 'I've gleaned this information from Crockford's *Clerical Dictionary* and the Methodist Archives and Research Centre.'

Faraday followed the colour coding again and the sequence of events, then compared and cross-checked the data from each matrix, double-checking with the information that had been coloured tagged. Satisfied, Faraday rested back in his chair thoughtfully.

'They thought that they would get away with it, Pippa.'

'They won't, will they, sir?'

'Oh, no,' he assured her firmly.

***

Minnie Sweet didn't receive many visitors, but she was content with the care she received and her memories, memories that softened her loneliness. Her room in the care home wasn't large but it was en-suite with French-windows allowing access to the gardens of manicured lawns, low shrubs and flowers selected for their scent.

Chief Inspector Kay Yin called, as suggested by the matron, at three o'clock as Minnie woke from her after-lunch nap and in time for afternoon tea. Minnie was fragile but her mind was alert although, as they talked, from time to time she confused Kay with one of the Chinese-Malay nurses. She talked of a life spent in service, firstly at Chelwood House, then for the Berkeley family and, finally as a lady's maid to the Duchess of Gloucester.

Minnie Sweet had been in service at Chelwood House between 1911 and 1927 and Kay Yin was certain that she would have more than noticed the handsome young Edward Haynes. Fully briefed at lunch time by Mark Faraday and Pippa Blanchard, Kay spoke to Minnie in generalities at first and then turned her attention to the young soldier. 'I am making some enquiries, Minnie, about a distant relative of someone you may remember at Chelwood House. Edward Haynes?'

There was a silence that seemed, for a moment, too painful for Kay to allow her to continue. 'I'm sorry, Minnie. Maybe we can talk of other things. Please, let me pour you some more tea.'

Kay poured the tea, added a little milk and placed the cup in front of her. The 109 year-old took the two-handled cup from the tray and drank a little as her memory took her back nearly a century. Like many old people, Minnie Sweet's long-term memory was much stronger and clearer than her short-term. Maybe the constant reflections on the past served to reinforce those memories, whatever, her tired eyes drifted over the young detective as if assessing her. Minnie had spent all of her working life with people, mostly as a silent observer of their strengths and weakness, their characters and personalities, their acts of kindness and their acts of wickedness. In Kay Yin she saw something, and what she saw made her feel safe in the company of this stranger, safe enough to talk. Finally she spoke. 'Edward was the only one I ever loved but he was taken in the Great War.' Kay listened as the old lady chose her words slowly as if desperate not to loose the memories. 'He was handsome. He was impish, not small you understand, but fun, always telling jokes, always with a happy smile.'

'Did he know how you felt about him?' she inquired so carefully.

There was no hesitation in her reply. 'Yes, he knew. He was kind to me but didn't know what to do.'

'Didn't know what to do?'

There was hesitation now as she thought of him. 'He was a kind boy, you see, and wouldn't hurt anyone. He knew how I felt but it wasn't to be. We were more like brother and sister really and I was content with that.'

'I suppose he confided in you, Minnie?'
'We did in each other.'

'Was there ever anyone else?' she asked, hoping to know if Edward Haynes had another love, but Minnie Sweet misunderstood the question.

'No, there was only ever Edward.'

'And what about Edward?' she asked fearful of distressing the old lady.

'Yes,' she replied, nodding her head together with a little smile that quickly faded as she added: 'but she was taken too.'

'And when was that, Minnie?'

'After, after the war. It was the flu, you see.'

'Do you know her name?'

She smiled again as she thought of Edward and how he would speak her name. 'He called her Lottie.'

'But that wasn't her proper name?' she asked although she already knew the answer, the grave stones had already spoken.

'No. It was forbidden you see, but the family were … they weren't unkind … but they were very cold and formal and Edward was so different, so much fun. That was the attraction for her.'

'And what was she like, Minnie?'

The old lady's face creased again with a smile, pleased to have been part of his happiness. 'She was so beautiful.' Minnie Sweet moved about in her chair and Kay tried to make her more comfortable.

'Is that better, Minnie?'

'Could you pull the cushion up a bit more for me, please, Miss?'
'Like this?'

'That's better. Thank you, Miss.' As Kay began to return to her chair, the old lady took her small hand and squeezed it. There followed a long silence as if Minnie was considering what was the right thing to do. She squeezed Kay's hand a little more tightly then let it go before speaking again. 'The box,' she said eventually, pointing to a polished cedar wood box standing all alone on an otherwise bare table. 'Could you get it for me, please?'

'Have you finished with your tea, Minnie?' but the old lady only nodded her reply. Kay removed the two-handled cup then picked up the box, which didn't appear to be very heavy at all, and placed it on the tray in front of the old lady.

Minnie Sweet opened the lid almost reverently, her arthritic fingers slowly searching through the contents. She removed one photograph and held it in both hands in front of her, her hands resting on the open box.

For a moment, Kay Yin thought that Minnie Sweet was about to burst into tears but, instead, her biggest smile creased her old face. 'My Edward,' she said.

Kay knelt besides her chair. The photograph she held was of a fresh-faced, handsome, smiling young man standing proud in an ill-fitting khaki uniform, polished boots and puttees.

'He was a handsome man, Minnie.'

Minnie Sweet didn't answer but passed the photograph to Kay as she foraged about in her little box and extracted another photograph. It was a larger photograph of over a hundred people, members of the Chelwood family seated in front of Chelwood House and, to the sides, arranged strictly according to position and status, were tenant farmers and members of the staff, the butler and housekeeper in prominent positions, together with estate workers.

Her crooked finger pointed to one young girl. 'That's me, Miss,' she said proudly. Then her finger moved along the rows of serious-looking faces and stopped on one of a young man with a broad grin. 'And that is dearest, dearest Edward.' After a few moments of tender reflection, her wizened finger moved back towards the centre of the photograph. She tapped the figure under her finger. 'But this was his real love, Miss.'

'Who was she?'

'Oh, a lovely, lovely young lady', she said with a ting of sadness.'

'Can you remember her name, Minnie?'

Without the slightest trace of bitterness she replied firmly. 'Lady Charlotte, Lady Charlotte Chelwood.'

Chapter 23

Friday, 6th April.

Police Headquarters, Bristol, England.

THE MORNING had not started off well. Inspector Silvia Glass had complained that on the 4th, when Faraday was out of the office, PC Blanchard had been insubordinate, refusing to carry out a task that she had allocated to her.

'I asked, *very nicely*, if Miss Blanchard would make enquiries with the bus company regarding new routes. She refused.'

'And what explanation did she give, Silvia?'

'She refused,' Inspector Glass repeated as if the reply was sufficient evidence of insubordination.

'Yes, but what did she say?' persisted Faraday.

'She *said*, in a haughty manner, that she was already fully committed.'

'Was the bus company enquiry a priority?' asked Faraday bluntly.

'It was important to me.'

'But Pippa had priorities, Silvia. I have already explained to all the staff that she is also assisting the murder enquiry.'

'But she is not a detective.'

'Whether she is a detective or not is nothing to do with you,' Faraday responded sharply. 'The tasks that she is performing are research-based, even if they weren't it has nothing to do with whether she is or is not a detective. You know as well as I do that Sergeant Weber works to you and Miss Blanchard is working to me.'

'Too closely,' she said but, seeing the anger in Faraday's dark eyes, quickly added, 'some would think.'

'Don't you dare. You get this straight, Silvia. Miss Blanchard is working closely with me and will continue to do so. I would also add that she is doing an exceptional job, much to the approval of the detective chief superintendent. You have the luxury of an experienced sergeant working to you, whilst Inspector Trench and I have relatively inexperienced constables working to us. I suggest you organise your commitments around the limited resources we have. If you want support, come and see me about it.'

'I asked for support the other day, and you ignored me,' she said defiantly.

'What are you talking about?' demanded Faraday at a loss to understand the meaning of Inspector Glass' comments.

'A couple of weeks ago,' she replied, 'I asked you about road closures and you ignored me and went off and had coffee with Miss Blanchard.'

Faraday racked his brain to recollect the incident but, typically of a dyslexic, the matter had completely gone from his mind, back into a little mental box, the lid tightly shut. 'I cannot recall what you are talking about. If I ignored you, I apologise, Silvia, but I'm not a magician. You know as well as I do that we are all juggling tasks and the work load that I take on is much greater than anyone else here. If I did ignore you then come and see me again or raise the matter at "Morning Prayers" or put it on the "Worry Board". Are the road closures still a problem?'

'I've resolved it now.'

'Excellent, then we don't have a problem do we.'

***

Mark Faraday and Kay Yin sat at the coffee table in Detective Chief Superintendent Perrin's office, their papers spread out in front of them. Perrin wore another immaculately-cut double-breasted suit and took up his usual position that alternated between sitting on the very edge of his desk, one foot on the carpet, and looking out across the Gordano Valley, hands behind his back.

'Can I suggest that I run through what we know and you interrupt as you wish, sir?' suggested Faraday. Like many dyslexics, he was superb at the set-piece presentation, Mark just hoped that Perrin would not interrupt him too often.

'Go ahead, Mark,' agreed Robert Perrin.

'Thank you, sir,' said Mark as he reviewed the documents before him. 'Some of what I will say is, inevitably, speculation and conjecture. Briefly, Edward Haynes was a Chelwood estate worker. When the First World War broke out he, like many other estate workers around the country, followed his master to war, in his case as a soldier/servant to Lieutenant Lord Tatton Chelwood. Lord Chelwood was soon promoted to the rank of temporary captain and we now know that he was the president of the Field

General Court Martial that sentenced young Edward Haynes to death.'

'You have the transcripts of the trial?'

'No, sir. What we do have, however, is the War Office form confirming his sentence of death endorsed with Edward's name and signed by Lord Chelwood. We also have the diaries of the army chaplain who was present at the execution, a man by the name of Patterson who was also the Chelwood's parish priest. Kay has now obtained these diaries from his grand-son, Dean Patterson. We also believe that Edward Haynes and Lord Chelwood's sister, Lady Charlotte Chelwood, were lovers.'

'How do you know that?'

'Kay,' said Faraday.

'PC Blanchard has carried out some excellent research work. As a result, I have been able to speak with a Minnie Sweet, a 109 year-old who was a maid at Chelwood House between 1911 and 1927.'

'How reliable is this elderly lady's recollections?'

'Better than most 109 year old, however, what was important was that Miss Sweet was able to show me some old photographs and what she recalls is now confirmed, or at least supported, by entries in Chaplain Patterson's diary. Crucially, Chaplain Patterson's papers include a note, seemingly written by Edward Haynes to Lady Charlotte, but not delivered. Also with this note is a photograph of Lady Charlotte. It is blood-stained and damaged in one corner.'

'Can we prove that the note was written by this young soldier?'

'We have arranged to have his enlistment papers forwarded to us from the National Army Museum. He would have signed these papers and so we should be able to confirm the writing as his.'

'And is the blood-stained and damaged photograph of significance?'

Perrin assumed that Kay would answer but Mark spoke. 'According to the chaplain's diary, Edward Haynes had the photograph in his left breast pocket when he was executed. It would have been customary for the execution party to be made up of his mates. They were probably nervous or bad shots. What the chaplain's diaries tell us is that he didn't die instantly and an officer had to administer the *coup de grâce*.'

'And you believe that his death was orchestrated by the young Lord Chelwood?'

'We could never prove that,' continued Mark, 'but it could have been so. There is no reference to the execution in the regimental history or in Chelwood's diary although another execution is described in some detail in his diaries and also referred to in the regiment's official history.'

'But there must be some formal record somewhere. You mentioned the War Office form?'

'Yes, the form was completed, it had to be, but Edward Haynes is merely listed in the regiment's history as "killed" and recorded in … ' He looked at Kay again.

'Recorded as "died of wounds" at the War Office,' she offered as if his faulty memory and her intervention were of no importance.

'Was that unusual?' questioned Perrin as he walked to the window. 'I'm sure I've heard that it wasn't?'

'No, you are quite right, sir, it wasn't unusual. There were many occasions when, to save the executed men's families more distress, the real cause of death was disguised.'

'So,' said Perrin turning from the window, 'why should the death of Private Edward Haynes be viewed any differently?'

'For a number of reasons,' replied Faraday. 'Firstly, the war memorial in St Matthew's church yard, in reality the Chelwood's private church and part of their estate, lists the name of Private Edward Haynes but, on the Chelwood memorial inside the church, his name is the only one absent.'

'And you believe that there is a reason for that?' asked Perrin returning to sit at the edge of his desk.

'Yes, I think the reason was that the Chelwoods couldn't bring themselves to allow Private Haynes' name to be on the same memorial as their heroic son and loyal estate workers who had laid down their lives.'

'Why not?'

'Because I believe that Lady Charlotte Chelwood was pregnant with Edward's child.'

Perrin stood up and sat with Mark and Kay at the low table. 'And how do we arrive at that conclusion?' he asked patiently.

'The priest that replaced Patterson at St Matthew's was a man called Downes, but he was vicar there for only ten months. Mrs

Downes gave birth to a baby boy, Daniel, whilst her husband was at St Matthew's, but the child died aged only four months. As could be expected, the child is buried there in the church yard.'

'You've been there?'

'Oh, yes,' replied Faraday.

'Go on Mark.'

'PC Blanchard has obtained all the documentation for us. We now have this child's birth certificate, his death certificate and record of the burial. We know that the Reverend and Mrs Downes moved to Beverley in Humberside a few months after his death. Surprisingly,' he continued but then corrected himself, 'well, it's not surprising at all really, the records show that a little baby boy was baptised in Beverley as Daniel Downes, the son of the Reverend and Mrs Downes. We have checked, sir. When Daniel Downes applied for a passport in the 1960s, there was no birth certificate as such.'

'As such?'

'As you know, the usual birth certificates are oblong and are actually a *Certified Copy of an Entry of Birth*, but Daniel was issued with a *Certificate of Birth*.'

Kay pulled a copy of the document from her file and handed it to Robert Perrin.

'You will see here,' she said pointing to the red coloured print, 'that this type of square certificate is endorsed "compiled from records" but it is in one sense meaningless because there are no official records of the birth of Daniel Downes, although there is a certificate of baptism.'

'You are suggesting that Lady Charlotte's son was spirited away to Beverley and unofficially adopted by the Downes as their own?'

'Yes, sir,' she replied.

'But you can't prove that, can you?' he enquired.

Kay was about to answer but Faraday replied in an uncompromising tone. 'Not at the moment.'

'That's OK. Maybe we can prove that later on,' he replied encouragingly. 'And what happened to Lady Charlotte?'

'She died in the outbreak of the so-called Spanish flu that swept the world during 1918 and 1919.'

'Nice story, Mark, and it may be of significance if you can prove it.'

'We can certainly substantiate much of what we've said,' he continued, 'although we can't prove at the moment that Lady Charlotte was pregnant nor that Edward Haynes was the father of Daniel.'

'But you hope to?'

'We, well I, have arranged to interview a descendant of Daniel Downes tomorrow.'

Perrin smiled at the persistence and determination of them both. 'OK you two, let us assume that your hypothesis is correct. Where does that get us?'

'Motive, sir.' interjected Kay Yin. 'We have examined the Chelwood family tree. Major Lord Chelwood was an only son. If Charlotte did have a child, the descendants of that child could have a claim to the Chelwood's wealth although not to the title.'

'You say "could have", Kay?'

'The passage of time makes any such claim weak, but I don't think that's it.'

'Go on.'

'What Lord and Lady Chelwood value is their reputation and social status.'

'And your hypothesis is that the enquiries by Nicholas Fry made the present Earl and Countess Chelwood uncomfortable, sufficiently uncomfortable to have the artist murdered?'

'It is a very real possibility,' she suggested.

'And by whom, Somers?'

'He would certainly be a candidate.'

'And his motive, Kay?'

DCI Yin looked towards Faraday. 'We were thinking, sir,' replied Faraday. 'When Somers retired, he would have collected a commutation of well over £130,000, together with a handsome monthly pension. I've checked with Personnel and, well some other people.' Perrin thought it best not to enquire who these *other* people where and allowed Faraday to continue uninterrupted. 'Somers was divorced three years before he retired and he had to hand over one-third of his commutation and half of his monthly pension to his ex-wife. Mrs Somers also kept the family home in Stoke Bishop whilst George Somers bought a two-bedroom dock-side terraced house here in the city. I spoke with Superintendent Waters who had served with Somers in the old Gloucestershire force. He said that Somers, whom he dismissed as pretentious, had purchased as an investment prior to his divorce a rather run-down house near Arlingham which had been formally owned by the local squire. Somers had grand ideas and spent a great deal on the house, re-roofing, re-wiring, new boiler, that sort of thing, only to be badly effected by the flooding. The result was that the value plummeted and he sold at a loss. We have also managed to access the Chelwood McBride web-site. In their social section, we found that under "Properties to Rent" Somers has a property in Kessering, near Serre-Kunda in the Gambia. From the "availability" section of his web page it is clear that he doesn't have many bookings.'

'Why not, I thought the Gambia was becoming quite popular with the new link with Bristol Airport?' Perrin asked.

'We have compared other properties there,' replied Faraday, 'and his problem seems to be that he is charging too much. There is another twist. When we checked with Gambian estate agents who also do lettings, we discovered that Somers has this property up for sale.'

'But the bottom line could read,' suggested Perrin, 'that Somers still has a police pension, is currently employed, and is the owner of three properties. If he has debts, and we don't know that to be the case, he appears to be in the process of selling one of his properties.'

'That may be so, but he is unlikely to make a great deal out of the sale of his Gambian property,' suggested Faraday.

'Why not?'

'Because, whilst UK estate agents charge about 2% commission, the Gambians charge 10% and this is rising to 15% at the same time as property prices around the world are falling.'

'Your suggestion is that Somers murdered Fry and was paid to do so. Yet, on the face of it, Somers is a respected ex-senior police officer who is employed by a prestigious bank on a good salary?'

'I accept that,' said Faraday. 'He has a company car, a Volvo V70 D5, and I would guess that his salary is probably £80,000, but he has little else.'

'You *believe* he has little else, Mark,' countered Perrin. There was a silence as Perrin relaxed back into his seat and raised both palms towards them as if to say that he was still on-side but needed to question and probe. 'Do we know anything about his life-style, who he lives with now?'

'We know that he is a complainer and lives with a girl friend, Judith Featherstone, a thirty-seven year old West Indian nursing sister,' offered the DCI.

'Anything known?'

'No, she doesn't even have a parking ticket recorded against her.'

Perrin rose from his chair and returned to the seat behind his desk, a manoeuvre that gave him time to digest all that he had been told. 'Look, I'm with you both and I would put Somers in the frame, but, after the adverse publicity surrounding the cash for honours scandal, we cannot afford a clumsy and public spectacle of arrests. So, what do you propose doing?'

'I propose to interview Francis Downes, that's Daniel's grand-son, tomorrow and then for us to interview Lord Chelwood.'
'Why?'

'I believe that Somers killed Fry at the behest of Chelwood. I propose that Kay and I interview the Chelwoods, but to confine our meeting to simply up-date them on some of our findings.'

'And?'

'I have no doubt that Chelwood will contact Somers and so we require the authorisation to tap Somers' phone.'

Perrin looked at them both without the slightest surprise at their request. 'And you think that the chief will be able to persuade the Home Secretary, Mark?'

'The Home Secretary would probably have a fit if we asked permission to tap Lord Chelwood's phone or his bank's. But I am sure that he will agree to us tapping Somers' phone, particularly if the chief says that we need his support so as to bring a corrupt former senior police officer to justice.'

Perrin smiled again, but he had read Mark Faraday's expression. 'You have no worries with this Home Secretary, Mark?'

'I think we can emphasise that we believe Somers murdered Nicholas Fry, although the Act makes it clear that our application mustn't be deceitful in any way, and so we will have to mention Lord Chelwood.'

'But not make too much of Chelwood's role?'

'We don't know what Chelwood's role in this is, sir, although there appears to be a connection. We will have to mention Chelwood's name in the application.'

'Yes, we must, although there is a chance that the Home Secretary will tip-off Chelwood, but it is a low risk, Mark.' Perrin picked up his telephone and pressed one key and waited. The wait was very short. 'Hullo, Claire. I need to speak with Sir John as a matter of urgency. It's for a wire tap, can I see him within the next hour, do you think?' There was a pause before he spoke again. 'Thirty minutes, that's fine. Thank you, Claire.' Perrin replaced the receiver and spoke to his two colleagues again. 'And your next move?'

'We should then invite Somers to Bristol Central,' replied DCI Yin. 'Arrest him, interview him, take his DNA and seize his car. Then bail him.'

'Why now, Kay?'

'We now have a motive, I agree that it is not directly connected to Somers, but it is a strong motive and is indirectly linked to Somers.'

'The problem is that the Chelwoods will very likely say that his family were aware of some sort of scandal surrounding Lady Charlotte, but these type of scandals are not new to the landed gentry, the Fitzroys, Fitzhowards and Fitzwilliams are all illegitimate descendants of the children of one king or another – so what?'

'I think we should interview Somers. If nothing else, he will contact the Chelwoods as a result,' said Kay Yin. 'I will invite him in again. He will come in because he needs to know what we know and he's arrogant enough to believe that it will be a walk in the park.'

'And what questions do you propose to ask him, Kay?'

'Where were you between the hours of 6pm and mid-night on the 2nd March?'

'And he will lie.'

'Of course he will,' she replied as if the reactions of Somers was a given.

'And what if the Chelwoods and Somers don't make telephone contact? Perrin asked.

'Mr Faraday has already authorised covert observations on Somers' dock-side home under the provision of Section 26(2).'

Chapter 24

Saturday, 7th April.

Bristol, England.

THE TITLE 'The New Room' is something of a misnomer. In reality this building was never a single room but was John Wesley's first chapel and home in Bristol, built in 1739 and enlarged in 1748. It consists of a large chapel with wooden pews and a lower and upper pulpit, all surrounded by a balcony. Above the chapel itself are now a series of five rooms leading off from a central Common Room, which acted as the quarters for John Wesley and his assistants.

Mark Faraday, in civilian clothes, entered from Broadmead, walking past Arthur Walker's equestrian statue of Wesley, through the double-doors. Faraday's first impression of the inside of the building was its austerity, its commanding feature the two pulpits, one above the other. He walked to the far end and up the wooden stairs, across behind the upper pulpit, up another flight of wooden stairs to the domestic quarters. As the policeman stooped to enter the Common Room he was greeted by the Reverend Canon Dr Francis Downes.

'You must be Superintendent Mark Faraday,' he said enthusiastically as he stretched out his hand and took Faraday's firmly. 'Welcome, welcome to The New Room. I am Francis Downes,' he announced, his parentage clear, the smiling face and ruffled ginger hair confirmed it all. 'Would you care for some tea, Superintendent?'

'If it's not too much trouble.'

'Of course not,' he said. Faraday studied this man. Francis Downes had a healthy, ruddy complexion with intelligent eyes set above what appeared to be a perpetual smile. 'Shall we go in here, John Wesley's study?'

Faraday followed Francis Downes into a small room containing three upholstered chairs set around a circular tripod table. There was also a bureau and the armchair used by Wesley as he wrote his sermons and hymns, together with a strangely square-shaped corner chair in which Wesley had sat as he delivered his very last sermon in 1790. The room was partitioned by a folding wooden screen behind which was his bedroom.

'It's quiet here, Superintendent.' He smiled as if he understood the delicacy of the visit. 'I think you would prefer privacy?'

'Firstly, it's kind of you to see me at such short notice,' Faraday said.

'I'm the chair of the District, like a sort of Methodist bishop I suppose, and up from Truro for a few days. Bristol is part of my district, so, it's no trouble at all, and it's good to be able to meet here where the Methodist movement has so many of its roots,' he said, making light of their meeting, but, he sensed that what was to be discussed would be a delicate issue. He allowed Faraday the opportunity to speak.

'I would much prefer to keep this discussion informal. Maybe we could use our Christian names, if I'm allowed to use that description in this pc world.'

'Of course, Mark. And it's Francis.'

'As I mentioned on the phone, I am making some enquiries regarding a recent case here in Bristol and, during the course of my enquiries, the names of your parents and grand-parents cropped up.'

'Is this what the police refer to as a "Cold Case"?' he asked, concern marring his smile.

'Oh no. My enquiries are in respect of a crime committed in the last four or five weeks.'

'But my parents both died some years ago and so I'm not sure of the connection,' he said, genuinely confused.

Mark chose to pursue a matter that could well be within Francis Downes' knowledge. 'Were you aware that your father had some difficulties in obtaining a passport?'

'Yes, I was.'

'Do you know why there were some difficulties?'

'Yes, I do,' he answered openly.

'Are you able to tell me what these difficulties were?' asked Faraday but the reply was interrupted by the arrival of tea and little packets containing three chocolate biscuits. Francis Downes poured the tea, Mark adding his milk and sugar. Ignoring the biscuits, Faraday sipped his tea and waited for the reply.

'I think I was about fifteen or sixteen at the time,' said Downes, a smile returning to his face as his thoughts drifted back to a happy childhood. 'I was with my father in our kitchen sat at the table. He suddenly told me that he was illegitimate and hoped that I wouldn't think badly of him.' His forehead creased in thought. 'It was the only time I saw my father frightened. Of course, I didn't think badly of him. I realised that he was not only being honest but also that he was prepared to trust me with a confidence. I just told him how much I loved him.' Francis picked up his cup and drank some of his tea. 'Is this important to your enquiries?'

Faraday answered the question with a question. 'Do you know who your father's parents were?'

'No I don't.'

'Do you think that your father knew their identity?'

He reflected for a moment. 'I don't think he did.'

'Francis,' said Faraday, returning his cup and saucer to the little table. 'I think that I may have some news about your father and grand-parents. You may be delighted to hear some of what I have to say but, I'm sure that you will be distressed with other ... other things.'

'That would appear to mirror the world we live in, Mark.'

'Your grand-father, Philip Downes,' continued Faraday, 'was at one stage the rector near here for about ten months in late 1914 and early 1915.'

'Yes, St Matthew's.'

'He and his wife, Elizabeth, moved from St Matthew's to Beverley in what was then South Yorkshire as rector. Your father, also a Church of England priest, later moved on to Newcastle.'

'Yes,' interrupted Francis Downes, either because of nervousness or because of pride, 'like John Wesley whose father was a Church of England priest, my father became a Methodist. He felt it more in-keeping with the poverty he encountered in the North-East amongst the families of coal miners, steel workers and dockers.'

'Francis, I believe,' said Faraday pedantically, 'in fact, I know, that your grand-parents had a son, Daniel.' Francis didn't interrupt as he realised that a tragic tale was beginning to unfold. 'That child died, probably of diphtheria, and is buried in the churchyard at St Matthew's. Your grand-parents then moved to Beverley where your father, another Daniel, was baptised as their own.'

Francis didn't want to ask but knew he must. 'Did they take the child from another family?'

'No. No, Francis. I believe they were given the child in the knowledge that they would be very loving parents - and discreet.'

'Do you know the true identity of my grand-parents?' he asked after a moment's hesitation.

'Do you have any letters or anything that might help us to identify your grand-parents?' asked Faraday avoiding a direct answer.
He considered the question carefully, imagining all the family papers he did have and had read. 'We do have all sorts of correspondence, but nothing like that.'

'What about an old family bible?' asked Faraday, aware that many families endorse bibles with details of births and marriages and handed them down the generations.

'Strangely enough, no,' he replied as if, on reflection, there should have been one. 'I have my grand-father's bible which was used by my father, but there are no endorsements of that kind.' They stopped speaking as a lady removed the tray and cups. When they were alone again Francis asked: 'You know who my grand-parents were?'

'I'm reasonably certain.'

'But to tell me would be … distressing?'

'Yes,' replied Faraday nodding almost solemnly.

'Please tell me, Mark.'

He hesitated for a moment but had already prepared his answer. 'I believe that your grand-mother was an exceptionally beautiful and kind lady and she had a child, your father. The father of this child was a happy, smiling, ginger haired young man.'

'And they died?' he asked, hoping that they had not committed suicide together or had died in horrific circumstances. Faraday saved him that pain – at least for the present.

'Yes, the young man, a soldier, died early on in the Great War and the young lady during the flu epidemic in 1919.'

Francis Downes was relieved, but he sensed that there were still dark clouds. 'And you believe that their lives, our lives, are somehow linked with the case that you are investigating at the moment?'

'I'm certain of it.'

'Can you tell me their names?'

'Not at the moment.'

'Then what do you want of me, Mark?'

'Your DNA.'

Chapter 25

Tuesday, 10th April.

Pall Mall, London, England.

WHAT REMAINED of the previous Friday had been occupied with preparing the formal application to wire-tap the domestic phone line of George Somers. E-mails had been exchanged between the chief constable, Sir John Sinclair, and the Home Secretary and approval was given with very few questions asked. As a result, British Telecom officials and the Post Office Special Investigation Branch had acted promptly. The wiretap and postal intercepts were now in place.

Monday had seen DCI Kay Yin's officers discreetly obtaining a short-term let on an unoccupied apartment overlooking the dock-side home of George Somers and Judith Featherstone, whilst Kay had attempted to arrange an interview with Lord Chelwood, deliberately seeking the help of George Somers when Chelwood's PA was less than helpful. The DCI had then contacted Lady Cecelia Chelwood.

Lady Chelwood had enjoyed her holiday. The *Odyssey* had sailed a further six-hundred and thirty-three nautical miles after leaving Curacao, arriving at Barbados via Grenada three days later. She had flown from that island paradise to London Gatwick six days after her husband had already returned from the United Nations. What Lady Chelwood had not enjoyed was her conversation with what she considered an impertinent and persistent DCI Yin, replying dismissively that her husband was already en route to the United Nations for his bi-weekly meetings.

Undeterred, Superintendent Faraday had contacted the Special Branch at Heathrow who were able to confirm Lord Chelwood's 10:25 British Airways flight number BA0175 to New York's JFK the following day. These officers were also able to provide His Lordship's contact address whilst in London.

Meanwhile, Kay Yin had liaised with the Financial Investigations Unit of the City of London Police whilst Faraday had spoken to the Thames Valley Police at their headquarters in Kidlington, Oxford as well as Scotland Yard, informing them of the urgency of their journey to London. Now he could relax in the *Valcona* leather passenger seat of his Audi A5 as Kay accelerated in the outside lane of the M4. Her speed was blistering, the blue strobe lights behind the black-mesh radiator grill warning others of her approach. As they neared the end of the motorway and entered Hammersmith, Kay switched off the strobes and reduced her speed. She drove purposefully along the Brompton Road and into Knightsbridge, circuiting Wellington Arch and along Constitution Hill, passing Buckingham Palace on her right and into The Mall where she pulled into the kerb and stopped a little past Clarence House.

Lord Chelwood had agreed to meet Superintendent Faraday at his club at one o'clock. Faraday was sceptical and prepared. The venue was Pall Mall, the significance of which had not eluded him. Pall Mall had been the home of the Dukes of Buckingham and the Prince Regent, it was also the home to the most exclusive clubs in the world, including The Athenaeum and The Reform Club, The Diogenes Club and The Carlton Club, the members of which had exercised world-wide influence throughout most of the nineteenth and twentieth centuries. An anachronism, maybe, but even in the twenty-first century the members of these clubs remained at the centres of power and influence, and had transformed the notion of networking into an efficient and ruthless art. Amongst their exclusive membership were former Prime Ministers and Princes, Foreign Secretaries and Attorney Generals, the chairmen of billion pound conglomerates and international bankers.

'12:15,' he said. 'Good driving and well in time for one o'clock.' He pulled his brief case from behind her seat, then kissed her on the lips. 'I will walk up through Marlborough Road. It will give me time to think. Good luck at Wood Street and, by the way,' he added with a mischievous grin, 'don't get rid of any of the goodies in the back.'

Pall Mall exuded distinction and sophistication, the ornate buildings bathing in the Spring-time sun, the entrance portals casting imposing shadows. He easily found the address. A few yards before the entrance, Faraday adjusted his suit jacket and checked his Royal Household Club tie for neatness, then mounted the steps as livered attendants opened the doors to allow Faraday to enter. The interior was opulent with glistening marble floors and carpets of luxuriant maroon pile. The Corinthian pillars gleamed in what seemed a thousand lights of the chandeliers and the air was scented by the most extravagant flower arrangements. A tall distinguished man approached unhurriedly wearing pin-striped trousers and a claw-hammer coat.

'Good afternoon, sir. Are we expected?' he asked not unkindly.

'My name is Faraday. I have a one o'clock appointment with the Earl Chelwood.'

'Oh, yes, Mr Faraday,' he said as if acknowledging Faraday as a regular guest whose name he had for a moment inexcusably forgotten. 'Could I invite you to await His Lordship in the Green Library,' he said gesturing to the right up a flight of three carpeted steps.

Faraday entered the library through glazed doors followed by his new, ever-attentive, companion.

'His Lordship is expecting you and will be with you shortly. Would you care for tea or coffee, sir?'

Faraday was confident that his wait would not be short. 'Coffee would be very nice. Thank you.'

'May I suggest Kenya Peaberry, it is very pleasant at this time of day, sir.'

'That will be fine, thank you.'

As anticipated the wait was not short but at least he enjoyed the silky taste of the creamy smooth coffee as well as the bite-sized shortbread biscuits - in total isolation. Faraday had moved one the chairs slightly so as to position himself near the doors leading into the Green Library. This allowed him a virtually unrestricted sight of the main entrance from Pall Mall as well as a clear view in one of the glazed doors of the library of the main staircase. At exactly 2.15pm the Rolls-Royce Phantom glided to a halt as Lord Chelwood descended the staircase. Miles Chelwood, already forewarned of Faraday's arrival, turned as the policeman approached from his left. He was completely unfazed and appeared confidently at ease.

'Ah, you must be Superintendent Faraday,' he said warmly shaking the policeman's hand. 'It was kind of you to wait. I have a meeting with the Foreign Secretary shortly, but I can give you ten minutes. Shall we walk?'

The liveried attendants opened the doors as the two men stepped out into Pall Mall.

'Thank you, Davies,' Chelwood said to his chauffeur. 'We are going to stroll, but be at the FCO for me.' The chauffeur returned to the Rolls-Royce as Lord Chelwood and Superintendent Faraday turned to their left.

'Now how can I help you?' he asked as if wishing to smooth the way of an acquaintance's son into the City. 'We can talk as we walk, it is such a pleasant day.'

'I have been investigating the murder of Nicholas Fry.'

'So you mentioned,' he said in the friendliest manner.

'I know that my colleague, Chief Inspector Yin, discussed with you your ancestor, Lord Tatton Chelwood.'

'That is so, Superintendent.'

'Did you know that Tatton Chelwood presided at a court martial?'

'No, did he?' he said as if fascinated by this revelation.

'Yes and sentenced a young soldier to death.'

'As did many other court martials,' he said sadly.
'There was a particular significance with this trial.'

'Was there?' he said at the same time as he acknowledged a pedestrian on the opposite side of the road.

'The soldier sentenced to death was his very own soldier/servant and a groom from the Chelwood estate.'

'My goodness… That must have been a very unpleasant business for Tatton.'

'You were not aware of this event, sir?'

'No,' he replied as if it were of no importance at all, adding: 'I suppose you have examined Tatton's diaries. I have but cannot recall any mention of this business. You are not a member are you?' Lord Chelwood asked as they continued to walk, completely changing the subject.

'A member, sir?' asked Faraday wary of the purpose of the enquiry.

'Yes,' he said pointing to number 119, 'the Institute of Directors. You are not a member I suppose?'

'No, I'm not, sir.'

'Oh well, never mind,' he replied as if disappointed, a disappointment that he could easily rectify. 'You were saying, Superintendent?'

'I have examined the diaries carefully, sir. There is something else not mentioned in his diaries.'

'And what might that be?'

'Lord Tatton Chelwood had a sister?'

'Yes, a beautiful girl, Charlotte,' he said raising his hand as if to halt any interruption to his thinking. 'But I am afraid that you are wrong, Superintendent. I think that you will find that Lady Charlotte is mentioned many, many times in the diaries. Tatton and Charlotte were always very close and exchanged correspondence on a very regular basis.'

'But there is no reference to the fact that Lady Charlotte was having an affair with this young groom.'

He stopped walking. 'My goodness, do you think they were?' he asked as if unexpectedly privy to gossip.

'I'm certain of it,' replied Faraday uncompromisingly as he tried to analyse the reactions of Lord Chelwood. 'More importantly, I believe that there was a child as a result of this union.'

'Do you? Well,' he replied with a amused smile, 'it wouldn't be the first time, Superintendent.'

'As I say, I'm certain of it. Indeed, I interviewed this child's grand-son last Saturday.'

For the first time Lord Chelwood was taken aback, albeit only for the slightest of moments. His lips moved as if to speak but nothing was said as he computed the implications of what he had just heard, but his recovery was rapid. 'I'm not too sure where this avenue of enquiry will take you, Superintendent,' he said, adding as if taking part in a private joke, 'you aren't going to ask me for money or go to the tabloids like Princess Diana's dreadful butler, are you?'

Faraday wasn't sure whether Chelwood was laying the ground so as to offer a bribe to the policeman or whether it was a remark in poor taste. He ignored the suggestion. 'I think that you can see the problem I have, sir. My concern is that we have an artist murdered who had a commission to paint a picture of Lord Tatton Chelwood, whose sister had a child, Daniel. It follows that this child, whilst illegitimate, could have a legitimate claim to part of the Chelwood estate.'

Lord Miles Chelwood was firmly back in diplomatic mode, the cool, astute pragmatist and Faraday detected not the slightest reaction at the mention of the child's name, although this would have further confirmed to Chelwood that the police enquiries were well advanced. Nor did Chelwood seem taken aback at the suggestion that the child's descendants could have a claim to his estate but, Faraday reasoned, Chelwood would have lived with the prospect of the existence of Lady Charlotte's child being revealed for much of his life.

'An interesting tale, Superintendent, but one that is quite new to me, although I am not really sure of the significance,' he said reasonably.

'The significance is that it provides a very compelling motive for murder.'

'Good God, you don't think me capable of murder do you?' he asked as if it was a light-hearted music hall joke.

'I *know* who committed the murder, Lord Chelwood,' said Faraday with a slight menace in his tone, a comment that for just a pico-second resulted in the smile leaving Chelwood's face. Faraday waited as his brown penetrating eyes fixed upon the other man, then continued. 'At the moment I don't have enough evidence to arrest him. Can you help me at all, sir?'

Chelwood began to walk along Pall Mall again towards Waterloo Place. 'How can I help you?' he asked as if it was a foolish request to make.

'Can you think of anyone who would gain from the murder of Nicholas Fry?'

'My wife and I have asked ourselves that question a number of times, but we can't think of anyone at all.'

'Well, thank you for your time, sir.'

'I'm afraid you have had a wasted journey, Superintendent.'

'My journeys are rarely wasted, sir.'

Chelwood did not like the ominous tone in this observation. 'Do you come up to town often?' he asked the policeman.

'Once or twice a year, sir, the theatre.'

'Ah, yes, the theatre. I like the City and Pall Mall, Superintendent,' he said reflectively. 'We used to have a house on St James Square, but it is Waterloo Place that brings back so many memories to me. I never tire of it.' Lord Chelwood turned to his right into Waterloo Place and approached the *Memorial to the Crimea* and stopped. 'The 2nd Earl fought in the Crimea.' He pointed up to the three magnificent bronze figures of a Grenadier, a Fusilier and Coldstream Guard. 'These were men who stood cheek to jowl and put country first, Superintendent. At the rear,' he said drawing Faraday's attention to bronze relief, 'is depicted a pile of broken Russian canons from Sebastopol, the canons from which the Victoria Crosses are struck, awarded to brave men who looked the enemy in the eye, fought belt buckle to enemy belt buckle, men with the faults of human beings who, at the moment of their greatest test, stood and did their duty.'

Faraday looked again at the proud and determined faces of the three soldiers and absorbed Lord Chelwood's words, but his lordship had already turned and began to walk toward the Duke of York's Column, stopping again below the equestrian statue of King Edward VII.

'The 5th Earl was an ADC to King Edward and was heavily involved in the medical reforms of the army instigated by the king.' He turned and faced Faraday at the top of the steps. 'It was George V, Superintendent, who in 1920 was so concerned that the recipient of a VC could forfeit his decoration, declared that, no matter what the crime committed by anyone upon whom the cross had been conferred, the VC could never be forfeited.' Was this comment made to exonerate Lord Tatton Chelwood or to put Faraday off the scent of the present-day murder of Nicholas Fry. Probably a mixture of both thought Faraday, thoughts interrupted by Chelwood.

'Let me say something to you candidly, I have no knowledge of a court martial or of any illegitimate child. If I had,' he added reasonably, 'I would simply tell you that I am not ashamed of Lord Tatton and, if there is evidence of an illegitimate child, I am sure that it would not have been the only one in my family. What I can also tell you, Superintendent, is that I do not have any knowledge of any connection between my family and the tragic murder of Nicholas Fry.' He took Faraday's hand and held it firmly as he would the dearest friend. 'Enough said I believe. Now, I must go.' He turned. 'Good luck, Superintendent Faraday,' he said and descended the steps to The Mall and walked across Horse Guards Parade towards the Foreign and Commonwealth Office.

Faraday crossed The Mall and walked towards the junction of The Mall and Horse Guards. He stood in front of the pale blue-coloured glass, ribbed pillar standing in a small reflecting pool. To the left was the black block with a glass vitrine containing the Roll of Honour of The National Police Memorial and the inscription: *'Honour Those Who Serve'*. Faraday looked at the open book and read down the names beautiful recorded in gold, red and black inks. One name in particular stood out for him:

Temporary Detective Constable Carl Norris
Severnside Police

Faraday backed away from the memorial deep in thought and absent-mindedly took his mobile phone from his pocket and called Kay Yin. He thought of Carl Norris, one of his young detectives murdered just three years before. If he had, for a fleeting moment, entertained any doubts about pursuing this case, the thought of people like Carl Norris, Edward Haynes and Nicholas Fry, put such thoughts completely from his mind.

Within minutes the Audi pulled to a halt in Horse Guards Road. He stepped into the car. 'You haven't eaten all the sandwiches and those little pork pies have you?' he asked as if chastising her.

'Of course not. The City police looked after me very well indeed at Wood Street,' she teased.

'And did their monitoring of bank transactions help us?' asked Faraday, referring to their powers under the Money Laundering (Proceeds of Crime) Act.

'Not of a financial transaction as such,' she said as she reached into the open briefcase behind his seat, pulled out a bundle of papers and placed them on her lap. She turned the pages and pointed to one page bearing the crest of the United States and endorsed *SECRET*. 'But this makes very interesting reading.' Faraday skim read the text. The contents of which were compelling.

'You're a gem,' he said kissing her on the cheek.

'Just a kiss on the cheek,' she teased again. 'Don't I deserve just a little more.'

'After I've had something to eat.'

'You didn't have lunch?' she asked indignantly.

'He was never going to invite me to lunch.'

'How did you know?' she asked quizzically.

'This was all about power, Kay, an exercise in power. He wanted to show me how important and well connected he was and how I was someone whom he would have no difficulty in sweeping aside. I think he was also sounding me out for a bribe. And, to cover all the bases, he tried to appeal to my sense of duty and my humanity.'

'And your opinion of him?'

'He's a diplomat, used to negotiating and not showing his hand. Whilst he would have a lot to lose if another heir suddenly popped up, I'm sure that he would know enough people, pull enough strings, prevaricate with skill and exhaust the finances of any claimant, then buy him off with a pittance. I can't see him hiring Somers to kill anyone, there would be little need.'

'Someone did,' she said but Faraday's thought were still with the financial stability of the Chelwood family.

'We know from Pippa's enquiries that Chelwood Kilbride is in good shape and the Chelwoods are worth about thirty-five million.' Kay didn't interrupt his thoughts. 'Chelwood is now in no doubt that we know the identity of the killer. If he's behind it, he must inform Somers. I don't know what he'll be talking to the Foreign Secretary about this afternoon but his mind will be pre-occupied with thoughts of the murder and your investigation. If he is involved then he will be mulling over what I have told him, what the implications are for his family and what damage limitation and crisis management plan he can enact. We have Somers closed down as far as phone, e-mail and post are concerned; we have to hope that Chelwood will make contact and be arrogant enough not to believe that we would have taps on Somers' home. If he does make contact we have in place the resources to cover Somers' premises and movements.' They looked at each other, pleased to be sharing each other's company. Any suggestions?' he asked.

'Yes, you need to eat.'

Chapter 26

Thursday, 12th April.

The United Nations, New York, USA and Police Headquarters, Bristol, England.

LORD CHELWOOD had arrived at JFK at 12:55 local time the previous day for his meetings at the UN. He was a key and highly regarded member of the International Bank for Reconstruction and Development, a part of the UN's World Bank Group, although this visit to New York was in his capacity as an advisor to the Economic Commission for Africa.

The meetings, which were scheduled to last until late Thursday, were part of a series that had commenced shortly after the formal resolution had been passed by the General Assembly. Principles had been agreed but even after seven meetings consensus had still not been reached in respect of pre-condition and the time-scale for aid. As always the devil was in the detail with junior officials preparing new briefs after sometimes heated debate over how binding should 'binding' actually be; what 'effective public financial management', 'fiscal discipline' and 'prevailing circumstances' actually mean in a drought-ridden country of few natural resources; and how the notion of democracy could, in practical terms, be applied to a vast country of disparate tribal communities.

Miles Chelwood – he always insisted upon being called Miles in these forums - in addition to presenting two papers, one in respect of sustainable development and growth, the other in respect of water, was a skilled contributor to these debates. He was knowledgeable, a persuasive speaker and experienced negotiator.

For him, as in all matters, it was all a question of balance and timing.

The meeting drew to a close well after mid-night, an eventuality anticipated by Lord Chelwood and entirely in-keeping with his timing. He made his first call from the twenty-ninth floor to the UK a little after 2am. As he spoke he looked out over the East River towards Queens, a borough like the rest of vibrant New York that never seemed to sleep. The recipient of his call, pleased to be on the periphery of a select group but also aware of his vulnerability, was already sat behind his desk in an office devoid of any vibrancy, occupied in methodically reading through briefing papers prior to the first meeting of his morning.

When Miles Chelwood replaced the receiver he was reassured that, as a result of what he had said, the investigation into the murder of Nicholas Fry would be stalled – better to have been halted altogether he thoughts, but, for the moment, stalled would suit his purposes.

***

Faraday arrived at the Deputy Chief Constable's office at ten minutes to five. There was an ominous air in the DCC's secretary's office – he could sense it. Nothing was said – maybe that was it – just slightly embarrassed and short-lived glances from the secretary. At five o'clock the secretary stood up without instructions, walked towards and tapped upon the DCC's door, opened the door and announced that Mark Faraday had arrived.

Faraday entered the office. The DCC was seated behind her desk, flanked by the standing figures of Assistant Chief Constable Wynne-Thomas and Detective Chief Superintendent Perrin.

'Mr Faraday,' she said formally, 'I will come straight to the point. A serious allegation has been made against you, namely that you attempted to solicit a monetary bribe from Lord Chelwood on Tuesday, the 10th.'

'Absolute nonsense,' Faraday replied instantly.

'Mr Faraday, before you say anything more, you will know that bribery is a criminal offence, therefore,' she said, picking up a printed form so as to ensure she quoted the words accurately, 'I must caution you that you do not have to say anything, but it may harm your defence if you do not mention when questioned something which you later rely on in court. Anything you do say may be given in evidence.' The DCC returned the form to the file before continuing. 'As this matter concerns Lord Chelwood, a member of the United Nations, I have already informed the Home Secretary and chairman of the police authority of the allegation. This is a criminal matter and I have asked Mr Perrin to take charge of the investigation and report to me within one week as to his initial findings. I am now serving upon you formal papers outlining the allegation.'

Faraday stepped forward and took the proffered papers. 'As I said, this allegation has no foundation at all.'

The DCC ignored Faraday's protestation. 'You will also see that, as a result of matters that have also been brought to Mr Wynne-Thomas' attention, there are additional allegations of gross misconduct, including bullying subordinate staff, namely Inspectors Trench and Glass; the improper use of police equipment, namely a dry-wipe board; and the inappropriate association with female staff, namely Constable Phillipa Blanchard and Miss Jade Hancock, so as to give rise to the perception amongst others of favouritism.'

Faraday looked at the papers in his hand but he couldn't focus on the words at all as his mind tried to grapple with the implications. The allegation by Lord Chelwood was, he knew, unsustainable, but the other allegations were to him worse, they represented betrayal. He recalled a poem, he thought written by Shelley. It was about the realistic acceptance by most of the inevitability of death during the course of one's life, although there was something that was always darker than death, and that was being let down by those in whom you had placed your trust.

'You are therefore suspended from duty,' the DCC droned on. 'You will now go with Mr Perrin and surrender to him your warrant card and all police issue equipment including keys. Mr Perrin will then escort you from the building. Meanwhile you will make no contact with any of the staff listed in those papers or any members of your *former* department.' She removed her glasses, adding abruptly. 'Carry on.'

Faraday walked out of the office in silence, his last image being of a triumphant Assistant Chief Constable Wynne-Thomas who was clearly having the utmost physical difficulty in restraining his vengeful glee.

***

An hour later, Detective Chief Superintendent Perrin called DCI Yin to his office and told her to take two days leave suggesting, that if this should be with Faraday, it would be better if they were both completely away from the force area.

Mark and Kay needed little urging. At Avon View Court they packed a single holdall and began their journey to Mark's cottage.

***

3,459 miles away in New York City, the last round of meetings attended by Lord Chelwood would continue for another eight hours until 7pm local time. It had been a tiring few days and he was thankful that he would be returning to the UK for a weekend break with Lady Cecelia.

According to plan he had called his personal assistant at Chelwood Kilbride saying that he had tried to ring his wife but without success. This of course was untrue. He then asked that the PA contact Lady Cecelia and say: *'Looking forward to the weekend, but could she make the final arrangement'.*

Lady Cecelia would understand the significance of the phrase 'final arrangements'. This would be her signal to warn George Somers to leave the country immediately in the knowledge that Superintendent Faraday would have already been suspended and the impetus of the murder enquiry stalled.

But, as Lord Chelwood discussed the issues of Africa, there was also another hastily convene meeting taking place, three floors below, in one of the secure conference rooms attended by six men. These business men, aged between thirty-four and sixty-two years, exuded success and ruthless power. They drank their coffees around the 'V' shaped table waiting for Peter Reeve to speak, oblivious of the spectacular night-time views towards New York's Central Park.

Peter spoke. 'I said that this meeting was important. You will *all* find it important, I know.' He stood up from his position at the point of the 'V'. He pressed a key on his lap-top and the full-width screen behind him illuminated. The screen only contained two words:

CRISIS MANAGEMENT

Peter had their full attention now. 'We are short on time so let me, if I may, remind you of our individual commitments to an enterprise that has been hard fought and won against probably the most formidable competition we have ever encountered in the seven years we have worked together.' Peter looked towards one of his colleagues.

'You, Bob,' he said. 'Your company's commitment for road building and infra-structure is seven billion over ten years.' Bob nodded, a smile of satisfaction on his face.

'David,' Peter said gesturing to another on his left. 'The commitment for your group of companies is four billion over the same period for dock facilities and rail connections, with the same amount, four billion, for you Al in respect of hospitals and schools.' Al said nothing but fiddled with his *Mont Blanc* pen as these men acknowledged the accuracy of what Peter said but they were, at the same time, wary of the implications of this unscheduled extra-ordinary meeting without secretaries and minute-takers.

'Philip, your commitment is the largest of us all,' he said to the only portly member of the group. 'Ten billion in respect of the extraction of minerals and other natural resources.'

Philip nodded as if humble but confident in the knowledge that he was very much the first amongst equals at this meeting. However, his self-assured composure would shortly change as the ramification of the meeting became clear.

'Bradley,' continued Peter, 'your organisation is committed to three billion with airport re-construction and facilities, the same commitment that I have in terms of the provision of internal security.'

'And Miles?' asked David.

Peter chose not to answer that question. 'Chelwood Kilbride has a remarkable track record in financing these sort of developments in Venezuela, Brazil, Iraq and India.'

'Shouldn't Miles be here?' persisted David.

'Let me explain his absence,' he replied as he pressed the button of his hand-held control and a standard text presentation for Crisis Management appeared on the screen.

'You will know the devastating effects that a crisis, if not properly managed, can have on any company. We only have to think of a relatively junior rouge trader in a French bank as an example, or a small amount of corrosion in an Alaskan pipe line, an earthquake in Indonesia or a world-wide hike in the price of crude.' He depressed the button again and more text appeared on the screen, words chillingly familiar to all six men.

'To deal with such a crisis, the prudent organisation has a business continuity plan. We have,' he paused for effect, 'a *major* crisis gentlemen.' He let the words resonate around the room then depressed the button.

'We all know that a continuity plan examines, amongst other issues, information, scrutiny and time.' As he spoke the word 'INFORMATION' was highlighted on the screen.

'Miles has told me but, for reasons that will become apparent, would prefer to distance himself from this meeting, that Chelwood

Kilbride had employed an artist to paint a picture of one of Miles' ancestors winning the British Victoria Cross. The painting was to be hung in their Bristol boardroom. The artist was brutally murdered on the 2nd March last and Chelwood Kilbride's Assistant Director of Security is soon to be arrested.' He pressed the button again and the word 'SCRUTINY' was highlighted as the other five men looked at each other, assessing the impact of this revelation upon them and their investments.

'All Crisis Management plans,' continued Peter in a matter-of-fact way, 'must take account of the scrutiny that will be attracted by the crisis and the *reactions* of governments, the press, our shareholders and our clients.' He made no further explanation. None was needed. All were beginning to compute the implications, particularly for their shareholders and the future viability of their companies.

The word 'TIME' was the next word to be highlighted on the screen. Peter pointed to this word and asked the rhetorical question. 'When do we have to respond?'

'You've posed some interesting questions,' asked Philip, 'but do you have any answers?'

'We all know that delay in dealing head-on with a crisis is costly. You will recall that delays by the management of Havinghurst Amsel Reitman resulted in a loss of five billion in just one quarter.'

'And the next step? asked Bradley. Each man leaned silently back in their chairs and awaited the response.

'We *know* what the next steps *must* be,' he replied as three words appeared on the screen:

'We know that at the end of the day, the survival of our companies rests on our reputation,' said Peter. 'This isn't a side-show or some sort of small lost-leader that we're involved in. All of us have already invested millions. Our companies are in too deep now to withdraw without catastrophic loss and irreparable damage.' Peter returned to his chair and sat down. He was sure that Philip would speak. He did.

'You're the security specialist, Peter. How do we make this crisis go away?'

'I mentioned rogue employees,' replied Peter reasonably. 'Miles has a rouge employee. If nothing else, the impact of any trial, if there is ever a trial, would need to be minimised. The problem with a trial is that it would be a high-profile event and would drag on for months. It would be prudent to assume that the press will turn the inconvenient murder of a nobody into the sensation of the year.'

'And the solution, Peter?' asked Al.

'The ideal position for us would be a situation that eliminates the threat to our reputations whilst at the same time portraying Miles as an exemplary figure of international standing, a hero like his ancestor, with his reputation and that of Chelwood Kilbride enhanced.'

'And how do you propose we achieve that, Peter?' asked Bob.
'There are two individuals that pose a threat to us,' replied Peter.

These six men were hard-nosed businessmen, ruthlessly prepared to advance their corporate enterprises. None was concerned about the detrimental effects upon the environment, the existence of towns and villages, traditional livelihoods or the stability of governments unless these issues impacted upon their bottom lines.

For the next thirty or so minutes they debated the threat to their interests and possible solutions, during which time Peter helpfully reminded them that 'he had people' in place. They considered their options and silently reminded themselves that their meeting was in secret and their involvement deniable. As they rose from their chairs and returned to their East 48th and Park Avenue hotels, no one voiced the slightest concern or objection to the measures that Peter would put in place.

Chapter 27

Friday, 13th April.

Bickenhill, Birmingham, England.

THE SIGNIFICANCE of the date eluded Brian. It was a Friday the 13th in 1307 that had been designated by King Philip IV of France for the European-wide arrest of the Knights Templar. By means of these arrests, Philip's debts to the Knights and the threat to the interests of the established monarchies by the powerful religious order were removed forever. But for Brian it was merely another working day.

First came the text call: *'Mother would like you to pay a visit this weekend at three'*. Brian duly rang the third mobile number on his list and was given an address and dates. That was all – just like the hangman receiving his telegram from the Home Office that simply contained the date and place of execution. He set about his work almost immediately in the sure knowledge that the money would come through as it always had done in the past.

The caller considered Brian a craftsman. Brian considered himself more of a magician, a magician who made problems disappear. He was a perfectionist and would have preferred more time but, there again, the urgency of the job meant the usual bigger bonus and he was used to working under pressure and to tight dead-lines. He sniggered at the thought of the term 'dead-lines' - most apt considering his line of work. He was also thorough. Residencies were always preferable with the targets resident either at their home address or in the country. It made little difference to Brian; their choice of residence would determine his means but the result would be inevitable.

He used a specially adapted vice in his garage workshop, the classical music playing in his earphones drowning out the noise of the aircraft on their flight path to Birmingham International Airport. The vice was bolted onto a sturdy wooden bench which was bolted firmly to the garage wall thus ensuring that, as he worked, the bench and vice would not move. The jaws of the vice were equipped with a wooden frame which, in turn, held a light bulb holder. Into the bayonet holder was fitted a standard 90w bulb and attached to the wooden frame was a cradle with a sleeve-bearing. He had favoured in the past an 800,000rpm dentist's drill with a bit of tungsten carbide-coated steel but he found that there had been too much wobble at the higher speeds and it had been awkward to clamp into place. As a result, Brian had recently changed to using the engraver's tool. With a lower rpm and high-torque, vibration-free operation capable of engraving egg shells, this tool was ergonomically better and provided the smooth and controlled cut required for his work. Clamping the electric engraving drill into the sleeve-bearing he turned a geared handle bringing the end of the drill-bit into contact with the glass. He began to cut a small elongated hole into the thickest part of the glass bulb where the glass globe met the metal screw base. It was a delicate task carried out with his usual patience. His experiments had shown that two elongated holes, one each side of the bulb, would ensure that gas seeped easily into the globe itself. Brian repeated the process on the other side and, satisfied, commenced his delicate work on another bayonet bulb. Once completed, he removed the bulb holder, replacing it with a screw holder and inserted another 90w bulb.

Chapter 28

Saturday, 14th April.

Grizedale Forest, Cumbria, England.

THEY HAD both arrived at the cottage before Brian could change the bulbs. He would wait, seated in his Land Rover Discovery, with his flask of black coffee, cheese and onion sandwiches, *Mars* bars and apples. From time to time he would raise his binoculars. This activity attracted no one's attention for no one would find a middle-aged man wearing a green *Barbour*, with National Trust and Royal Society for the Protection of Birds badges on his windscreen, at all unusual in this area of outstanding natural beauty and renowned for its wildlife.

At a little after six-thirty his targets left the nineteenth-century cottage on foot. He waited again but only to follow them when sensible to do so. As the couple entered the *Duke of Westmoreland* public house, Brian pulled his Land Rover into the car park. He too entered the public house and made his way through the lounge bar to the toilets. As he walked back through the bar, his targets were already seated at their dining table. They seemed morose and pre-occupied he thought, in stark contrast to the lively babble and animation of the other patrons.

Brian returned to his vehicle and drove up the main road and turned off along a track, avoiding the docile sheep grazing on the verge, and parked about three-hundred yards from the rear of the target cottage amongst the pine trees. He walked across the field at the rear, around the side of the cottage to the front porch. Brian should have been surprised at how easily he was able to enter the cottage, but he wasn't. Over the years he had found that professionals and holiday makers were quite sloppy when it came to security. And that was good.

He entered the flag-stone hallway. He looked around and assessed that the cottage was probably well over one-hundred and fifty years old. That was also good as the thick walls would serve to contain the blast wave within the building ensuring maximum destruction. He firstly walked down the hallway and into the kitchen which was sympathetically fitted with modern *Bosch* appliances and gas hob together with a *Blanco* stainless steel sink unit. He surveyed the scene checking for smoke and gas detectors as he went. He found none. The kitchen was always a possibility, he considered, but he re-entered the hallway, opened the fifteen-pane door and walked into the rustic lounge. This was much better, he reasoned. In the stone fireplace that dominated the far wall was a gas log-effect fire in a dog-grate. He checked the lighting. There was a double switch near the door leading back into the hallway. One of the switches operated a ceiling light of two 60w bulbs, the other the two table lamps, one to the left-hand side of the fireplace, the other on a side table behind a luxury cream-coloured settee.

Brian removed the two ceiling light bulbs from behind their glass cover and gently crushed the glass without damaging the filaments, replacing them in their holders and re-fixing the glass cover in place. Satisfied, he then concentrated his attention upon the table lamps, removing the bulbs and placing them in his pocket. He then took two of his 90w bulbs from the individual padded *Jiffy* bags and carefully inserted the bulbs into the holders. He looked around the room and gauged the volume. He knew that the room would have to be filled with at least 14% of gas for an explosion to occur. There would, of course, be a greater build-up of the lighter-than-air natural gas towards the ceiling but, if the concentration of gas was in excess of 70%, the light bulb filaments would simply glow much brighter but without causing an explosion. The accumulation of gas would, however, be less concentrated at the lower levels of the lounge, almost certainly within the range of 14% - 70%, thus the table lamps were at the very best height and position for his purposes, the heat generated by the filament of a 90w bulb ensuring the auto-ignition temperature required for the explosion. Brian knew that there was no guarantee of success but his remit, as always, was to ensure that death appeared to be by way of a tragic accident without leaving any damming forensic evidence. He was confident that reliance upon both the ceiling light and table lamps would ensure success. He crossed the room and opened the transom window a little, creating a gentle circulation of air, then, removing some books from the bookshelves he scattered them onto the floor so that they would be seen from the light in the hallway. He returned to the door and surveyed the room noting with professional satisfaction that he could clearly see the tops of the innocent-looking bulbs just visible above the shades of the table lamps. Finally, he approached the fireplace and knelt before the fire, turned on the gas control and then walked back across the lounge to the hall, closing the lounge door carefully as he went.

***

At quarter to ten, the morose couple left the *Duke of Westmoreland* and walked back towards their cottage, their heads bowed against the drizzle. As they reached the dark porch, he fumbled with his keys, opened the front door and turned on the hallway lights.

Old fashioned coal gas had a very distinct smell but, the North Sea gas is methane and hardly smells at all. It was particularly difficult for either of them to detect the smell of the natural gas when their nostrils had been assailed by the sweet smell of forest pines although, in the hallway, they both felt that they could smell something.

They walked towards the open kitchen door to investigate, but both stopped as they saw through the glazed lounge door their books scattered on the floor. Without comment he pushed open the door and entered the lounge as her beautiful fingers felt for the light switches. If the table lamp bulbs had been broken this may have served as a warning to them both, but, other than the scattered books, nothing appeared amiss. She pressed both switches on simultaneously. The explosion was instantaneous, devastating and fatal, the flame front enveloping them both in a consuming, searing heat.

Chapter 29

Monday, 16th April.

Wells District Police Headquarters, Somerset, England.

GEORGE SOMERS was arrested at 09:20 at Bristol International Airport as he was about to board a charter flight to the Gambia and taken to the police station at Wells. At the same time, other officers raided his dock-side home, one team discreetly removing his company car and taking it by a non-descript low-loader to Police Headquarters.

At two thirty-five in the afternoon, the two officers entered the interview room and activated the recording machine. George Somers looked sullen and resentful seated behind the grey-coloured metal table in an ill-fitting white forensic suit.

'For the purpose of the tape, I am Superintendent Mark Faraday,' he said pulling out a chair and sitting down opposite Somers.

'And I am Chief Inspector Kay Yin,' she added as she took her chair to his right. 'Will you please announce yourself, Mr Somers?'
'Neither of you can interview me,' he replied.

'Thank you Mr Somers. That will do nicely,' she said then, looking at the lawyer. 'And you, sir.'

'I am Derek Headington and I am representing Mr George Somers.'

'You can't interview me,' Somers said angrily, 'neither of you can.'

'Oh, and why should that be, Mr Somers?' asked Kay.

'Because,' he said with a self-satisfied smirk as he leant back in his chair and folded his arms, 'the protocol, *Miss*, is that I can only be interviewed by someone of my previous rank or higher. It is all about showing respect for the rank I held.'

'I think that you have misunderstood the purpose of that protocol,' she said dismissively.

'What do you mean, *misunderstood*?'

'The intention of that protocol is to ensure that an interviewing officer would not be intimidated by a prisoner who had previously held a rank higher than the interviewing officer.' DCI Yin looked the former head of CID directly in the eyes and held his stare. Somers became unnerved. He had always dismissed female officers as being of no match to their male colleagues, at best they could be useful when dealing with women and children, little more. But this female detective was the type of officer he had not encountered before. 'And you don't intimidate me, Mr Somers.'

'My client has already been here for nearly four hours, Chief Inspector.'

'I have explained to your client at the time of his arrest, and I explained to you before this interview, that I am awaiting the results of the forensic teams, meanwhile, now that you are here, I wish to put some questions to your client.'

'I shall say nothing.'

'That is your right, of course, Mr Somers,' she said, 'but a jury is always disturbed to learn that a prisoner failed to take the opportunity to provide a reasonable explanation when asked reasonable questions at an early stage in a police enquiry, only later to manufacture some half-baked excuse.'

'My client has found his very public arrest this morning unnerving and distressing,' said Mr Headington, gesturing to placate his client, 'and is willing to answer your questions as best he can in the circumstances.'

'Mr Somers,' continued DCI Yin, 'you will be aware that we are investigating the murder of Nicholas Fry.'

'Yes,' he replied as if bored by the whole process.

'Did you know Nicholas Fry?'

'No, I did not.'

'But you knew *of* him?'

'Yes.'
'How did you know of him?'

'I knew that he was painting a picture for the boardroom.'

'The boardroom at the head office of Chelwood Kilbride bank in Bristol?'

'Yes,' he replied impatiently.

'Do you know where Nicholas Fry lived?'

'In Clifton somewhere,' he said, adding, 'I don't know the exact address.'

'Did you ever drive Lord Chelwood to that address?'

'I told you, I don't know the address.'

Kay Yin shuffled some papers and extracted one, pretending to check the contents. But this was only a pretence. What she needed to do at some stage of the interview was to establish his exclusive use of his car. This was a suitable time to make the subtle enquiry. 'You have a blue Volvo V70 don't you?'

'Yes.'

'And that's a company car, the bank's car, isn't it?'

'Yes.'

'I am thinking here of blue Volvos that might have been sighted at Royal York Crescent and York Gardens. I know that Nicholas Fry often invited his clients to his studio to see his work in progress. All I'm thinking of is that it would be quite reasonable to assume that you would have driven Lord Chelwood to Nicholas Fry's home?'

Somers began to drop his guard assuming that the young detective was following a lead in connection with the sighting of another Volvo near Nicholas Fry's home. 'I've told you, I didn't know where he lived.'

'Maybe Lord Chelwood used your car or some other member of staff did and drove to Nicholas Fry's home.'

'Lord Chelwood has a Roller and no one ever uses my car.'

'And you have never taken any documents or sketches, things like that, to Nicholas Fry's address,' she added before Somers would realise the significance of what he had just said.

'My client has already made it clear Chief Inspector that he doesn't even know where Nicholas Fry lived.'

'Is that correct, Mr Somers?'

'Yes.'

DCI Yin also knew that the evidence of the courting couple outside of Nicholas Fry's home at the time of his murder was weak but she needed George Somers' denial of ever being in Royal York Crescent. 'My problem, Mr Somers, is that I have two witnesses, a courting couple, Peter Weaver and Sandra Bennett, both of whom have identified you as the person leaving the home of Nicholas Fry via his front door. What do you have to say to that?'

'They must be mistaken.'

'Are you saying that you have never visited the home of Nicholas Fry or, in fact, any house in Royal York Crescent?'

'That's correct.'

'I am now showing Mr Somers Exhibit KY/19. This is a frame from CCTV footage,' said DCI Yin, 'taken at 21:52 on Friday the 2nd March at Princess Victoria Street. It's a picture of you, isn't it?'

He looked at the picture. It seemed bizarre, he was looking at himself. He didn't realise that he had been captured on CCTV but had bought the hat in anticipation of such an eventuality. Damn, he thought. 'That's not me,' he said, moving the picture one way then another as if to examine it more closely. 'It could be a hundred different people.'

'I am now showing Mr Somers Exhibit KY/62. This is your Police Personnel Record photograph is it not?'

'Yes,' he replied but seeing the photograph took his mind back to the time that he had been, as the Americans would say, the Chief of Detectives.

'Our forensic people have made photoanthropometry measurements, those are the measurements of "landmarks" on these photographs. They are prepared to tell the court that these "landmark" measurements show that these photographs are of the same person.'
'Chief Inspector,' interrupted Mr Headington, 'you are trying to trick my client. You know that the evidential value of such comparisons has not been accepted by the courts.'

Kay ignored the lawyer and directed her remarks to the prisoner. 'No one is trying to trick you, Mr Somers. I am pointing out to you at an early stage the nature of the evidence that will be presented in court and offering you the opportunity to comment.'

'Well, I've commented. I wasn't in Princess Victoria Street.'
'Can you tell me where you were between 6pm and mid-night on Friday the 2nd March this year?'

'I think I was at home,' he said pretending to think back in time. 'Yes I was. It was Judith's night out with her girlie friends.'

'Judith Featherstone is your partner?'

'Yes.'

'Does she usually go out with her friends on Fridays?'

'Most Fridays,' he said as if that detail would not convict him.
'How well do you know William Harding?' asked Faraday suddenly, knowing that Kay had concluded her agreed phase of questioning. The change of interviewer surprised Somers.

'I told your junior here that I hadn't seen him for years.'

'Other than in the street, once or twice, apparently?'

'But not to speak to,' clarified Somers.

'You see, this is another of our problems, George. You had arrested Bill Harding … ', DCI Yin drew Faraday's attention to the highlighted writing on a piece of paper, '… eight times and he was also an informant of yours.'

'Yes, that's right. It should all be in the records,' he said as if this fact would also be of no evidential value at all.

'You know that he died recently in hospital?'

'Your junior told me that, too,' he said condescendingly.

'And that he had written a note confessing to the murder of Nicholas Fry?'
'Yes.'

'But we now know that he could not have committed the murder.'

'So I've been told,' he replied disinterestedly.

'But you visited him in hospital?'

Somers could not disguise the shock of this unexpected revelation which shook him out of his complacency. 'Visited him? What do you mean "visited him"?' he said, playing for time, adding: 'I've never visited him in hospital. I didn't even know he was ill.'

'I am now showing Mr Somers Exhibits SP/16 and 17 which are stills taken from a CCTV camera at 18:11 and 19:14 on the 14th March in the corridor leading to William Harding's hospital room.' Faraday placed the photographs on the grey metal table in front of Somers and slowly turned them around towards him. Somers knew that all eyes were on him as they awaited his response. 'That's you, George. I think that you will agree that all four photographs show a startling similarity.'

'Only a similarity, Superintendent,' interjected the lawyer.

'You work for Lord Chelwood?' asked Faraday, changing tact.

'I work for Chelwood Kilbride Bank.'

'In what capacity?'

'I am the Assistant Director of Security.'

'*One* of the Assistant Directors?'

'Yes,' he replied, his annoyance showing through.

'And what duties do you perform as an Assistant Director?'

'The overall management of the UK's security staff, about one hundred and thirty all told. Internal security audits in compliance with the Financial Services Act; security reviews and data and information protection,' he replied more confidently and assured.

'To whom do you report?'

'The Director of Security.'

'That's Sir Tim Metcalfe?'

'Yes.'

'So you wouldn't report directly to Lord Chelwood?'

'No, although he might call me in to his office in the absence of the Director.'

'You wouldn't accompany Lord Chelwood to meetings or on visits to London for example?'

Somers couldn't quite understand the purpose of these questions and felt uneasy again. 'I have once or twice. Went up to London once and to Edinburgh, but as a stand-in for the Director.'

'Or carry out any tasks or errands for him?'

He didn't like the implications of the question. 'Of course not. I'm not an *errand boy*.'

He certainly didn't like the implications of Faraday's next question. 'I see. And what about Lady Chelwood, have you carried out any tasks for her?'

'What do you mean?' he asked defensively.

'Don't take offence, Mr Somers. I am merely trying to establish your relationship with the Chelwood family, that's all. It might be that Lord and Lady Chelwood would have sought your advice in respect of, I don't know, maybe the alarm system that protects their home,' adding in order to anger, 'or Lady Chelwood might wish to collect some jewels from her jeweller and you happened to be to hand?'

'I told you, I'm not an errand boy,' he replied as he attempted to control his anger, knowing that angry men often reply spontaneously and make mistakes.

'How often do you see Lady Chelwood?'

His heart rate increased at this question and he could feel the perspiration under his arms. 'I see her sometimes when she visits the bank and sometimes at the bank's social events.'

'And you have had no other contact?'

'No,' he replied sharply.

Faraday was going to ask further questions but was interrupted by a knock on the door. A uniformed officer whispered in his ear.

'I think,' said Faraday, 'that this is as good a time as any to have a short break. Tea and biscuits will be arranged for you both. I suggest that we recommence in thirty minutes. This interview is terminated at 14:55.'

***

At three thirty that afternoon, the interview of George Somers recommenced. 'Can I return to Royal York Crescent, George?'

asked Faraday. 'You say that you have never, ever visited the house of Nicholas Fry?'

'That's correct.'

'George. We took the break because we have now received by phone the preliminary results from our laboratories. I can tell you,' said Faraday almost light-heartedly, 'we've had dispatch riders racing up and down the motorways of England, to Force Headquarters and the forensic science laboratories at Chepstow and Birmingham,' adding in a more serious tone: 'and the results are quite conclusive.' Faraday opened his leather file slowly and extracted various pencilled notes which he arranged on the table in front of him and DCI Yin. 'Chief Inspector.'

'When we searched your home this morning,' said Kay Yin, 'I was keen to have examined one pair of dark-grey trousers, particularly as a little dry cleaning stub was still affixed to the sweat band with those annoying little pieces of plastic.' Somers' shoulders sank as he visualised the square purple tag. I should have removed that, he thought as he controlled his inner anger. 'These trousers were taken by you to the cleaners on the 3rd March. Is that so?'

'I can't remember,' he answered defensively.

'It is our belief, Mr Somers, that the man who savagely killed Nicholas Fry by beating him repeatedly over the head, broke the window in a basement door of Mr Fry's home in an attempt to convince the police that the killer entered the premises by that door.' DCI Yin paused for effect. 'You see, Mr Somers, Royal York Crescent was built between 1791 and 1820. The glass in the basement door is original and was made by Powell and Ricketts, the famous Bristol glassmakers. Their glass was of very good quality but, significantly, was made of a particular composition of sand, kelp and clay. You will also know from your CID days that glass can be identified by way of its density and its refractive index. In the turn-up of your left trouser leg and in the foot-well of your car, particles of glass were found that are identical to the glass in the basement door of the home of the murder victim, Nicholas Fry.'

'Cross-contamination,' he said quickly.

'Cross-contamination?' asked Kay Yin with a frown.

'Yes, the forensic teams who examined this artist's house could have accidentally contaminated my trousers and my car.'

'Our evidence will be that different teams where involved and Nicholas Fry's home, you, your house and your car were all treated as separate crime scenes.'

'But it could have happened, Superintendent,' said Somers smugly hoping to distract the DCI.

'You are denying ever being in the home of Nicholas Fry or using your car in the commission of his murder.'

'Yes I am, Miss, and you've got nothing here,' he said in an assured way, but he couldn't mask his anxiety. 'Samples could easily have been cross-contamination and the glass could have come from anywhere. If Powell and Richetts were so famous in Bristol, as you say, they must have made glass for loads of house.'

Faraday removed a collection of horrific photographs from his file. 'I am now showing Mr Somers Exhibits NE/3, NE/4 and NE/5.' Headington leaned forward to inspect the photographs, withdrawing back in his seat in shock. Somers looked away.

'These pictures are of Nicholas Fry, a gifted and unassuming artists.' Faraday pushed one photograph forward across the table top. 'You can imagine the savagery of the attack, George, can't you? Look at the distorted shape of the head, the matted hair in congealed blood, the cold staring eye.'

'I think you've made your point, Superintendent,' said the lawyer. 'This means nothing to my client.'

'Oh, I think it does mean something to you, Mr Somers,' said DCI Yin. 'You see, Mr Somers, your DNA was found at the scene. Do you have any comment to make about that?'

'What do you mean, found at the scene?' he blustered looking at Faraday. But Mark remained expressionless, Somers turning his anxious gaze back towards a pensive Kay Yin.

'When you were arrested,' said the DCI, 'a DNA swab was taken from you. That has now been analysis and compared with spittle mixed with the blood of Nicholas Fry found on the back of the settee in which he died.' Faraday passed a photograph to Kay Yin who continued her questioning. 'I am now showing Mr Somers Exhibit NE/46. You will see the forensic maker, number 118, Mr Somers, indicating Nicholas Fry's blood and your spittle. Do you have any explanation to offer, Mr Somers?'

Somers ignored the direct question. 'What motive would I have for killing an artist?'

'I will ask you again, Mr Somers. Can you explain how your spittle mixed with the blood of Nicholas Fry was found on the back of his settee?' Kay persisted.

'What motive would I have to kill him?' he said, his voice beginning to sound croaky.

'Greed, Mr Somers. Greed,' suggested DCI Yin.

As pre-planned, Faraday spoke. 'George, I said that we have received the preliminary forensic results. These will be confirmed shortly. It is now twenty-five minutes past four and this is as good a time as any to terminate this interview.'

'I am asking for my client to be released on police bail,' said the lawyer.

'Certainly not,' snapped Faraday. 'This is a murder enquiry, Mr Headington. There will be no bail. Your client will be detained over night and interviewed again in the morning. Shall we say nine-thirty?'

'But that will mean that he would have been detailed for longer than twenty-four hours. You can't do that?'

'Oh yes I can, Mr Headington,' he replied uncompromisingly and turned to the DCI. 'Would you care to ask Mr Miller to step in, please?'
DCI Yin left the interview room. Somers and his lawyer didn't protest, they knew only too well the procedure that was about to take place.

Within minutes, the door opened and a uniformed officer entered with a clip-board under his arm, followed by Kay Yin. 'Mr Headington?' he enquired.

'Yes, I'm Headington,' replied the lawyer. 'And this is my client, Mr Somers.'

'Thank you, sir. And I'm Superintendent Miller, the Police Commander for the District of Wells and, in compliance with Section 42(1) of the Police and Criminal Evidence Act 1984, I am the officer responsible for this station,' he said reading from his clip-board, 'and am now authorising the detention of Mr George Somers for up to thirty-six hours on the grounds that there is not sufficient evidence to charge your client but, I am satisfied that this investigation is being conducted diligently and expeditiously and that Mr Somers' detention is necessary so as to secure and to obtain evidence by further questioning.' He finished reading from the sheet, adding: 'Do you understand?'

Somers shrugged his shoulders.

'Will you sign here please, Mr Somers?' he asked as he offered George Somers the clip-board.

'I'm not signing anything.'

'I will endorse the record that you have declined to sign,' said Superintendent Miller as if it made no difference to him at all whether Somers signed or not. 'If you wish to speak privately with your client, Mr Headington, those arrangements can be made now and for any time you wish between now and nine-thirty tomorrow morning. Meanwhile, a cooked tea will be made available to your client within the next half-hour. If you would also care for a meal, this can easily be arranged.'

As Miller left the room, Faraday spoke. 'This interview is now terminated at four thirty-eight.'

***

Superintendent Faraday and Chief Inspector Yin met with Detective Chief Superintendent Perrin in the vacated District Commander's office. They talked whilst they drank coffee and ate ham salad sandwiches.

'Well done, both of you,' said Robert Perrin who had been seated in the observation room throughout the interview. 'We have him now at the scene, we have his continuous denials and we have his sole use of the car.'

'But we do have the difficulty in … *presenting* … motive,' Faraday added.

'We know what his motive was - money. Our problem is: How do we introduce that without upsetting our American cousins?' asked Perrin.

All three officers knew from the information obtained from the City of London Police that members of the US Coast Guard, on board HMS *Iron Duke*, a Type 23 British frigate on station in the Caribbean, had been monitoring the drug-running activities of Captain Frederik Jelstrup. A call to Lady Chelwood on board the *Odyssey* from Chelwood Kilbride Bank had been intercepted. The call had been a simple enquiry by Lord Chelwood's PA enquiring about Lady Chelwood's anticipated date of return, but, the caller's number had been fed into the National Security Agency's headquarters at Fort Meade, Maryland and computer-stored. When Somers had used his office phone at the bank's head office to call Lady Chelwood on her mobile, this call had automatically been monitored by NSA and the content known.

'Frederik Jelstrup is using his position as captain of the *Odyssey* to ferry millions of dollars worth of cocaine from Colombia to Florida via the Caribbean islands. The Americans are not ready to arrest all the main players yet, so, we can't reveal our source of information. Our major problem is that we know Somers was paid but we don't know how much or where it is. What you two have to do is provoke Somers into telling us. Can you do it?'

'If you don't mind, I think that I should interview Somers alone tomorrow?' suggested Faraday.

'Do you think that will work?'

'I want to speak with him man-to-man. Kay in fact suggested this approach. We think it is more likely to work than if Kay is present and it will help that the deaths of the Chelwoods hasn't been hinted at yet.'

'The Cumbrian Constabulary have told the local press that the explosion was so severe that it has not been possible yet to positively identify the remains, which is absolutely true. There is little doubt that the remains are those of the Chelwoods and dental records will confirm that but, as the Chelwoods let out their cottage to holiday-makers, it cannot be assumed that the Chelwoods are the victims, and that suits us at the moment. The bank's Director of Security is keen to keep this under wraps until they have conjured up an announcement that is scheduled for ten tomorrow morning. I am told that the UN will make an announcement at three o'clock our time. But the bank is agitated.'

'Agitated at any connection between the Chelwoods' deaths and George Somers?' asked Faraday.

'Yes. Whilst the explosion does seem to have been an accident, they want to make their announcement quickly. I have asked them to delay until you start your interview of Somers. They have agreed and I have said that we will attempt to portray Somers' arrest as a coincidence and keep it low key, but I have told them that, Cumbrian accident or not, Somers will be charged with the murder of Nicholas Fry. I've left it that if there is a connection between Lord Chelwood and Somers, then this will have to come out in the trial.'

'Are you happy that I interview Somers tomorrow?'

'Go with it,' replied Perrin confidently with a smile as he picked up the large oval plate. 'Another sandwich anyone?'

Chapter 30

Tuesday, 17th April.

Wells District Police Headquarters, Somerset, England.

FARADAY ENTERED the interview room at 09.42. 'I'm sorry I'm a little late.'

'You are late, Superintendent. I hope this isn't a silly police interview tactic?' said the lawyer.

Faraday was unperturbed by the aggressive opening comment. 'Oh no Mr Headington, I have now received the written reports from our forensic people and I was also awaiting the draft press releases.'

'Press releases?' asked Somers.

'Yes, but I will come to those in due course. You are still under caution, George, so let me cut to the chase and ask you about your girlfriend, Judith Featherstone.'

'She's my partner.'

'But you do have a girlfriend, don't you, George?'

'I don't know what you're talking about.'

'I think you know full well what I'm talking about, George, but, it's more a question of what Judith knows. Judith is rather upset.'

'Upset?'

'Well, I think it's understandable, don't you?' he said.

'What do you mean, understandable?'

'Going off to the Gambia George and with another woman... What's her name? Oh, yes, Kadi Fakonda.'

'I don't know what you mean?' he replied, involuntarily biting his lower lip.

'Judith has had her suspicions that you have had a girlfriend tucked away in the Gambia, and she is very unhappy that you intended to fly off to Africa to be with this twenty-eight year old. She has made a statement to DCI Yin that on the 3rd, 4th and 5th March, you were ... ' he read from his notes, 'as she puts it "like a hippo on heat, all wild and snappy".' He let Somers digest the implications of Judith's comments. 'I understand, George, that more people are killed in the Gambia by the hippopotamus than any other creature. If that's the case you must have been really agitated late on the 3rd and on the 4th and 5th. Why should that have been, George?'

'Judith's always very melodramatic.'

'Well, this very melodramatic Judith goes on to say that on the evening of the 2nd, she had prepared food for your supper but you hadn't eaten it ...
'

Somers interrupted. 'I didn't feel too good.'

'Did you seek medical attention?'

'No. I wasn't that bad.'

'I think you have been bad, George. I believe that you took the opportunity of Judith's absence from your home to murder Nicholas Fry?'

'I haven't murdered anybody.'

'I believe you murdered Nicholas Fry,' he said as he produced the gory photographs of the murder victim again. 'You did this, George?'

He was going to push the photographs away, his hand hovering over the pictures of death, but he couldn't bring himself to touch them. George Somers just stared at his inquisitor with a blank expression.

'Since you moved to your dock-side home, you have made eight complaints about noisy parties. Yet, on the evening of the 2nd March there was an eighteenth birthday party. It was very noisy, George, but you didn't complain as you would normally. Can you explain that?'

'I was watching TV with the windows shut.'

'But the police were called to this party at 9.33pm because of the noise. Yet you heard nothing. You weren't at home, were you?'

'I told you, I was unwell. I told Judith so when she came back on the 3rd.'

'Let me tell you what else Judith has told us. She also says that she saw a trilby hat in your spare room, similar to those captured on CCTV, but now it's missing along with an expensive pair of black leather shoes.'

'She's mistaken.'

'George, you're in trouble.' Faraday stopped speaking as if he had concluded the interview. He moved in his chair and crossed his legs as if sat in front of a cosy fire. 'I can't understand how you got yourself into this mess, George. For God's sake,' Faraday said with understanding and sympathy, 'you were a respected detective chief superintendent, what, one of maybe not more than one-hundred and thirty in the whole of the country. You had a huge police pension, an impressive house in Arlington, a nice place on the dock-side, a villa in the Gambia.' He moved in his chair again so as to face his prisoner allowing thoughts of what he had thrown away to flood through his mind. 'You had a prestigious job at an internationally famous bank with all the perks. Now you are here, George.'

Bitterness began to ferment in Somers' mind as Faraday continued. 'You had to sell your Arlington house; your ex-wife is sat in the big house in Stoke Bishop counting out half of your hard-earned pension every month; Judith is staying at the dock-side house; Kadi will now surely take up residence in your Gambian villa and Chelwood Kilbride will repossess your top-of-the-range Volvo. They, all those former colleagues at Chelwood Kilbride that is, won't give you a second thought whilst you rot in prison. You're going down, George.'

'Not alone,' he said spitefully, grasping at straws.

'Not alone?' Faraday said as if not comprehending what he had said. 'I can never understand how it is that, on the rare occasions that police officers commit crime, they are so stupid as to get caught. I think it is just arrogance or you're just a cretin, George.'

Faraday rearranged some papers as Somers tried to rationalise his situation, to grapple with his resentment at what he saw as disrespectful investigators; his jealousy of the privileges enjoyed by Lord and Lady Chelwood; his anger at Judith Featherstone; his frustration with himself and his very real fear for his future survival in a prison. 'Are you really suggesting,' said Faraday eventually, 'that others were involved, George. Anyone involved with you in this murder of yours would need psychiatric therapy.'

'The Chelwoods are involved,' he said, desperately playing his final hand. 'They paid me, paid me to do it, alright. You won't touch them and that means you won't touch me.'

'The Chelwoods you say?' Faraday said as if the suggestion was utterly preposterous.

'Yes, both of them, but she was the one behind it.'

'That's rather cheap, George, even for you.'

'What do you mean, cheap?' he sneered.

'Both Lord and Lady Chelwood were killed in an accident on Saturday, George.'

Somers was not only shocked but frightened as he began to quickly calculate the implications. 'Killed?'

'Yes, they were taking a weekend break at their holiday cottage and there was an explosion, faulty gas heater or something, but both killed,' Faraday said in a matter-of-fact way.

'But they paid me £200,000. It's in a Cayman Island account.'

'I don't think anyone is going to listen to your ramblings about the Cayman Islands, George, not now,' he replied pulling faxed copies from his file. 'I have here the press release that is about to be made by the bank and another to be made by the Secretary-General of the United Nations.'

Faraday read the first statement to George Somers issue by Chelwood Kilbride.

'It is with great sadness that we have to announce that Lord and Lady Chelwood were tragically killed this weekend in a gas explosion at their weekend cottage in the Lake District.

Lord Chelwood had been the effective and charismatic chairman of the board for eleven years and steered the bank through turbulent times with such skill that Chelwood Kilbride remains a world-class leader.

I am informed by those at the scene that early indications confirm that Lord Chelwood, totally in-keeping with his heroic ancestors, sensing danger as they entered their cottage, stepped in front of Lady Chelwood at the very moment of the explosion. Sadly, both died.

The Deputy Chairman has now assumed responsibility for the board, meanwhile, our thoughts are with their son, Charles.'

Somers was speechless as he listened to the words, resentful that, even in death, the Chelwoods were being acknowledged as honourable people. His resentment multiplied as Faraday read the statement from the United Nations.

'The tragic death of Lord Chelwood, with his wife Lady Cecelia, has robbed us of a brilliant and gifted man.

His mind livened debate; his imagination inspired thought; his leadership galvanised the cautious and his wisdom fortified resolve.

Miles Chelwood would be the first to recognise, however, that the strength of the United Nations is to be found in all of its members. He would not wish for our work to falter as a result of his death, but he would urge us ever onward – that is his legacy and we will respect that.'

Somers leant back in his chair for support as Faraday had read the words of acclaim. He was unsure of how to respond, his stomach felt as if it was being twisted in a mangle and he was finding it difficult to breathe. Then Faraday spoke again.

'You say that the Chelwoods' paid you, George, but I find that difficult to comprehend. £200,000 into a Cayman bank account, no one will believe that?'

But a smile crossed Somers' face. The press statements had given him renewed confidence and a light at the end of his darkening tunnel – as Faraday knew it would. 'The British government won't want a scandal nor will the UN, Mr Faraday. The Attorney-General won't sanction my prosecution. "Not in the public interest", you've heard of that, haven't you?'

'I've heard of it, George, but all I've heard from you is an outlandish claim that the Chelwoods have made a payment to you. I'll need much more than that, George.'

'I can prove it,' he said desperately as Faraday stood up from the table.

'How can you prove it, George, you're in custody?'

'I have the account details in here,' he said tapping the side of his head with his forefinger, 'and the code.'

'And how do you propose to access the account?' asked Faraday as if mystified.

'All I need is a phone.'

Faraday opened his diary at the page giving the world's time-zones. 'George, banks in the Cayman Islands won't be open for business for four or five hours.'

'I'm not going anywhere, Mr Faraday,' he said with a smirk. 'Well, not yet.'

'OK. If Mr Headington is in agreement, I can get a phone line in here, together with a fax machine. I will want to know who paid the money in, the date of payment, the amount paid in, the account number and account holder's details to be confirmed by fax. If that is received then, OK, your story will have some credence.'

'It's alright with me. You see if I'm not right,' said Somers, his lawyer nodding in agreement.

***

At two forty-five, Somers made the telephone call from the interview room to the Cayman Island bank. Three other people were present: his lawyer, Superintendent Faraday and DCI Yin. All listened intently at the conversation on speaker phone, as the interview room tape machine whirled again. The clarity of the speech was near-perfect. Somers gave his full name and account number, followed by a series of letters and figures: '6842121KF', a combination that included the number of the house in which he had been born, the number of his Arlington house, his former warrant card number and the initials of his Gambian girlfriend. Finally, George Somers gave the police fax machine number for the reply and replaced the receiver. They all took their respective seats around the grey table and waited.

At three-seventeen, the fax machine, placed upon a little wooden desk-like table, wires trailing along the skirting board, made a buzzing signal followed by a clunking sound as it slowly ejected a single sheet of A4 paper. DCI Yin stood up and walked to the machine, picked up the paper and read the contents expressionless, although she was completely surprised and ecstatic at what she had seen. She sat down and handed the paper to Superintendent Faraday. He read the message, his face also devoid of expression.

'I will read out to you the content, George. There is the usual preamble, I suppose, the name of your bank,' Somers smiled at the use of the word 'your', 'with its address and phone numbers.' He looked at the text again then read the content:

Account No: *44298-674536-681*
Account Holder's Name: *George Derek Somers*
Date of Deposit: *26th March*
Amount Deposited: *200,000 UK£*

But it was the last entry that shocked George Somers.

Deposited by: *Shane Ward on behalf of Nicholas Fry of Royal York Crescent, Clifton, Bristol, UK.*

Lady Chelwood had indeed covered her tracks and ensured that George Somers would be implicated.

'The bitch,' Somers shouted like a wounded beast. He stood up and, for a moment said nothing further. He leaned onto the table, knuckles on the table top. He didn't look up as he spoke again. 'She stitched me up. She stitched me up,' he repeated almost quietly in utter amazement.

'Who stitched you up, George?' asked Faraday calmly.

Somers slowly brought his head up and stared at Faraday with eyes filled with intense anger. 'That bitch, Cecelia bloody high-and-mighty Chelwood.'

Faraday understood what had happened but feigned ignorance. 'But how could she, George? She's dead.'

Somers was silent again, like a trapped animal knowing his fate. 'She knew what she was doing, the ... *bitch*.'

'Wasn't £200,000 enough, George? Is that why you went to Nicholas Fry's home on the 2nd March and beat him to death?'

Somers lowered himself into his chair, all arrogance gone now, the fight in him draining away as he realised his impossible position. 'I'm fucked aren't I?'
He was, but Faraday still needed his confession. 'Why did you have to hit Fry so many times, George?'

Somers' mind drifted back, almost dream-like, to that evening in early March. 'He shouldn't have turned around,' he said. 'The silly fool turned around and I didn't hit him right first time, I ………' but his words were lost in a series of self-pitying sobs.

Chapter 31

Thursday, 26th April.

Police Headquarters, Bristol, England.

AT THE request of the Cumbrian Constabulary, Mark Faraday had visited Chelwood House. His enquiries had confirmed some of the personal details for the team investigating the deaths of Lord and Lady Chelwood at Grizedale Forest. At the same time he had acted as a liaison point of contact with Lord Charles Chelwood, the 8th Earl. During his first visit, an examination of the 7th Earl's diary quickly revealed the contacts that he had had with Assistant Chief Constable Wynne-Thomas and Dean Patterson.

As a result of the content of the diary and an interview with the new Bishop of Lincoln, Chief Superintendent Jim Logan, head of the force's Professional Standards Department, had interviewed members of Operational Planning. Four days later, Deputy Chief Constable Mary Priestly summoned Wynne-Thomas to her office, along with Logan. Detective Chief Superintendent Robert Perrin was also present at this meeting.

'John, take a seat. This won't take long,' said the DCC. Wynne-Thomas had not expected the call and the attendance of Logan and Perrin was ominous. Their presence was a warning, but of what he couldn't fathom. He would soon know. 'I had asked Mr Logan to investigate the allegations that you had made against Superintendent Faraday. The bottom line, John, is that your allegations have been found to be either without the slightest foundation or simply spurious.'

Wynne-Thomas fidgeted in his chair with indignation. 'I must object that my judgement has been brought into question.'

'Listen, John. There is no doubt at all that both Inspector Trench and Inspector Glass have not been performing to standard. This has been well documented by Faraday and Fowler. Both have given advice to these two inspectors but to no avail. In fact, both inspectors are seen by junior staff as a bit of a joke.'

'That has certainly not been …' he was going to say perception but thought better of it, '… the information that I have been given.'

'We will come to the way that you have obtained your information, in a moment John. You also suggested, in fact you asserted, that Faraday's behaviour towards PC Blanchard and Miss Hopkins was inappropriate.'

'He … he was perceived to be far too close to these young ladies.'

'John, the perception was yours and yours alone. The facts are, if you had chosen to ascertain the facts, that Miss Blanchard has helped Mr Faraday and Mr Perrin enormously with the recent murder enquiry and Mr Faraday is listed by a university as Miss Hopkins' work-based mentor.'

'I should have been informed,' protested the ACC.

'Informed? You were privy to all Chief Officer Group meetings. You knew perfectly well that Faraday was playing a key role in the murder enquiry and the delicate nature and far-reaching implications of that enquiry.'

'But what of his associating with Miss *Jade* Hopkins?' he demanded hoping that the emphasis on her first name would imply that Miss

Hopkins was probably a pole dancer in her spare time. 'And how was I to know that he was acting as her *work-based mentor*?'

'It's very simple, John. You come to work every day and we trust you to get on with your job. What you should have done was to have trusted Faraday and allow him to get on with his job, unless, there was clear evidence to the contrary.'

'But there was.'

'Was there? Let's examine that evidence, John. Chief Inspector Fowler supports Mr Faraday's assessment of Trench and Glass and Inspector Hogkiss is complimentary regarding Faraday's leadership. I think he said,' she thumbed through a thick sheaf of paper looking for the paragraph as Logan quickly drew her attention to the third paragraph on page 17, 'yes, thank you, Jim. Here it is. "Mr Faraday gives me freedom to act", a sentiment I would encourage. Disturbingly, Sergeant Weber felt that you had pressured him into making a critical written statement against Mr Faraday because you implied that if he didn't, he could very well be invalided out of the force.'

'I have to protest,' he replied angrily. 'You are suggesting that my conduct has been inappropriate, yet you agreed to Faraday's suspension in the full knowledge that you had not suspended him at all, allowing him to continue on duty and thus undermining my authority.'

'John, you lost your authority a long time ago.'

'What do you mean?'

'You have never understood, John,' she said wearily. 'Wearing an ACC's jacket doesn't make you an ACC.'

The remark deflated this pretentious man, but he managed to weakly challenge her again. 'How dare you speak to me like that in front of subordinate officers'.'

'These officers are both fully aware of the manner in which you have recently conducted yourself. They have first-hand knowledge of your vindictive blundering about. In particular, your irresponsible contacts with the late Lord Chelwood and Dean, well now, Bishop Patterson, which could have so easily been detrimental to the delicate and complex enquiries being undertaken by Superintendent Faraday. In short, your conduct during the past weeks can be seen as either misguided or totally unprofessional. I tend to favour the latter.'
'What are you saying?'

'John, you have thirty-two years' service. You could have retired on full pension two years ago. I am suggesting that you retire as of today.'

'And if I don't?' he said with a weakening defiance.

'As you are an ACC, you know that we would have to invite a senior officer from another force to investigate your conduct,' she said, adding in a no-nonsense tone, 'I have already spoken to the Chief Constable of Sussex and he is prepared to send his Deputy here.' Mary Priestly closed her file and handed it to Logan, then appealed to Wynne-Thomas' ego. 'We would have to await his report, of course, but it is likely to be unpleasant and leave your reputation in tatters. I am prepared, however, to accept your resignation now and you can leave the Severnside Police with your reputation intact.'

***

In the presence of all members of Ops Planning, Mark Faraday had congratulated PC Blanchard on her forthcoming Special Branch course but, for Inspectors Trench and Glass, he had waited until his staff had all gone to lunch before speaking to them privately. He had suggested the most dignified course of action. Now, at twenty past five, he waited until the last of the Ops Planning staff had left the office to go home, leaving only Gordon Trench and Silvia Glass at their desks. Alone, they quietly cleared their desks and emptied their lockers. The process was embarrassing and took much longer than he had thought, with Trench constantly banging drawers shut or dropping papers onto the floor. Eventually the painful task was completed.

'I've left detailed notes for PC Haverlock, sir,' said Trench in as confident an air as he could muster. 'I think everything is up-to-date and as it should be.'

'Thank you, Gordon.'

'And I've done the same with Max Weber and left another note with Ray who will be looking after the Carnival,' added Silvia Glass, but still with a spiky edge to her voice.

'Thank you, Silvia.'

Trench stood in front of Faraday's desk determined to make a final excuse. 'If only we had known what was going on, sir, maybe this unpleasantness could have been avoided.'

'Gordon, you both knew that Pippa and I were working with the murder enquiry team.'

'But we didn't know about her boyfriend,' interjected Silvia Glass. 'If only we had been made aware of that we could have been more supportive.'

'Why should you have been told?' replied Faraday calmly. 'When I came here you were undergoing tests for breast cancer, Silvia. You told me but made it clear that you didn't want anyone else to know, that is until all the tests proved negative, which was the case a few weeks later. I respected your request.'

'But we are senior officers, sir, and should have been confided in,' said Trench.

'If you were incontinent, Gordon, would you really expect me to announce to everyone during "Morning Prayers" that you might have to absent yourself suddenly and ask everyone to be understanding? No you wouldn't.'

'If only we had known the complexities of the murder enquiry, sir,' Trench persisted.

But Faraday would not compromise. 'You might not have understood the complexities of the investigation, Gordon, but you both understood the difference between loyalty and disloyalty, didn't you?'

Chapter 32

Wednesday, 9th May.

Chelwood House, Bristol, England.

BADMINTON HORSE trials had been a great success from the event organisers' and a police point of view, less so the arrangements for a meeting at Chelwood House between Charles Chelwood, Mark Faraday and Francis Downes that had been fixed for Monday, the 7th May. This meeting had been cancelled due to the murder of George Somers whilst on remand at HM Prison, Horfield.

On the 4th May, a knife had been smuggled into the prison and passed between prisoners concealed in a bar of soap. On the 6th May, twenty-one prisoners where finishing their showers as a similar number were quietly waiting to take their place. The wardens should have recognised the unusually subdued queues but they either didn't or chose to ignore this warning sign. One of the prisoners queuing was George Somers. As one group trooped out of the showers, the other group trooped in. As one column passed the other, Somers was stabbed repeatedly in the inner thigh. All the prisoners gathered around and engaged in a pre-arranged pantomime of rendering first-aid. Their efforts were completely successful in that all forty-two prisoners were covered in blood. George Somers bleed to death in less than four minutes.

Thoughts of the death of Nicholas Fry, Lord and Lady Chelwood and George Somers were in Mark Faraday's mind as he and Kay drove along the gravelled drive to the front of the house and parked. Already there was Canon Francis Downes.

'Francis, how are you?' said Faraday shaking his hand.

'I am well, Mark,' he replied with his usual enthusiastic optimism. 'And you?'

'I'm fine, Francis. Can I introduce you to my colleague, Chief Inspector Kay Yin.'

He took her hand gently in his. There was a smile on his face, a little larger than normal, thought Mark as his eyes flitted between them both. 'It's a great pleasure, Kay,' he said. He thought that he might say something else but decided that the time wasn't right. 'Shall we go in?' he suggested.

The three walked towards the front portico of the house. As they approached, the doors were opened by Gribble and Lord Charles Chelwood walked out and began to ascend the steps. He met his visitors half-way. A good start, thought Faraday.

'Superintendent,' he said, 'it's good to see you again.' He shook hands before turning his attention towards Kay Yin who was wearing a *Michael Kors* trouser suit.

'Chief Inspector. Welcome to Chelwood House,' he said, his hand shake brisk and courteous. 'At our last meeting I was disrespectful to you. I'm sorry for that. It was inexcusable of me.'

'You were flirty, sir, that was all,' she said not unkindly holding her head proud.

'Maybe, but it was nevertheless inexcusable.' He seemed embarrassed, the arrogance had gone, she thought, although there was still a confidence in his manner and bearing. He turned to Francis Downes. 'And you must be Canon Downes, sir?'

'I would be much more comfortable with Francis.'

'Then first names it must be,' he said as they shook hands. 'Let's go inside and have some tea.'

They took their tea in the Library overlooking the gardens and estuary, their talk being mainly about the history of the house and its paintings. But the visitors were waiting, waiting until Lord Chelwood was ready to speak as they knew he would.

'I had hoped that the inquest,' he said at length, 'would have provided some sort of closure for me, but it hasn't. I have been appointed a junior member of the board, which was kind of them. But, sitting in the board room is a constant reminder of my father. When I walk around this lovely house, every step I take brings back memories.'

'You have commissioned another artist to paint the picture for the board room, I understand?' ventured Kay, breaking the ice.

'Yes,' he replied reflectively, 'I think my father would have like that.'

'I'm sure that would have been his wish,' said Kay.

Lord Chelwood looked at the beautiful Kay Yin. The truth would be more hurtful if spoken by her, he thought, and so turned to Faraday. 'Was he a bad man, Mark?'

'Who?'

'My father ... my father and my mother?'

'Both came under our scrutiny during the enquiry. In all murder enquiries there is speculation and innuendo, but there was no concrete evidence that your parents were involved in the murder of Nicholas Fry.'

'And Lord Tatton?'

'It is difficult to know with the passage of time but, I think that he was genuinely very protective towards his younger sister. At that time, things, social norms, were very different. I suspect that he saw his sister as beautiful, yet vulnerable. I have no doubt that he was angry, but we don't know that he manipulated the court martial so as to have Edward Haynes shot. Maybe he did, that's always a possibility. It wouldn't have been inconceivable. Certain it is that, thereafter, his behaviour became more extreme and his actions increasingly reckless. But that does not mean to say that he wasn't a brave man.'

Charles Chelwood recognised the diplomatic and sensitive answer for what it was. 'I've thought that I should dismantle Tatton's room and restore it to use as a bedroom.'

'I wouldn't do that,' replied Faraday without hesitation.

'But you believe Tatton did manipulate the court martial, don't you?' He leaned forward, almost challenging the policeman for the unpleasant answer.

'Charles, I think that there are some hard and unpalatable truths. What I think we can be certain of is that young Edward went to war in the confident knowledge that he was in the service of his master. Facing death was one thing, but a poet once wrote that being let down would be something darker than death.'

Lord Chelwood smiled a knowing smile. 'You are being kind, Mark.' He lowered his head as he thought of the importance of

the words that the poet had written, then spoke again. 'I think that Percy Shelley wrote of *betrayal* being darker than death.'
'Yes he did,' replied Faraday making no pretence of denial.

'I have a lot of mixed feelings right now. I feel that I have been betrayed, yet, I live in this lovely house and can expect to live a full and comfortable life. But, to have been alone and betrayed, like young Edward, must have been virtually unbearable for him.'

'But he wasn't entirely alone, Charles,' said Francis Downes. 'A very, very caring army chaplain was with him and he had the comfort of a photograph of Lady Charlotte.'

'Not much, was it?' he said almost angrily.

'It was a great deal, Charles,' Faraday said.

'How do you mean?'

'My father was a fire fighter all his professional life. I asked him once, what was the best thing that he had ever done during his thirty-eight years of service. I thought he would talk about the time he rescued a man from the debris of a collapsed building or when he was in charge at the scene of a large oil fire in the docks. But no. He said that the most important thing he ever did was when he had crawled through mud under an up-turned car that had been involved in a road accident. The car had gone over an embankment and was wedged in a dried-up drainage ditch. The driver, a young girl, was trapped. They couldn't get her out and she slowly bleed to death, but he held her hand.' The emotion of what Mark was saying began to affect all that heard him speak. 'You see, he didn't want her to be alone.'

The little group were silent for a few minutes and busied themselves with pouring more tea. Then Charles Chelwood spoke again.

'I know I am being selfish, but you, Francis, don't wish to make any claim on the title, and I need to do something.'

'Worldly riches mean nothing at all to me unless they can serve the needy,' he said without pomposity. 'You have a job to do, and I am sure that you will do that job much better than I ever could.'

But he needed to do something. 'Mark, you spoke at our previous meeting of a charity?'

'Francis has a suggestion,' Mark replied.
'Yes, I do, if it's agreeable to you, of course.'

'Go on Francis.'

'Well, part of my parish, so to speak,' said Canon Downes, 'includes St Ives in Cornwall. The town is in desperate need of a new lifeboat. Mark has made some tentative enquiries. A *Mersey* class lifeboat would cost about £2.4 million and then there would be the annual running costs and a quarter of a million refit every three to five years. You might think that such a generous gift would be appropriate and worthwhile.'

'Would that be enough?' he asked.

'Charles,' replied Francis kindly, 'it is not for you to shoulder the guilt of others – if guilty they were.'

'But is it enough?'

'Since 1861 the St Ives lifeboats have rescued ...' said Faraday, but then needed to look towards Kay.'

'Over six-hundred and eighty people, I think,' she offered as if the exact number would not be easily known, although she knew the precise figure.

'Yes,' continued Faraday, 'and I believe that one lifeboat alone had rescued over two-hundred people during its service. Charles, the present lifeboat will be taken out of service and must be replaced. To fund a new lifeboat would seem a good thing to do. A lifeboat would be something I would thoroughly recommend. And Kay has another thought, too.' He turned to her. 'Kay.'

Epilogue

Saturday, 29th September.

St Ives, Cornwall, England.

THEY SAT in comfortable wooden chairs on the balcony of the *Ocean Rooms*, the mid-morning sun still warm on their bare arms. Their elevated position immediately above The Wharf allowed Mark and Kay a perfect view across the harbour between the West Pier to the right and Smeaton's Pier with its two lighthouses to the left.

They had been here in St Ives for the past week. They had walked through the woods towards Portminster Point amongst the wild *Toadflax*, *Mallow* and *Alexanders*, across Carbis Bay to Carrack Gladden; through the 'downalong', the maze of narrow cobbled streets to The Island and the chapel of St Nicholas; and barefoot along Porthmeor Beach, always to return to the sanctuary of their harbour-view room with its pristine white sheets. As often as not, they sat on the balcony content in each other's company, without national or local papers, just up-turned books in their laps, empty coffee cups on the floor. Here, the *Ocean Rooms* provided a temporary respite from the harsh world that they had chosen to move within.

Now, the late summer sunlight danced on the water as the masts of the slumbering boats began to shift upright in response to the incoming tide. The number of holiday-makers had lessened now as the season drew to a close but the ever-present gulls dived or hovered on the in-shore breeze. Just a little way back from the quayside, the bells of the fifteenth-century parish church sounded the quarter as two police constables appeared in front of the blue doors of the lifeboat station. Grey gates were pushed closed across the road at the end of the West Pier as the blue doors rose to reveal the RNLI *Mersey* class lifeboat on its caterpillar-tracked trailer. The caterpillar tractor's engine came to life with a rumble and a belch of exhaust smoke and began to push the new thirteen-tonne, thirty-eight foot long craft with its white-helmeted six-man crew out onto the quay and down its slipway. Crowds began to gather at the grey gates and along Wharf Road, leaning over or peering through the railings as this monster made its stately procession down the slip-way to be manoeuvred, bow facing towards the open sea, stern towards the Salvation Army's citadel, in this especially cleared part of the harbour.

As the incoming tide swirled around the lifeboat's trailer Mark and Kay looked at their watches. They said nothing, words were unnecessary as they stood and held hands. The previous day they had met with Canon Downes for lunch at the *Porthminster Hotel* and, although invited to the naming ceremony, they had declined and would remain where they were. 'This is your family's day, Francis,' they had said.

From the balcony of the *Ocean Rooms*, Mark and Kay had a near perfect view of Wharf Road, the West Pier and the lifeboat. Some of the holiday makers realised that something was different today as pedestrians stopped to peer at the lifeboat whilst others were more attentive to their children or restaurant menus but, as the church bells sounded another quarter, two police vehicles drove along Wharf Road towards them, one a coach, the other a van. These stopped near the *Sloop Inn* and the Old Slipway. From the coach emerged uniformed members of the Devon and Cornwall Constabulary's band. Each member retrieved their precious instruments from the accompanying van and assembled into marching order. The band master spoke to each member; he waited as the bass drummers and tuba musicians adjusted their straps and others checked their music in the clips.

Timed as if to perfection the incoming tide lifted the lifeboat from its trailer and ass it did so the tractor moved forward and the coxswain engaged both diesel engines to guide his boat to the end of the West Pier as the tractor chugged back over the spit of sand to the Old Slipway. Once the tractor's engine had been silenced, the bandmaster called his musicians to attention and adjusted their dressing. He checked his watch – and waited. He had paced out the distance and knew the time it would take to march to the West Pier and had selected the music accordingly. He checked his watch again and took up his position at the head of the band.

This band, playing *Heart of Oak*, made a magnificent sight as they marched forward in their ceremonial uniforms, boots shinning, helmet badges gleaming proudly in the mid-day sun; children waving and some of the adults clapping as they marched past. Observed amongst the spectators by Mark and Kay were Charles Chelwood and Pippa Blanchard, but they were both too engrossed in each other to look up and see their friends standing on the balcony.

At the lifeboat station, the royal standard flying above the Royal National Lifeboat Institution's flag, the grey gates were opened again to allow the band to march forward and take up its position. As the bells marked 11.30am the mayor, the chief constable and officials of the RNLI arrived, followed moments later by the Lord Lieutenant. At 11.40 the duke's car appeared proceeded by police motorcycle outriders to stop immediately outside the lifeboat station. Salutes and greetings were exchanged and introductions made as the police band played *Salute to Heroes*.

His Royal Highness the Duke of Kent, president of the RNLI, acknowledged the crowds and spoke to all the dignitaries and officials, spending much longer in conversation with Canon Downes. As he did so the lifeboat moved to the end of the West

Pier and was made fast against the stone steps. After his private words with Francis Downes, His Royal Highness, the operations director of the RNLI, the mayor of St Ives and other dignitaries walked along the bunting-lined West Pier followed by the chaplain to the St Ives lifeboat and Canon Downes, their black cassocks tossed by the breeze. At the top of the stone steps, the duke stood at the microphone. He read from prepared notes and spoke of the proud history of the lifeboats that had served St Ives since 1861, of the six-hundred and eighty souls saved and the brave members of crews lost. He thanked an anonymous benefactor who had made the purchase of the lifeboat and its continuous maintenance possible. Then he handed his notes to an aide. He paused and looked across towards Francis Downes. For a moment their eyes met before he spoke again.

'I now have great pleasure in naming this lifeboat the *Edward and Charlotte*.'

Then the duke and the official party stepped aboard the lifeboat. Once they had assembled, Canon Downes walked down the steps, the sea water lapping around his shoes as the vessel cast off fore and aft, the coxswain skilfully manoeuvring his boat to pivot on her bow so as to allow Francis Downes to lean forward and trace the sign of the cross on the glistening blue paintwork of her bow. As the blessing ended, the *Edward and Charlotte* moved slowly astern, then stopped perfectly still as if waiting for permission to proceed to sea.

Francis Downes remained on the stone steps oblivious to the cold salt water above his ankles as the coxswain was about to go half astern, but the duke stayed his hand on the throttle controls. The crowds became silent and a hush descended upon the ceremony as if all became aware of an untold significance.

Slowly, The Reverend Canon Francis Downes, the great-grand son of Private Edward Haynes, raised his right hand, made the sign of the cross once again and spoke. As if this gesture and his words had at long last finally re-united Edward and Charlotte, the lifeboat went astern then made its way forward out into St Ives Bay and the Atlantic Ocean, his words unheard, his tears unseen.

******

The second **Mark Faraday Collection** crime novel

International intrigue and brutal murder

DIRTY Business

by Richard Allen

IN THE absence of his superintendent, Chief Inspector Mark Faraday takes command of the Bristol Central District just as MI6 move in to conduct a covert and unauthorised surveillance operation on his district. To make matters worse, Faraday is required to share his office with the beautiful Helen Cave of MI5.

But when one of Faraday's best young officers is murdered an intricately woven plot is uncovered involving secret bank accounts and a dissident Irish terrorist group. From County Wicklow and the rarefied atmosphere of an exclusive London club to Salisbury Plain and the streets of Bristol, and against a background of brutal murder and international intrigue, a deadly clock is ticking as Mark Faraday and Helen Cave race against time to prevent the nuclear devastation that threatens the West Country.

Available as eBook or paperback direct from
www.amazon.com or www.amazon.co.uk

The second **Mark Faraday Collection** crime novel

Heartless murder and ruthless self-interest

DIE Back

by Richard Allen

WHEN SUPERINTENDENT Mark Faraday defies orders and begins to investigate the disappearance of a local lorry driver, a top secret US and UK intelligence operation, designed to destroy the poppy fields of Afghanistan, is unwittingly undermined.

As Faraday is drawn deeper into the secret world of intelligence, he confronts his own senior officers and foreign law enforcement agencies, cynical self-interest and murder.

From the splendour of the House of Lords and the beauty of the Venetian palazzos to the vastness of the deserts of Western Australia, Mark Faraday relentlessly pursues his investigation, haunted by the murder of one colleague and mesmerised by the beauty of another.

Available as eBook or paperback direct from
www.amazon.com or www.amazon.co.uk

Printed in Poland
by Amazon Fulfillment
Poland Sp. z o.o., Wrocław